The skin at the back of her neck prickled with alarm.

"Sassy?" Nick said in her ear. "Are you there?"

She cupped her hand around the phone's receiver. "I think...I think someone might be in the house," she whispered.

"What?" he hissed back. "What do you mean?"

"The back door's open. And there are tracks, like before. Only these come all the way in..."

"I need you to get the hell out of there. Now. I'm dialing the police..."

She felt the urge to run. Hide.

But this was her house. Her own.

She muted him, slowly placing the phone back in her pocket with the call still in progress. She found her cordless nailgun under the sawhorse near the archway and picked it up.

The light in the bedroom was off. She could see the tender blue strokes of dusk painting the walls of her room.

A voice crept out of the darkness. "Hello, Haseya."

Her blood went cold. It was him.

Dear Reader,

Would you like to know a secret? Friends to lovers is my absolute favorite trope. It's like Reese's Pieces. I cannot get enough. Enemies to lovers is great, too, but there's something about a character realizing that the person they've always known is their actual soulmate... Cue that bubbly champagne feeling that keeps us coming back to romance, right?

Sassy Colton and Nick Malone's friendship has lasted forever and nothing can stand in the way of the relationship they've built since grade school... unless they fall for each other. Nothing like a series of unfortunate events and some danger to make these two realize that the heat between them has nothing to do with the weather in Dark Canyon, Utah.

I hope you have enjoyed books one and two in the Coltons of Dark Canyon series. Are you ready for Sassy and Nick's journey? They've come so far together in every aspect of their lives. Will their strong bedrock of friendship survive the very real feelings they have for each other, or will it all collapse underneath them?

Read on to find out...

Amber Leigh

COLTON STORM WATCH

AMBER LEIGH WILLIAMS

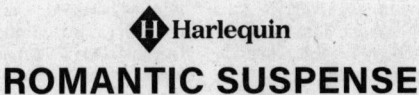

ROMANTIC SUSPENSE

If you purchased this book without a cover you should be aware that this book is stolen property. It was reported as "unsold and destroyed" to the publisher, and neither the author nor the publisher has received any payment for this "stripped book."

MIX
Paper | Supporting responsible forestry
FSC® C021394

Special thanks and acknowledgment are given to Amber Leigh Williams for her contribution to The Coltons of Dark Canyon miniseries.

Recycling programs for this product may not exist in your area.

ISBN-13: 978-1-335-47183-3

Colton Storm Watch

Copyright © 2026 by Harlequin Enterprises ULC

All rights reserved. No part of this book may be used or reproduced in any manner whatsoever without written permission.

Without limiting the exclusive rights of any author, contributor or the publisher of this publication, any unauthorized use of this publication to train generative artificial intelligence (AI) technologies is expressly prohibited. Harlequin also exercises their rights under Article 4(3) of the Digital Single Market Directive 2019/790 and expressly reserves this publication from the text and data mining exception.

This is a work of fiction. Names, characters, places and incidents are either the product of the author's imagination or are used fictitiously. Any resemblance to actual persons, living or dead, businesses, companies, events or locales is entirely coincidental.

For questions and comments about the quality of this book, please contact us at CustomerService@Harlequin.com.

TM and ® are trademarks of Harlequin Enterprises ULC.

Harlequin Enterprises ULC
22 Adelaide St. West, 41st Floor
Toronto, Ontario M5H 4E3, Canada
www.Harlequin.com

HarperCollins Publishers
Macken House, 39/40 Mayor Street Upper,
Dublin 1, D01 C9W8, Ireland
www.HarperCollins.com

Printed in Lithuania

Amber Leigh Williams writes pulse-pounding romantic suspense and sexy small-town romance. When she's not writing, she enjoys traveling and being outdoors with her family and dogs. She is fluent in sarcasm and is known to hoard books like the book dragon she is. An advocate for literacy, she is an ardent supporter of libraries and the constitutional right to read. Learn more at www.amberleighwilliams.com.

Books by Amber Leigh Williams

Harlequin Romantic Suspense

The Coltons of Dark Canyon

Colton Storm Watch

Fuego, New Mexico

Coldero Ridge Cowboy
Ollero Creek Conspiracy
Close Range Cattleman

The Coltons of Arizona

Colton's Last Resort

Southern Justice

Escape to the Bayou
Crossing Deadly Tides
Vigilante Honor

Hunted on the Bay

Visit the Author Profile page
at Harlequin.com for more titles.

Friendship is built around the table.

The making of this book made me very, very hungry.
If you choose to read on, the reason why
won't come as a shock to you. It's no coincidence
that Sassy and Nick's meet-cute happened
at a lunch table. So this one goes out to
my fellow foodies who KNOW how to eat.

Now will sombody please pass the hot wings?

Prologue

Stealing was like heroin. It lit the night on fire.

The fact that he was stealing from Haseya Colton…that made it even hotter.

The cuff sat on her gallery desk, the sterling silver shining in a beam of moonlight from the transom windows. Ten turquoise stones were encased along its slender length, coupled with detailed stamping.

The piece felt warm to his touch, as if Haseya had just taken it off. It was small. Someone on the nearby reservation had customized it to fit the delicate circle of her wrist.

The craftsmanship was stunning, much like its owner. It was a one-of-a-kind piece, the type that went for hundreds of dollars. People paid in excess just to say they'd bought their window dressing from an authentic Navajo artist.

However, it wasn't the monetary value of the piece that called to him. It was the thrill of the break-in, an illicit frisson along his spine. It was knowing that Haseya had worn it—that she would miss it.

It was a tacit connection to her. He could no more resist pocketing the cuff than he could stop himself from smelling the air, gathering one last sip of the scent she carried on her skin. "Good night, Haseya," he murmured before slipping out of that pool of moonlight and merging into the shadows.

Chapter 1

"No," Haseya "Sassy" Colton mumbled when the piercing shriek of an alarm interrupted a perfectly good dream. She'd been dreaming of the warmth of the sun. It had felt glorious after a long winter.

She desperately held on to that feeling.

The alarm grew louder, rending the dream in two.

"Nope," Sassy said, trying to shake her head...and failing because the warmth on her face felt...heavy?

Sleep slid through her fingers. It was desert sand disappearing through a grate.

She realized she couldn't breathe. Her mouth felt furry.

Reaching for her face, her palms confronted the soft, warm form of her sleeping cat.

"Rogue," she said, muffled. "Get off my face!"

The full-grown Maine coon growled low in her throat as Sassy nudged her. The growl turned into an aggrieved *mew* as Sassy sat up in bed.

Sassy gulped air. She gaped at the cat-shaped lump on the bed next to her. "Trying to smother me in my sleep again?"

Rogue lifted a dignified paw to her mouth and regally began to cleanse herself.

The volume of the music increased so loudly Rogue retreated from the bed. The racket made Sassy's eyes water.

"What the actual *hell*?" she demanded, rolling over to squint at the phone on her nightstand. Fumbling blearily for the display, she rapped her knuckles on the corner then accidentally swiped the clock off the nightstand altogether—not before she caught sight of the numbers on its face.

3:23 a.m.

"You've got to be kidding me," she groaned. She shoved the hair back from her cheeks, realized half of it was pasted there, and winced. Picking up the phone, she tapped the screen several times before the alarm fell silent.

She sighed, using her thumbprint to unlock the phone.

A black-and-white security feed instantly popped up. Words flashed across the screen.

There is a person at your back door.

"What?" Sassy asked, bewildered. She brought the screen closer to her face.

The display showed a back alley. She recognized the vacant three-space parking lot.

It was showing her the back of her art gallery in town.

Her heart lurched. She was awake now. Tearing off the bedcovers, she angered Rogue further as they piled on top of her cozy form. Scrambling to her feet, Sassy snatched up the flannel sweater she'd left on the side chair and a pair of fur-lined, slip-on boots.

As she dressed, she thought wildly of the fine art she'd carefully curated from a pool of local artists, mostly Indigenous and female crafts folk. She thought of the priceless artworks sprinkled throughout the gallery and felt a hot flush crawl up her neck. She grabbed a flashlight from the nightstand drawer and her purse from the dresser.

As she wove out of the bedroom to the front door, Rogue trailed behind, yowling her displeasure.

At the threshold, Sassy turned. "I'll feed you when I get back," she promised.

Rogue let her disappointment be known with the flick of her tail.

"Don't look at me like that," Sassy said. She was jittery with nerves. Holding up the flashlight, she added, "Mama's got to go fight crime."

The cat gave her a deadpan look.

Sassy glanced down at her mismatched pajamas—the oversize bright pink T-shirt that warned she was Cute but Feral and the pj bottoms with faded koala bears.

As an afterthought, she grabbed a trapper-style hat off the coat stand and jammed it over her bedhead. "Don't wait up," she told the feline before rushing out into the chilly night.

A wise person would have called the police. They'd have phoned a friend—or any one of her brawny male cousins, all of whom would have laughed at the idea of Sassy fighting crime. They'd more than likely chew her out for confronting it on her own.

The only person Sassy could think of as she drove into downtown Dark Canyon, Utah, was her best friend, Nick Malone. Normally, Nick was her go-to partner in shenanigans.

She began to punch his number into her phone and then remembered that he wasn't home. He'd taken the week off from his job as a Dark Canyon first responder to go on a solo camping trip, the one he took every year around his birthday—and the anniversary of his father's death.

"Okay," she reasoned, gripping the cracked leather wheel

of the 1976 Ford Bronco Wagon. The tires hummed loudly and the springs of the old driver's seat squeaked as she sped through the turn signal onto Elm Street. "I have no backup, but I'm armed and dangerous." She eyed the flashlight alongside the hornet spray she'd snatched off her front porch. As improvised weapons, they'd do.

Still, she lifted the phone again and dialed her cousin Ryan—firefighter by day…and most nights.

Praying he wasn't on a callout, she waited through the drone of ringing before his voicemail picked up. "Hi, Ry," she greeted. "It's Sassy. I know it's…" She glanced at the dash clock and made a face. "…forty winks past midnight. Ew. But I got this weird notification from security at the gallery saying someone was at the back door. If you get this message within the next few minutes, would you mind heading over to Zephyr so you can check it out with me?"

She realized that she'd futilely waited for an answer. She swerved into the little alleyway that ran between the gallery and the bakery next door. The windows of the boxlike 4x4 barely fit between the walls that hugged either side. "Never mind," she decided. "Just…call me back, 'kay?" Ending the call, she tossed the phone on the passenger seat.

Should she switch off her headlights?

What would be the point? Unless the intruder was stone deaf, they'd heard the deep-throated Bronco coming from a mile away. They'd probably hightailed it by now.

She stepped on the brake as she reached the alley's end and eased the Bronco into the small parking lot behind the gallery. Two blue dumpsters shared the space, one for the gallery, one for the bakery.

As soon as the driver's mirror cleared the alley wall, she opened her door. Leaving the truck on, she kept the headlights blazing so that every square inch of the area was lit up. Holding the flashlight out in front of her, she uncapped the hornet spray. "Hello?" she called.

The words cascaded back to her on an echo. The security light over the back door of the gallery flickered drunkenly, another problem that needed fixing.

She inched toward the door. It wasn't open. It wasn't even ajar. She caught herself breathing a little easier.

The flashlight beamed off something on the pavement. Sassy looked around, checking her surroundings. Then she crouched to pick it up.

The item was silver. It lay heavy across her palm.

It was a bar rod, the kind found at the end of a chain lariat.

She turned the rod, looking for an artist's mark. The light overhead flickered again, buzzing in and out. Angling the flashlight, she examined it more closely.

It wasn't a signature or initials. It was a brand. She frowned at the grim face of the longhorn bull skull. The empty eye sockets were prominent slashes of black.

She knew most every jewelry maker in the Four Corners region of southeastern Utah. A good many of them resided between Dark Canyon and Moab, and Sassy had learned to distinguish one artist's style or mark from another's.

She'd never seen this one.

The sound of tinkling glass made her jump out of her skin. The can of hornet spray fell from her grip. It rolled across the ground before she picked it up and faced the dumpster. "Who's there?" she demanded, wheeling the light around. "Come out or I'll…" She considered her options, eyeing the dead hornet on the can's label. "…blind you with insecticide."

Her steps faltered at the sound of more glass tinkling. It was definitely coming from the dumpster.

If the intruder was hiding out inside, he didn't have much for standards. Trash collection wouldn't be until the day after tomorrow. Between the gallery, the bakery and the Tex-Mex eatery two doors down that used it for overflow, the gallery dumpster would be loaded at this point.

The smell coming off it was enough to put Sassy on her heels. The light shook slightly and her pulse jackrabbited as she approached the flip-up lid from the side. If a criminal was going to pop out like a jack-in-the-box, she'd prefer to be out of reach.

She steeled herself, silently counting to three. Then she threw back the lid. It bounced against the side of the dumpster, making a racket worse than the screaming alarm that had woken her. The banging echoed endlessly down the alley as Sassy held the flashlight and can in a two-handed hold in front of her like it was a real weapon.

The chittering broke through the noise in her head. The unblinking reflective eyes of the furry creatures sitting tandem in a bed of torn garbage bags washed over her.

Both she and the raccoons left the staring contest unbroken for several moments. Sassy's mouth formed into an O of understanding. "Right," she said finally. "Sorry." She cleared her throat. "You two…carry on." She nodded toward the high beams of her vehicle. "I'll be over here." Backing away from the dumpster, she left the lid open so the mammals could crawl out when they were ready.

Chastising herself for being overly jumpy, she stalked back to the gallery's rear exit. She cranked the knob of the door. It didn't budge. "Locked," she assured herself. She eyed the unblinking red eye of the security camera over the door and said again, louder this time, "It's locked."

Still, the feeling of uneasiness wouldn't leave her. She

dug into the pocket of her flannel sweater for the bar rod with its skull brand.

Who could have dropped it here? No one came out the back exit except her and her assistant, Soledad Yazzie. Artists, clients and customers entered and exited through the front entrance unless there was a major event that involved catering. Even regular deliveries didn't come through this door.

Despite all evidence to the contrary, she couldn't shake the disquiet she'd felt at the thought of an intruder.

She went back to the Bronco and cut the engine. The headlights dimmed until the area behind the gallery was enveloped in darkness. Sassy rattled the keys companionably as she approached the back door again. She fumbled for the right one and shoved it into the lock. The satisfying clicking of releasing tumblers answered as she turned it, then flung the door wide.

It was pitch-black inside.

She flipped on the light.

The storeroom was as she'd left it, everything in its place. The organization here had more to do with Soledad. Sassy was notoriously untidy.

She caught a glimpse of herself in the plate-glass window on the wall.

It was a good thing Ryan hadn't answered...and that Nick was out of town. With her pillow-creased face, messy hair sticking out of the trapper hat, rumpled clothes and wild eyes, she'd probably scared the raccoons more than they'd scared her. It was a wonder their souls hadn't left their bodies at the sight of her.

Tugging off the hat, she looked around again, double-checking that everything was as she remembered. Then she moved on to the next room, the gallery itself. She wandered from one display to another until she assured herself there wasn't a dust mote out of place. The only faces that greeted her were those of the subjects in the paintings or the wooden and ceramic sculptures atop pedestals.

The cash register behind the front desk, Soledad's domain, lay undisturbed. Sassy had taken the day's earnings to the bank before she'd headed home for the night. The front doors, too, were locked tight.

With a sigh, she climbed the narrow, winding staircase to her upstairs office.

She didn't keep cash here, so she never locked the door. Stepping into the room, she switched on the light and leaned heavily against the jamb.

The adrenaline was leaving her body. She felt cold, sapped and a little sick to her stomach.

She hadn't overreacted, she told herself. The body of a woman had been discovered in Dark Canyon Wilderness a few months before. Sassy's friend Fern Hensley had been restrained and almost burned alive in a house not far from town and was still recovering at Baldwin Memorial Hospital. Sassy's cousin Ava had survived an attempted kidnapping only a few weeks before.

Something was happening to women in and around Hall County. The attacks didn't seem to be random. Sassy sensed from close conversations with her cousins—Ryan, the firefighter, Noah, a search and rescue dog handler and investigative journalist, Jacob, who was a National Parks SBI special agent, and Ava, Fern's psychologist, plus Ava's partner, Chayton Benally, an officer with Navajo Tribal Affairs—that these incidents could be related.

Trouble had come to Dark Canyon. Chances were it hadn't left.

But for now, the gallery was secure and Rogue needed to be fed.

Before Sassy left, she opened the desk drawer and dropped the bar rod into the clutter inside. She switched off the light, descended the stairs and shut off more lights as she made her way to the rear door.

As she locked up for the second time that night, she again eyed the camera above. A commotion from the dumpster followed the sinister sound of an animal scream. She made a note to call her father, Dr. Richie Colton, the local veterinarian, in the morning to send someone early to check if the animals were still there. If they were, they needed to be screened for rabies. The last thing Dark Canyon needed was an outbreak.

As she clutched the flashlight, her head swiveled right, left and back.

It didn't matter how scary she looked. She could use some company right about now, a distraction from all the scenarios running through her head. She wished Ryan had answered the phone. She wished Nick had made it back from his hiking trip.

Nothing sliced the dark in half like her best friend's boyish grin or the way he knew just by looking at her that she didn't want to be alone.

As soon as she was back in her vehicle, she checked her phone, half expecting to see Nick's name in her notifications.

There was nothing.

Her brow furrowed. She wished he was back in cell phone range. She wished he'd been with her when she'd flipped back the lid of that dumpster and confronted those raccoons. She'd have been able to laugh over the situation then. Laughing was always easier with Nick, no matter the circumstances.

She checked the date—March 12.

She counted the days since his departure.

He normally spent four nights in Dark Canyon Wilderness, following the trail he and his father had once hiked together. She wouldn't lie and say it unnerved her that he always made the trip solo.

So far, he'd been gone three nights.

"Malone, if you're not back in twenty-four hours," she muttered as she cranked the Bronco, "I'm going in after you."

The engine sputtered. She tried again, cooing encouragements until the pistons fired. She mashed on the gas to hear the comforting roar of the engine. "Thatta girl," she murmured before putting the Bronco in Reverse and watching her rear window as she backed out the way she came, leaving the night critters to their dumpster fight.

Chapter 2

Don't freak out.

The worst thing a solo hiker could do was panic in situations like this.

The mixed-breed rescue dog who'd nestled beside Nick during the five-minute breather whined in consolation.

Nick ran his hand down Riot's short, spotted coat. "It's all right, bud," he assured him, his voice rough. The feel of the coarse hair beneath his palm quieted some of the doubts in Nick's mind over whether they would make it back to the trailhead before dark.

They were already a day behind. They didn't have the supplies to make it another night in Dark Canyon Wilderness.

Nick cursed himself silently. Their situation wasn't dire, but it wasn't encouraging, either. Nick had let Riot drink the last of their water hours ago. Nick knew dehydration was becoming a problem for himself. His lower lip had cracked down the middle. His mouth felt as dry as the loose-sand trail. A small headache bored at his temples, and he was feeling more and more sluggish.

He and Riot had come several miles from the last water source. They hadn't been able to use it, thanks to the buildup of moss and the risks of giardia, cryptosporidium and E. coli. Nick had chosen not to boil the water and purify it, knowing how far he and Riot were behind schedule and how many miles they had to go before dark.

Nick knew they wouldn't meet another water source before he got back to his truck. Despite recent snowmelt and the plentiful pools they'd found closer to the canyon deep in the wilderness, Dark Canyon was notoriously dry. Pools and streambeds were widely separated. Many had dried up, thanks to droughts in previous years.

Nick was an experienced hiker. He was no stranger to Dark Canyon Wilderness and its challenges. Thanks to rising insurance costs, the bills for his mother's treatment and the facility he'd chosen for her had soared, so he had been taking extra shifts as a Dark Canyon paramedic. As a result, his preparations for this year's hike had been rushed. He'd thought he'd brought enough liters of water to last him and Riot the entire hiking trip.

Clearly, he'd been wrong.

His pace, normally a decent two and a half miles an hour, had slowed. The sun had started its steady crawl toward the horizon.

He would not panic. Riot would pick up on Nick's negative feelings. He probably already had. The low whine continued in the back of the canine's throat. Nick picked up the rhythm of his petting to comfort him. "Not much further, boy," he murmured, scratching Riot behind the ears.

It felt like a lie. Ten miles wasn't much. Usually. But with the threat of dehydration-related sickness lurking, those ten miles to the trailhead seemed like twenty.

Nick had taken more time at the ruins this year. Too much time. His father, Dr. Lincoln Malone, an archaeologist who had settled his family in Dark Canyon, Utah, after his retirement from the field, had loved nothing more than exploring the Ancestral Puebloan Indian structures and uncovering artifacts that had not been touched by human hands since the time of the Ancestral Puebloan people. He was the leading expert on ancient American rock art and petroglyphs.

Or, he had been. Until one morning in March fifteen years ago when he'd said goodbye to Nick's mother, Margot, and left for his and Nick's annual hiking trip to celebrate his son's twelfth birthday. Far into the canyon, they'd been set upon by thunderstorms, followed by a flash flood. The rushing water had scoured the canyon floor. Nick's father had gotten caught in the surge. Once the water levels settled, his body washed up amid a debris pile of ponderosas and aspens.

Nick had barely survived the ordeal. His father's last words to him had been for Nick to stay on the small, slippery ridge where he had been safe from the floodwaters. He'd hugged the canyon wall as the rain fell, frozen with fear. He'd been terrified he, too, would slide off the ridge and get swept downstream.

Days later, Search and Rescue had found him in the same spot. He'd been so weak, he hadn't been able to walk away from the canyon on his own.

Fifteen years. It wasn't enough time to forget his father's quiet laugh or the contemplative lines around his mouth or the light in his eyes when he'd made an archaeological discovery. Nor was it enough time to forget the towering wave of terror he'd felt at seeing his father plunge from the ridge where they'd taken shelter or the sight of him flailing, helpless to fight the unstoppable current.

He could remember too much of the intervening years. His mother's sorrow, her mental breakdown and later decline. He could remember the self-blame that had lurked in the heavy, dark corridors of depression.

It had taken him a long time to pull himself out of that depression. It had taken even longer to learn to live with what had happened to his father.

His mother had never learned how to live without her husband. Nick had had to in order to take care of her. The idea of losing her, too, was intolerable. Watching her mind begin to slip away and her constant care wasn't easy, but she was still a big part of his life.

He threw himself into work helping others. Saving lives. It wouldn't bring his father back. It wouldn't erase what had happened to his mother as a result. But he thought if he could save enough people…maybe he would be forgiven for not saving his father.

Maybe he could forgive himself.

Nick stood from the boulder he and Riot had been resting on. He picked up his pack and slung it on his back, making adjustments.

Riot sprang to his feet, panting and looking a good deal more ready than Nick felt.

Nick wrangled an encouraging smile onto his face. "Back on the trail."

Riot bounded forward, leading the way.

Nick squinted against the sun. He preferred to hike west to east in the afternoons to keep the low-hanging sun out of his eyes. Lowering his chin so the bill of his ball cap cut the angle of the harsh rays, he followed his dog.

Riot's past was as linked with Dark Canyon Wilderness as Nick's. Three years ago, Nick had been camping near the Ancestral Puebloan ruins when he'd seen the dog loping across the canyon floor. At first, he'd thought he was a coyote. But as the animal crept closer to Nick's tent and the smell of food, he'd realized that he was a young mutt with a gray face, a white speckled coat, one brown ear and bicolored eyes. Riot had been skin and bones. Nick had shared his dinner with him. The dog had eaten like he hadn't seen a scrap of food in days. He'd lingered at the campsite long after moonrise.

When Nick woke the next morning, the dog was still there. As Nick had cooked breakfast, he'd waited patiently, tail wagging. When it came time to pack up and head out, the animal had followed.

Nick thought he would branch off to hunt or search for pack members somewhere along the trail. But when he reached the trailhead days later, the dog had been with him still. After Nick had loaded his gear into his truck, he and the dog had engaged in a brief staring contest with Riot's tongue lolling out the side of his mouth, eyes round with expectation, and Nick's restraint had crumbled like a rock ledge. *C'mon*, he'd said, opening the passenger door of the cab. Riot had had no qualms about leaping into the seat. He'd spent much of the ride back to the town of Dark Canyon with his chin propped contentedly on Nick's free arm.

I guess I've got a dog now, he'd thought. His grin hadn't been forced then. It wasn't often he drove away from Dark Canyon Wilderness after his annual hiking trip smiling. That year, it had been as inevitable as his and Riot's connection.

But by rushing to get ready for this year's trip, Nick hadn't just potentially endangered himself. He may have endangered Riot, too.

Shame coated his parched throat and he struggled to swallow. He kept walking at a steady pace, following the tracks Riot left on the narrow, sandy path.

They trekked another half hour before the nosebleed started. It began as one drop of blood in a slow crawl from his left nostril. Then the other joined in. Riot whined as Nick stopped again to dig out his handkerchief. He dropped his head back, trying to stanch the flow.

Nosebleeds happened in dry climates, particularly when the subject lacked hydration. Nick knew that. Still, his pulse knelled ominously against his eardrums. He could feel it in the back of his head.

He looked up to see that Riot had wandered off the path into the sagebrush to sniff the remains of a dead elk.

"Riot!" Nick called. "Get away from there."

Riot reluctantly padded back to him. He planted himself at Nick's feet, resting his rump in the space between Nick's well-worn hiking boots.

"Stay," he instructed, trying not to look at what remained of the elk. He and Riot had passed it on the way into the wildlife zone. It'd been there for some time. There were patches of fur and skin left in places, but the line of its stark white jawbone and the ladder of its ribs jutted out in distinction.

Another casualty of the wilderness. A reminder that nature took everything back eventually.

"We should move on," Nick said, wiping the space beneath his nose once more with the handkerchief. He sniffed wetly.

Riot let out a low woof. He rushed forward with a cadence of barks.

"No!" Nick cried, sprinting after him. "Riot! Come back!"

Riot ran full tilt up a small rise and stopped, tail wagging madly.

Nick raised his hand to block the sun. A figure stood at the top of the rise, small and slender.

The figure raised a hand. Then a voice called out to him, "Yá'át'ééh!"

He recognized the voice and the traditional Navajo greeting. His shoulders sagged in relief. The muscles of his back eased. His lip cracked again as his mouth split wide in a grin and he raised his hand in return. "Aoo' yá'át'ééh!" he called.

Sassy, decked out in a desert-brown button-up and cargo pants, her long braids climbing down her shoulders, beamed as she scratched Riot's back. The flash of her bright white teeth caused a weak sensation around the joints of his knees. She broke into a run, her backpack bouncing noisily against her spine and Riot fast on her heels, skipping in all his excitement.

Nick let her come, fighting the urge to sink to his knees in gratitude.

"Where have you been, Nick Malone?" she asked, close enough that he could see the square points of her jaw and the perfect round apples of her high cheeks. "Never mind." She threw herself at him.

"*Oomph!*" The impact of her body meeting his set him back a full step. When she wrapped him in a bear hug, he responded readily.

He'd needed to see her. He'd needed the sight of her like water.

"You said you'd be back yesterday." Her voice sounded muffled against his shoulder.

"I did say that," he acknowledged, unwilling to release her. Still, he set her back on her heels so she wouldn't feel the slight quaver in the muscles of his arms. "We got hung up at the ruins."

"Something bad?" she asked, her impossibly dark eyes clouding with apprehension.

He shook his head. "I lost track of time."

Her brows came together as she zeroed in on his upper lip. "What happened there? Boxing match with a coyote?"

Before she could reach up to where blood stained the skin beneath his nose, he raised the dirty handkerchief again and swiped. "Nothing. Minor nosebleed."

"Nick," she said, gripping his shoulders as her gaze trekked across his face. "Are you okay? You look…"

"Fine," he finished. "I'm fine." He dismissed his headache, allowing a smile to play again across his lips. "You came looking for me?"

"You're over twenty-four hours behind schedule. What else was I supposed to do?"

"You set out late," he pointed out. "What if I was further up the trail? What if you lost the way? That's easy, even with a map."

"I would've found you," she said stubbornly.

Dammit, she would have. "You should have waited till morning," he advised.

"I brought a tent."

"I didn't know you had a tent," he said, amused. "Can you pitch it?"

"I would've figured it out," she claimed.

He didn't give voice to his doubt. Seeing her silhouette pop over the hill had been like witnessing a miracle.

Her frown grew. She dug in her pocket, producing a clean handkerchief. "You're a mess," she said as she brought the cloth up to his nose.

He didn't wave her away. Normally, the break from the real world did him well. As a paramedic, he rarely had any free time. While he loved his job and valued the relationships he'd built with coworkers, the firefighters who worked out of the same station, the medical personnel and the people he and his team had helped through the years, sometimes he longed for the solace of nature—for forest, mountain, desert terrain... He was an adventurer at heart, just like his father.

This year, however, something was different. He hadn't realized how much until he'd seen her. While she wiped his skin clean, he tried not to breathe her scent too deep. He tried not to dwell on the beauty mark near the corner of her left eye or the silver chain that disappeared underneath the unbuttoned vee of her shirt. Even in nature, Haseya Colton liked a little shine.

The flash of metal stood out against her dusky skin. He saw the faint dewy tinge of perspiration at the hollow of her throat and tried to ignore the stir beneath his navel he'd managed to mute for the better part of their friendship.

"There," she said, satisfied, pocketing the handkerchief once more. She tilted her head, narrowing her eyes in an intuitive manner so like her mother, Bly Colton, it was striking. "Something's wrong."

He attempted to swallow. The muscles of his throat refused to work again. "Got any water?"

Her eyes widened. "You ran out of *water*?"

Embarrassment flustered him. He shrugged his pack off his shoulders, letting it slide to the ground. Never mind his advanced hiker status. He was a medic. He knew what the human body required and what happened when it lacked proper fluids. More, he knew Dark Canyon Wilderness. He knew it almost as well as the pattern of spots on Riot's hide. Its long stretches without water were no stranger to him. He should've known he wasn't packing enough for him and Riot. "I've got some left." *Not enough.*

She, too, shrugged off her pack and pulled out her thermos. "Here."

He wrapped his fingers around it, dipping his head

gratefully to her. "Ahéhee," he said—"thank you" in her mother's native tongue.

Concern puckered the corners of her mouth. The rarely seen divot in the middle of her chin appeared. She saved it exclusively for times of true turmoil.

He drank, lifting his face to the tufty clouds gone neon bright in the late afternoon, and closed his eyes as the water hit his parched throat. The water tasted clean. It felt cool. Cold enough, he almost couldn't stand it. He drank, drank, drank, making his Adam's apple work in fast reps.

When he came up for air, his lungs shoveled air in and out and he couldn't fight the loose smile on his face or the worry hanging around her mouth. He knelt down next to Riot, poured enough water into the cap to fill it and offered it to him. The dog lapped lightly at the cool drink, his thin, pointed tail stuck in a happy windshield-wiper motion.

"How long?" she asked as Nick came to his feet.

"How long what?" he countered, handing the thermos back to her.

She took it. "How long have you two been out of water?"

He ignored the pounding behind his temples. "We're good now."

"Nick," she said pointedly.

He made a noise in the back of his throat. "Since this morning."

She cursed under her breath. "You have a radio. You could've signaled a park ranger."

"It was only a few miles back to the truck," he told her. "We have extra water there. We would've been okay."

"Are you sure about that?" she asked, incisive.

"Sassy," he said, trying to broaden his smile into a lie he couldn't even fool himself with. He'd always found lying to her difficult. They'd known each other since grade school. Since before that fateful spring when his father had passed.

They'd bonded over the fact that they were both only children, they were both wild about buffalo wings and they both dreaded Mr. Sarcowski's algebra class. They'd had to study with the same tutor after school. They were both invited to all the same birthday parties, since she was a Colton and he'd been good friends with Ryan.

The house he grew up in had been down the street from hers. They'd spent their summers helping out her father in his veterinary practice until she went off to New York for art school.

The separation had felt strange. How do you live without someone you saw every day for years on end? Whom you'd learned to lean on—who leaned on you in return during the hard days. She'd gone a long way toward helping him overcome those years after his father's passing, the worst years of his life. She'd been there for his mother, too. She'd gotten her whole family involved in regular check-ins. They'd brought him and his mother into the Colton fold, making Nick and Margot feel like they belonged to the clan, too.

After art school, Sassy had returned to the Coltons and Nick in Dark Canyon. He often wondered why she'd left the New York art scene she'd once thought so exciting and intriguing. What kept her coming back to Dark Canyon?

He'd felt incomplete while she was away...though he'd needed a break from her, because he'd been lying to her about the very real feelings he'd been hiding for her beyond their friendship.

He'd needed the separation to get his head on straight. To erase all that. So he could feel normal around her again.

When she'd returned, he'd been able to convince himself that the mission had been a success. They'd gone back to being friends...*just* friends, with no underlying weirdness on his part.

He reached out and gripped her shoulder, leveling with her. "We would've made it back to the truck. If I thought for a moment we wouldn't have, I'd have radioed for help." The idea that he would have risked putting his mother through more heartbreak...or left Sassy in that position... It hadn't been all that long ago since her aunt Kate had died. And with everything happening around their hometown, including Ava Colton's kidnapping, she didn't need more turbulence in her life.

He'd stopped pushing his odds right around the time he'd come to understand that his mother wouldn't be able to take care of herself much longer. These yearly hikes weren't about pitting himself against nature or risking his life. It was about reconnecting with his dad.

He eyed her pack, desperate to shift her worries away from him. "Are there any wings in there?"

She scoffed at him, but the grin that took over the lower half of her face made it sound like she was holding back a laugh. Barbecued wings had been another long-standing birthday tradition. One of their own. "You wish."

He picked up his pack once again and slung it around his shoulders. "Do we still have that reservation at the Sauce Spot?"

"You know it."

"Don't want to miss that." He felt sapped, but the promise of wings and Sassy's company galvanized him.

She planted a hand against his chest and gave him a good-natured shove. "*After* you shower. You smell like Riot."

Riot let out a chorus of barks at the sound of his name, pleased at the attention. He trotted off, leading the way as Nick's and Sassy's laughter chased him.

Chapter 3

They missed their reservation.

"Maybe they'll still be open," Sassy said, feeling optimistic as she and Nick speedwalked through downtown Dark Canyon.

Nick, hair wet from his shower, checked his watch. "They closed ten minutes ago."

She could see the display windows of the Sauce Spot ahead and ignored the fact that they had already gone dark. "Tony knows we have a standing wing appointment." Breaking into a run, she prayed the Sauce Spot's owner, Tony Vasquez, a classmate of theirs from high school, would hold out. She booked every one of Nick's birthday dinners at the Sauce Spot twelve months in advance. Every February, she tracked Tony down to make sure the reservation was still on the books.

Nick groaned. "I'm so hungry at this point, I'd eat a squirrel."

Unbidden, the image of two raccoons wrestling over a rotten, half-finished can of Spam flashed before her eyes. "Question."

"Go ahead," Nick said, not taking his eyes off the Sauce Spot's windows. The neon Hot Wings sign was off.

"Did you change the security notifications for the gallery to an alarm?" she asked.

That got his attention. That signature half smile of his tugged at one corner of his mouth. His light brown eyes flashed mischievously. "Maybe."

She'd had her suspicions. He and Ryan had installed the security system in the first place. Nick had access to her phone and knew the numerical passcode to unlock it. She was notoriously forgetful and often forgot important dates, meetings, appointments... He'd been setting reminders and alarms for her for years.

"Thanks," she offered with a sardonic lilt.

He smirked, which tugged the other half of his mouth up. The full-toothed gleam of his grin and the humor dancing in his eyes were nothing short of disarming. "Don't mention it."

Sassy was aware that her best friend was attractive. She also knew there was a running rumor around town that the two of them were more than just friends. Because how could two single twenty-seven-year-olds spend all the time they did together and not bump uglies on occasion? Especially when the two of them were notorious for discarding members of the opposite sex after only a handful of dates.

Sassy was aware her and Nick's individual dating histories featured a long list of seemingly compatible contenders who for some reason hadn't made the final cut. The people of Dark Canyon assumed just because they knew each other like peanut butter and jelly that intimacy...the kind that made clothes hit the floor...was inevitable between them. They thought she and Nick were incapable of remaining friends.

What happens when he gets married? she'd been asked on several occasions. *How are you going to feel watching him build a life with someone else?*

Do you really think his wife will want you *around? Or*

that she won't feel threatened by you? That you won't have regrets?

She hadn't known how to answer those questions. She still didn't. Probably because she was a one-day-at-a-time kind of girl. She lived in the present, embracing every moment.

Just because Nick spent a lot of those moments with her didn't mean their futures were tied up in marriage, kids and joint tax returns.

She loved Nick. He was a great guy. He was equal parts brawn and brain. He cared deeply for others, and he was more loyal than anyone she'd ever met. He could climb mountains and white-water kayak. He'd jumped out of planes with nothing more than a Hail Mary and a parachute strapped to his back. Even his bad jokes, combined with his killer smile, could summon women in hordes.

She'd once accidentally overheard that he was excellent in bed. *Playful...attentive...could last for days* had been the exact words exchanged in front of a ladies' room mirror by two unidentified women while Sassy had been trapped awkwardly inside a bathroom stall. For some undefined reason, those words had bored into her skull and made a home there.

But Sassy loved her messy single life. And she *was* messy, while Nick was... Well, a neat freak. Organized to a fault. He'd organized his own life to such a degree that he'd started organizing hers. The notations in her phone. The reminders. The texts when he was too busy to drop in and he knew she was swamped at the gallery. Did you remember to grab lunch? or It's Soledad's birthday today or Don't forget: Rogue needs cat food.

She should've found it annoying. His type-A tendencies should have driven her type-B personality up the wall a long time ago.

The funny thing was, she loved them. She loved the dynamic they'd built. There was no way in hell she was going to ruin that by throwing herself at him when she was horny.

She had any number of other single male friends' numbers she could dial when she reached the point of no return.

She and Nick had never spoken of the rumors about them. They'd been mutually shrugging or laughing off comments made to them in public for the last decade. The *So, how is she? Wink, wink*, or the *We know you've tapped that*.

Once...only once when Nick had had a few too many drinks at a party had he responded to crude comments made about them with his fists. But they'd been sixteen at the time and he'd still been dealing with his father's absence.

The growling of his stomach made her eye the taut line of his abs beneath his shirt. "If you pass out from hunger..."

"You'll catch me. Right?"

"Right." Movement beyond the windows made her snatch Nick's hand up in hers. "Did you see that?"

"Someone's inside," he hissed.

Together, they broke into a run, her limping slightly. Those hiking boots she'd borrowed from Sabrina West, US Forest Service officer and her cousin Noah's girlfriend, had rubbed a blister on her heel.

Sassy all but ran into the door in her desperation. She knocked furiously. "Tony!" she called, peering into the seating area. The peanut shells had been swept off the floor. The Ms. Pac Man machine in the far corner had been unplugged. The dining room lights had been dimmed. *Not a good sign.* "Tony Lorenzo Vasquez, open this door before I break in and raid your fridge!"

She kept knocking and calling as Nick stepped around the building to see if he could spy Tony's vehicle or catch someone coming out the side door. Her hopes were slipping away like smoke. Then she saw the metal door to the kitchen swing open and Tony emerge. He approached the door with a measured tread. Sassy bounced on her toes in anticipation. She could already taste the Sauce Spot's signature barbecue blend. "Nick. Nick! Get back here! He's coming!"

Through the glass, Tony's narrowed eyes passed over her face. He didn't look happy. Nonetheless, when he unlocked the door and opened it, she nearly threw her arms around him.

He stopped that notion by opening the door a few bare inches, enough to peer at the two of them. "Colton," he drawled.

"Hi," she greeted quickly. "Feed us."

Tony gave her a slow blink. "It's after ten."

"So?" she challenged.

"On a Tuesday," he added. "During the slow season."

She shook her head. "I'm missing the point."

"And we're super hungry," Nick chimed in.

"*I'm* hungry," Sassy amended. "Nick here is about to start gnawing on his own arm."

Tony's brow arched. "You two don't have food at home? There's a grocery store up the road—"

"We need wings," she told him. "*Your* wings. Feed us." She clasped her hands together. "Please."

He flicked a glance from her to Nick and back again, shaking his head. "You two are worse than a pair of raccoons."

"I resent that," she said.

"Don't knock raccoons," Nick commented. "They aid in pest control, seed distribution, composting..."

"Nick, focus," she advised. "Tony, wings. Don't make me say please again. It pains me."

"Read the sign," Tony said, pointing to the placard in front of her nose. "We're closed."

"We had a reservation."

"Two *hours* ago."

"It's Nick's birthday."

"Happy tidings, Malone."

"Appreciated," Nick said with a nod. Then he offered him the most boyish smile he could muster. "Wings?"

Tony scowled, but Sassy saw him soften.

How could he not? She'd felt the impact of that smile, too. It was so sweet, it wormed its way into her joints, where it did a tingly tap dance.

What the hell, Haseya? she asked herself when a shiver went up her spine. That was the happy little shiver of anticipation of a first date coming to an end and the kiss that came after...

...the kind of kiss that left her knees quaking, her back pressed against the beveled glass of her front door and her mind empty of everything but *oh, yes, more, please*...

Tony heaved a resigned sigh. He parted the door wider. "Come on in."

"*Yes*," Nick said, the boyish smile morphing into something triumphant, almost wicked, something she recognized from their shenanigans through the years. This was the Nick she knew best.

As Tony held the door open for them, she turned her attention fully on him and gleaned a tiny glimmer of amusement. "You were going to let us in all along, weren't you?"

"There's something about watching the two of you beg," Tony said as he flipped the lock on the door again.

"You're pure evil," she muttered.

"What can I say?" Tony asked. "It's my new kink."

"Whatever keeps you warm at night, Tony, my friend," Nick said magnanimously. The chairs had been stacked upside down on the tables. He pulled two down and righted them. Pulling the first out for her, he kept his hands braced on the backrest as she lowered to it.

It was a courtesy he'd offhandedly performed for her countless times. Had she ever dwelled on it before?

She could feel the thought tumbling around in the messy hamster wheel of her mind.

There wasn't room in there for this. She'd have to demo, rewire and reimagine everything.

Everything she and Nick were and ever had been to each other.

No, she thought. That wasn't right. That wasn't what either of them wanted. Their friendship had been the touchstone that had kept her life in order. It made her world make sense. She knew it was that way for him, too.

Nick lowered to his seat.

Standing over them, Tony clasped his hands behind his back. "Menus?"

"Bring us each a plate of hot wings with a side of your Whoa Daddy sauce," Nick said readily.

"And loaded crinkle fries," Sassy added. "Don't forget the ranch." Then she dug a one-hundred-dollar bill from her purse and extended it to him. "For opening the doors for us after hours." She threw in a saucy wink for free.

Tony took the edge of the Benjamin between his first and middle fingers contemplatively. "You two want bibs with that?"

"Ha," Sassy tossed back. Then she thought about it, eyeing Nick's retro T-shirt—his favorite—and glancing down at the pretty square-neckline blouse with floral print and balloon sleeves she'd recently splurged on at Wagon Wheel, the pricey new boutique downtown. She changed her mind, sobering. "Yes, please."

"I'll get right on that," Tony said before turning for the kitchen.

Sassy caught the faces pressed against the small round window in the kitchen door. They scattered as Tony crossed the room. She leaned toward Nick. "I don't think he was the only one who stayed late to cook for us."

The light in Nick's eyes wasn't something she'd miss for the world. He'd been spread so thin before the camping trip, working too many shifts, too many long nights and spending most of his free time with his mother at the medical facility where he'd secured a place for her. Over Christmas, he'd moved into an apartment complex across the street from it so he could be as close to her as possible.

According to her doctors, Margot's Alzheimer's disease had taken a turn. Nick wasn't willing to take any chances if she needed him at a moment's notice.

He looked thinner than he had five days earlier. The structure of his face appeared more rugged. After hours under the harsh Utah sun, the mesas of his cheeks were stained red, bringing stony canyon walls to mind. His cheekbones were now fine-cut, shadows living in the slight hollows underneath them.

She should be the one sending him reminders for breakfast, lunch and dinner. *Eat your Wheaties, Malone... Don't skimp on the carbs... The bakery's gone BOGO on doughnuts. Treat yo'self!*

She eyed the hand he'd placed on the table. The urge

to cover it with her own gnawed at her. He cared so much about others. Not enough about himself.

Thank God she'd gone looking for him and Riot in Dark Canyon Wilderness. Would he have really radioed for help if he had needed it? Or would he have convinced himself that park rangers had more important things to do than get him through the last leg of his journey back to the trailhead?

Her pulse picked up because she wasn't sure. The thought of his star fading out burned like acid in her throat. The bridge of her nose prickled, as it often did at the onset of tears, and she did reach for him.

His eyes skimmed up to meet hers. They looked almost golden in the light from the kitchen window—tawny lion eyes.

There was so much she wanted to say, too much building up inside her. She settled for "I'm glad you're back."

His smile was soft. His hand flipped underneath hers to clutch her fingers. Despite the cold outside, his skin warmed hers. "Me, too."

Maybe one day he wouldn't hike alone. Maybe one day he'd take someone with him…like her. She wasn't the best hiker. She'd spent nights out in the elements, but she'd never pitched her own tent. She'd had to borrow Sabrina's hiking boots because she didn't have a decent pair of her own. Though how could she say no to sleeping under the stars or spending days in isolation exploring Dark Canyon Wilderness with the person she felt closest to?

Nick carefully let go of her hand. He gripped the table's edge. "You got a security warning from the gallery?"

"What?" It took a moment for her thoughts to reset. She shook her head to clear it. "Oh. Yeah."

"Anything I need to know about?"

She could tell him how she'd sped across town in the middle of the night to catch two raccoons in a dumpster raid. She thought of the bar rod she'd found outside the back door to Zephyr Gallery with its unidentified skull brand. More than likely, it meant nothing. "It was just wildlife doing their thing."

He frowned. "I set the alarm for a breach at the back door, not motion in the parking lot."

"It was nothing," she assured him. "The door was locked. I checked the gallery floor and the office upstairs. There was no sign of an intruder."

"You checked it out yourself?"

His voice had darkened. So had his eyes. She sighed because she recognized this part of him, too. She saw it all too often with her male cousins. Because she didn't have brothers of her own, they all felt obligated to protect her. "It was nothing," she repeated, slower this time.

"You didn't call anyone?"

"I called Ryan," she informed him. "He was on a callout so he couldn't answer. He checked in the next morning to make sure everything was all right."

"You could've called Noah," he pointed out. "Or Jacob. Your dad or Chay."

"Nick," she said, raising her voice slightly. "It's fine. I'm fine. Nothing actually happened. I told you. It was a glitch."

He lifted his chin, arms crossed over his chest as he studied her. "Next time, call somebody else."

She checked the urge to roll her eyes. Her sarcasm was harder to curb. "Yeah, you never know when those raccoons are ready to throw down against someone four times their size."

"It could've been a black bear," he pointed out. "They've been seen around town recently."

"Sure," she said, unwilling to engage in this debate with him any longer.

He thrust his pinkie finger toward her. "Pinkie swear you'll call someone until you get an answer next time."

Now she did roll her eyes, but offered her pinkie anyway and twined it around his. "Okay, Nick. I pinkie swear I'll drag someone out of bed to spy on trash pandas with me."

He shook it, binding her to the pledge. "Weird things have been happening around Dark Canyon over the last few months. People have started locking their doors for the first time in years. This may no longer be the safe environment we've counted on all our lives."

She knew that—had thought of that herself. "I'll call," she promised.

He drew in a relieved breath and slowly funneled it out through his nose. "Good."

The door to the kitchen swung open, and Tony appeared carrying a tray over his shoulder. The smell of barbecue walked with him. "All right," he said, dragging a foldout from the corner. He shook it until the legs extended and set it and the tray down. "One mega-size wing platter," he said, setting the basket in the center of their table. "Side of fries. Extra sauce and ranch dressing. And two large Cokes to wash it all down."

Nick rubbed his hands together as he surveyed the feast. "We're going to need extra napkins."

"Thank you," Sassy said as she dug into the wing basket without preamble. "You're the best."

"I am," Tony agreed, picking up the tray, removing the foldout and flipping the cleaning rag he carried over his shoulder. "You two are the Sauce Spot's best customers. You've talked this place up so much, I owe most of my regulars to you. Just do me a favor."

"Anything," Nick agreed.

"Show up before closing next time," he requested.

"No promises," Sassy tossed back playfully.

Tony eyed her with something like wariness. "Be nice, Colton, or I won't bring you those napkins. I can't get better advertising than you two walking around Dark Canyon with Whoa Daddy sauce all over you."

"She's been warned," Nick stated, his mouth full. "Thanks, Tony. Really. This is amazing."

Tony clapped him on the shoulder. "Happy birthday, big dog."

Chapter 4

Holding on to the turquoise silver cuff was a risk, and an unprofessional one at that. He wasn't a psychopath; he didn't take trophies. He'd stolen from people he knew before—acquaintances, friends and, even in moments of desperation or weakness, family.

Attachments meant nothing in this business but trouble. Yet he'd chosen Zephyr Gallery knowing it belonged to Sassy Colton. Knowing full well he had unfinished business with her.

He'd thought the years since he'd last seen her would have cooled the resentment.

He ran his thumb over the cuff's rounded edge and felt the pleasant stir in his belly, the one he'd felt when he'd spotted it in that shaft of moonlight on her desk.

The job had been to leave everything as it was. No sign of a break-in. No forced entry. No indication that he'd been there at all.

And yet he'd known as soon as he'd laid eyes on the bracelet that it was hers and he wanted it.

He'd lifted the piece like an amateur thief with no street cred. Like an idiot who never considered the consequences. Who chased the thrill and nothing else.

He didn't make mistakes. He hadn't. Not in years. So

much was riding on his presence here in Dark Canyon. He couldn't afford complications.

His old feelings for Haseya Colton would not be his downfall. He'd come too far for that.

He set the cuff down and ignored the tingling at the tips of his fingers he always felt when he fondled the piece. He pried on the black nitrile gloves, one finger at a time. On jobs, he used them in place of latex because they were less likely to transfer the natural oils of his skin or sweat onto anything he touched. Thanks to the mistakes of his youth—when he'd chased thrills and danger like a kid possessed—his prints were in the system. He could leave none behind during tonight's visit to the gallery.

There would be no need to visit her office upstairs, no reason to touch anything that belonged to her or smell her scent on the air.

He only needed to access the back half of the lower floor. That would be the safest place for the transaction to take place during the Coltons' famous silent auction in a few weeks.

He would leave his feelings for Haseya Colton at the door. He hadn't come this far to allow her to lead him down a path of disaster once more.

"That dog can't be here."

Nick dropped his hand from the handle of the door leading into River House, a long-term care facility just outside Dark Canyon. The man sitting on a nearby bench frowned so deeply that the lines cut sharp diagonals across his pale cheeks. He raised a arthritic finger to the leash in Nick's hand.

At the end of the leash, Riot's perked ears lowered a

fraction. He gave a whine, looking from the man to Nick and back again, waiting for instruction.

"Mr. Kincaid," the nurse said as she approached the bench with a cluster of wildflowers clutched in her hand. She extended them to him, gently wrapping his fingers around their stems. "That's Riot. He's the therapy dog that goes round residents' rooms."

"What for?" Mr. Kincaid asked, narrowing his eyes on Riot distrustfully.

In response, Riot plopped onto his rear and hung his tongue out of the side of his mouth, as if he were trying to look as harmless as possible.

Nick petted his boxy head. "He's a real people person," he explained to Mr. Kincaid patiently. "He likes being around everyone and meeting new people."

"What if he jumps on them?" Mr. Kincaid asked. "People fall down all the time in there." He jerked his thumb to the building at his back. "My neighbor broke three ribs last week just getting out of bed."

"He's well trained," Nick assured him. "He's got his certifications. He's been volunteering here and at other homes for years and he's never jumped on anyone. Never so much as barked at anyone, either." Nick had been as surprised as everyone else when he'd discovered Riot's knack for comforting people, particularly the sick and elderly.

"Is he clean?" Mr. Kincaid asked, the edge of suspicion in his voice undiluted.

"He just had a bath yesterday," Nick replied. "No fleas or ticks, the groomer assured me. And he's up-to-date on all his vaccinations."

The nurse gauged Mr. Kincaid's pinched expression. "Would you like to pet him?"

Mr. Kincaid's lips pursed as he and Riot engaged in a

stare down. Despite the man's unwelcoming facade, Riot's tail wagged happily against the sidewalk.

"Oh, hell, why not?" Mr. Kincaid muttered.

Nick exchanged a smile with the nurse. Carolyn, he recalled. He whistled to Riot, who rose to all fours and followed Nick to Mr. Kincaid's side, where he sat again.

"Don't be shy," Carolyn prompted when Mr. Kincaid only stared at the animal. "My favorite spot is behind his ear."

"His, too," Nick noted.

Mr. Kincaid lowered his blue-veined hand to the back of Riot's head. Riot tilted his ear into Mr. Kincaid's receiving palm and gave a low groan as the touch morphed slowly into a caress.

Nick fought to keep his lips from twitching when moments later Mr. Kincaid raised the opposite hand to Riot's other ear and Riot's foot tapped against the ground in answer.

A quiet, high-pitched sound rose from Mr. Kincaid's throat. Laughter, Nick realized with a start. His face hadn't transformed with humor, but his eyes crinkled at the corners. "You like that, do you?"

Again, Riot answered for himself by laying his snoot on Mr. Kincaid's thigh.

"He's not a purebred," Mr. Kincaid observed.

"No," Nick admitted. It was a common question. "I found him while hiking Dark Canyon several years ago."

"I had a mutt once," Mr. Kincaid said, running his hand almost absently down Riot's back. "Ugly-looking thing. Best companion I ever had. Old boy outlived my first marriage. Went with me everywhere, even to church. He and I met when we ran across each other one day. He was living rough out near Elephant Hill. You know it?"

Nick nodded. "I do."

"Sometimes I think he found me when I needed him," Mr. Kincaid mused. "Not the other way around."

Nick looked to Riot's close-lipped smile. "I know exactly what you mean, sir."

Carolyn's hands were folded in her lap as she watched Mr. Kincaid's face. "Would you like to see Riot when he comes back next week?"

"Suppose I wouldn't mind it," Mr. Kincaid said almost ruefully as he smoothed the fur on Riot's face. He glanced up at Nick. "What'd you say your name was?"

"Nick," he said, extending his hand. "Malone."

"Malone," he repeated. "You aren't related to Margot?"

"She's my mother," Nick said.

"She has the room across the hall from mine," Mr. Kincaid noted. "Sweet lady."

"Riot and I think so, too," Nick said.

Carolyn chuckled as she reached out to pet Riot. "She tells everyone that Riot here is her 'granddog.'"

"Granddog." Mr. Kincaid gave another one of his quiet, high-pitched laughs. "You're here to see her then."

"How has she been?" Nick asked, directing the question to Carolyn.

Her smile melted a few degrees. "She's missed you."

Nick felt a sharp stab of regret. "Is it a bad day?"

"She had PT this morning," Carolyn explained, "so she's a little tired."

"Riot and I won't wear her out too much," Nick promised.

"I won't keep you," Mr. Kincaid said as he gave Riot a final pat between the ears.

"We'll see you next week, Mr. Kincaid," Nick replied,

then clucked his tongue. Riot lifted his head from Mr. Kincaid's pant leg and followed Nick inside.

Reilly Porter, River House's administrator, greeted both man and dog with a broad grin. "I was wondering when you boys would show up today."

"Ms. Porter," Nick said with a nod, folding the end of the leash around his hand. "How are you doing?"

"I'm fine, just fine," she said. "Have either of you had a chance to rest since you got back from canyon lands?"

"For the most part," Nick fibbed. When they'd finally returned home from the hiking trail, Nick had had only enough time to shower, change and guzzle another jug of water before meeting Sassy for dinner at the Sauce Spot. He'd returned late and found Riot exactly where he left him, curled up in a nest of throw pillows in his favorite spot on the couch, chasing z's to the tune of raucous snores. They'd gone to bed shortly after. However, Nick had slept fitfully, his mind on everything he needed to do before he went back to work. "I thought we'd start today with the patients who aren't able to leave their rooms. Then Riot can socialize more freely with others in the activity room."

"We've got the chairs set up already," she explained, pulling her sweater closed tight over her generous bosom as she led him down the hall to the suites. "You'll want to see her first."

His mother. "Yes."

"She missed you two," Ms. Porter noted.

"I hear that," he said, trying to swallow the heavy well of guilt. Had his mother watched the calendar in her room, counting the days until his return? Or had his trip slipped her mind, leaving her with the vague sense of absence she fell victim to on days that were worse than others?

He was the child Margot Malone had thought she would

never have—the one she'd wanted with all her heart and soul. He'd arrived late, to her and his father's surprise. They were both in their midforties when he was born. The pregnancy had been high-risk. Margot had admitted to coddling him often throughout the early years of his life. *If you'd waited all your life to hold your child in your arms*, she'd told him often, *you'd have wanted to save him from the world, too.*

His father had countered Margot's overindulgence with regular trips to Manti-La Sal National Forest. He'd been as at home in the great outdoors as he had been on the lecture circuit or in the classroom.

He'd been a kind and attentive husband. When he died, the hole he'd left in her life had been impossible to fill. Trying to step into his father's shoes had been an exercise in futility.

The shock of losing him had led her here. At first, the signs had been subtle. She'd stopped caring for herself. Once a social person and a regular volunteer in the Dark Canyon community, she had stopped leaving the house. She'd stopped seeing people, ignoring those who had come to the door.

Nick hadn't known she'd stopped paying the bills until the debt collectors had started calling him, day and night.

They'd lost the family home. Nick hadn't been able to save it for her. Her depression had taken a hard left turn. Her prescription drug abuse had started.

She'd quietly resented Nick for moving in and trying to stem the worst of it. By that point, the intensity of loss and everything that came with it had whittled her down to the bones of a stranger. He'd started to notice what the pills had been masking. She'd stopped bathing or dressing. Her inability to get out of bed had been less to do with doldrums and more to do with decreased mobility.

She'd become more withdrawn from him, increasingly agitated and, worse, aggressive. When she'd started losing touch with reality altogether—often referring to Nick's father in the present tense, as if he were away on a business trip—his constant worry for her had morphed into full-blown fear.

A consultation with a neurologist, followed by the results of an MRI, had confirmed it. She was in the early stages of dementia.

The savings from his father's life insurance hadn't been enough to make her comfortable in the only long-term care facility in Dark Canyon, where Nick felt his mother would receive the best treatment. He'd considered transferring to Moab—the need for paramedics wasn't limited to his hometown, and his mother's living situation may be easier to solve and afford elsewhere.

But he couldn't fathom leaving. During her more lucid moments, she'd balked at the idea, too. She and his father had planned to retire in Dark Canyon, live out their lives there. Nick was determined to see to her wishes. Even if it meant working himself to the bone to keep her installed here at River House.

Ms. Porter escorted him down the well-lit hall. They passed a woman in a wheelchair being pushed by an orderly. The older lady beamed at Riot and reached out to brush her hand across his back. "Hello, Riot. Nicholas."

Nick nodded politely to her. "Good to see you, Ms. Redmont. We'll be in the activity room shortly."

He and Ms. Porter bypassed several more doors and turned right down the corridor. The second door to the left was closed and decorated with a daisy and lavender wreath at its center, a gift from Sassy. She delivered a new wreath to his mother every season. The last had been fir with red berries.

Ms. Porter rapped her knuckles lightly against the door. "Margot? You have some visitors."

The first thing Nick saw was his mother's dainty feet appointed on the needlepoint footstool she'd brought from home. Someone had painted her toenails a spicy red—again, probably Sassy. There was no swelling around her ankles, but the veins in the tops of her feet stood out in stark relief.

He stepped into the room, Riot beside him. She was awake, a book open across her lap, her knitting needles on top of it. She'd once been a voracious reader. Before his father had published his work, she'd edited his manuscripts. They'd spent hours together locked inside his study working at the same desk, her on one side, him on the other, their toes touching underneath, heads bent close over the desktop…

Nick knew she now struggled to organize her everyday thoughts, much less read more than a few pages at a time. Dementia had taken so much, even in its early stages. To take her enjoyment of reading as well…it felt like another betrayal of the mind.

As his mother blinked at him in the bright stream of sunlight through the lace curtains he'd hung over the room's single window, her eyes were so blue they looked watery. He waited for recognition…prayed for it. He didn't know what he would do the day she didn't recognize him. She glanced down at the leash in his hand, then at Riot. A smile touched the corners of her mouth and bloomed across her thin lips. "My boys," she said in the same quiet tone he'd known since birth.

"Mom," he murmured, bending down to touch a kiss to her cheek. When she'd first come to River House, the skin there had stretched taut across the bones, thanks to her inability to feed herself properly in the months previous. Her plump apple cheeks had returned since she'd settled under Ms. Porter and her staff's care. With time, circles of healthy pink had reappeared there as well.

Ms. Porter helped her into her house shoes, but when Margot made to stand, Nick held out a hand, squatting low to park himself on the footstool. His mother reached for him. He grasped her hand. "I'm late," he acknowledged.

She leaned forward in the comfortable tufted armchair and touched the hair starting to slant across his brow. In a practiced motion, she swept it back, only to grin fully when it stubbornly fell back into place. Like his father's hair, she often said. "Where've you two been off to?"

He tried not to frown over the question. "We went on a hike," he said, affecting an easy tone he didn't feel.

Her smile dimmed noticeably. "The canyons?"

He nodded. Her concern was evident in the furrowing around her mouth. "We're fine. We just got back a bit later than planned. I would've been here yesterday if I could have."

"As long as you're safe," she replied, patting the underside of his jaw. Her hands fell from him to pet Riot, who patiently sat in the space next to her chair. She lowered her brow to the flat of his head and whispered, "I've been trying to talk them into letting me keep this one for a couple of nights a week."

"He'd enjoy that," Nick noted. He looked up at Ms. Porter.

She folded her lips and gave a slight shake of her head. While therapy animals were approved after an extensive application process, pets were strictly forbidden for patients of River House. If they made an exception for his mother, they'd have to allow others the same privilege. While his mother hadn't had a dog of her own since her King Charles spaniel, Hamlet, had passed away two years after Nick's father, he knew the longing for a companion was there.

Riot stared adoringly at Margot as she fussed and tutted over him. Nick glanced around the room, spotting a new blanket folded neatly at the foot of her bed. Its pattern was authentically Navajo, handcrafted. He'd seen Sassy's mother's textile work. This looked similar. "Sassy's been here."

"She visited every day you were gone," Ms. Porter said as she fussed around the room, plumping pillows and hanging Margot's soft pink robe on the hook by the door to the en suite bathroom.

Nick was grateful. He'd asked Sassy to peek in on his mother. The fact that she'd taken time out of her busy schedule to sit with her every day…

Old feelings worked their way to the surface, warming his chest and winding up through his upper arms. He curled his toes inside his boots when he felt the impact. He rearranged his feet on the floor and rubbed one palm against the other. "Level with me," he said, lowering his chin. "How've you been?"

Margot hesitated, and he knew she was running through all her silent issues in her head. When he'd approached her about moving into River House, she hadn't been thrilled. It had been like saying goodbye to the house she'd built with his father, a life choice she wasn't mentally or emotionally ready for. Her physical limitations had forced his hand, however, and while he had no doubt River House was the best place for her, he still carried his guilt around like a change purse of weighted coins. "I can't complain," she said quietly, not meeting his eye.

He rubbed the space on his jaw she had caressed moments before. She *could* complain. She just wouldn't. At the end of the day, they both knew the reality of her situation. Even if some part of her wouldn't forgive him for failing to save his childhood home or making her transfer to River House, she'd bury her complaints. Nick noted the way her eyes averted from his, bouncing back to Riot, who asked no questions. She went back to petting him, and Nick knew to close the subject.

She waited until Ms. Porter stepped out of the room to speak again. "They don't know this," she said in an undertone, "but Sassy snuck Rogue in to see me, too."

Nick's lips twitched. That sounded like something Sassy would do. Only she could sneak a gigantic Maine coon into his mother's room without anyone the wiser just so Margot could spend a few minutes with the animal. "She's mad at me."

Her gaze snapped to his. "What have you done, Nicholas?"

"She doesn't want me going back to work tonight," he explained. "She thinks it's too soon."

"She may be right," Margot cautioned. "Are you not rested?"

He didn't know what it meant to rest anymore. Not really. "I was always scheduled to go back to work today," he pointed out. "It doesn't matter if I got back later. There's no giving away my shift at this point."

"I'm sure something could done if you asked."

"Mom," he said, then stopped and breathed carefully. He couldn't tell her about the extra shifts. Not without her knowing why he'd volunteered for them. They couldn't lose this spot at River House. He'd do anything to keep that from happening. He owed her that much. "It's fine. I don't want you worrying about me."

"Worrying is every mother's prerogative, Nicholas."

He took her hand again. "It's time you accept the fact that it's me who worries about you."

"A mother doesn't stop being a mother," she told him. "If I lose our memories together, that won't stop it, either. You know this. Don't you?"

It was a bitter pill to swallow. Still, this was an argument he knew he couldn't win, so he said simply, "The only thing I want you to worry about for the time being is you. Trust me to take care of everything else. Okay?"

She searched his face. When Riot placed his paw on her knee, she diverted to him, pointing to the glass biscuit jar on the edge of the dresser. "I've got some treats in there. Grab one, won't you? This boy deserves at least three before he goes to the activity room."

Nick debated arguing, pushing her for an answer. But he sensed she didn't have the fight in her today. One day, his mother would see him as nothing more than a stranger. That day wasn't today. For that, he dropped the subject, rose from the stool and followed her directions.

Chapter 5

"Soledad," Sassy called through the doors of her office downstairs into the gift shop. "Have you seen my turquoise bracelet? I thought I left it here on my desk."

The sound of her second-in-charge's footsteps rapping up the stairs on a set of toothpick heels made Sassy's feet cry in sympathy. The tips of Soledad's straight black hair were touched with electric blue. There was a thin silver ring in her nose and a matched bead above her left eyebrow. Based on appearance alone, people in Dark Canyon often misconstrued her as a troublemaker. Sassy knew Soledad had a heart of gold and a sweet nature.

Sassy had given her the job at the gallery because she was one of the few people in the world who could manage the chaos of Sassy's mind. Soledad was the method to her madness and a big part of the reason Zephyr Galley was the outstanding success that it was.

"I saw it on your desk, too," Soledad pointed out. She dropped to her knees. "Did it fall on the floor?"

"I checked there," she said, riffling through each drawer. In the topmost one, she caught a flash of silver. Grabbing it, she realized it was the bar rod she'd found outside the back door after the alarm had tripped. She eyed the top of Soledad's head as she searched the patterned rug beneath the desk. Would her friend recognize it? Soledad's father was a silversmith living on the rez. She might know more about the skull brand on the rod than Sassy had been able to discern.

"Did you take it home?" Soledad asked.

"I may have..." Sassy considered it, shoving the bar rod into the desk. That creeped-out, intrusive feeling had stuck with her since the night she'd checked for burglars. But she'd been over the security footage again and found nothing. No intruder. No one casing the joint. Not even a back-alley drug deal inadvertently caught on camera.

The brand on the bar rod wasn't a harbinger of night or death or anything dangerous and/or nefarious.

She shoved the drawer closed and stood up. "I must have carried it home," she reasoned. "Are the paintings I set aside ready for travel?"

Soledad adjusted one of her large hoop earrings as she rose to her knees and peered across the desk. "I just finished packaging them. Do you want me to run them to the hospital for you? You said your truck was running rough this morning."

Sassy had had to borrow her neighbor's jumper cables to get the Bronco running. "It's the cold," she excused. "She's had a long winter, just like the rest of us. Plus, those old bones aren't what they used to be."

"You'll call if you need a lift?" Soledad pressed.

Sassy nodded. "If I can't reach you, I'll call Nick or..." She trailed off, remembering that he hadn't canceled tonight's shift. She'd seen the half-moons of fatigue under his eyes last night and doubted they were much improved after one night's sleep. She tried not to dwell on how stubborn he was...or how concerned she was about the amount of work he piled on himself regularly or where that might lead.

He placed too much on his own shoulders—too much responsibility, blame and guilt he refused to process...no matter how many years it had been since his father's passing.

The guilt and blame weren't his to carry. That was something she'd never been able to make him understand. He'd spent years fighting his mother's grief and negative coping mechanisms and hardly any time dealing with the trauma he had walked away from Dark Canyon Wilderness with as a fatherless boy who'd seen and experienced far more than any child should.

As for his mother...no one wanted him working himself until he was sick, least of all Margot. He couldn't take care of her without taking care of himself first.

She'd offered to help him pay for his mother's tenure at River House, even if it was just a loan. Any one of her cousins, his friends, would have been happy to do the same for him.

He hadn't accepted, no matter how many times she'd pushed the issue.

Soledad helped her carry the paintings for the new pediatric wing of the hospital to the Bronco. She danced on her toes as a cold wind whistled through the back alley, shoving a strand of her bicolored hair behind her ear. "Hey, I don't know if you remember me mentioning that guy? The one I've been seeing."

Sassy thought about it. "Yeah. What was his name? Fletcher?"

"Yeah." Soledad bit her lip. "It's still new—the relationship, I mean. But I've seen some of his work."

"That's right," Sassy remembered suddenly, setting the paintings carefully in the cargo bed and shutting the back hatch of the Bronco. Pulling her gloves from her back pocket, she tugged them on one at a time. "You said he was an artist."

"I know we primarily showcase women's and Indigenous work," she pointed out. "And he knows you own a gallery and hasn't hinted even once that I should ask on his behalf. But I think you should check him out."

"Is he local?" Sassy asked.

"Sort of," Soledad said measuredly. "He's Utah-born. He left shortly after high school to study out of state."

Sassy had done the same thing. Her art studies in New York hadn't panned out—her career as an artist hadn't launched the way she'd wanted it to. But she'd walked away with a career in business that had led to Zephyr Gallery becoming what it was, so she had few regrets on that score. Especially when she got to nurture and curate local artists. "What medium does he work in?"

"Metals," she said. "Like Dad."

Sassy shook her head. She'd never heard of a local metalworker by the name of Fletcher. But Soledad had an uncanny eye for artistry. "If he's willing to let me look at some of his pieces, I'd be happy to consider them for the gallery. Does he have representation?"

"No. He says life got in the way of the dream."

"I can understand that," Sassy said with a nod. "Talk to him and see if he's interested. If so, help him pick out a few pieces for consideration. We'll have dinner, the three of us." She offered her friend a sly grin. "This isn't the first time you've brought him up. You must really like him."

Soledad grinned sheepishly. "Maybe I do."

He better treat her right, Sassy thought. *If not, he'll have to answer to me and mine.* "I should probably meet him then, anyway." Soledad was practically a sister at this point. The sister Sassy had never had.

"As long as you promise not to challenge him to a hot dog–eating contest," Soledad cautioned. "Like the last man I dated."

Sassy spread her arms. "The guy said there was no way I could eat more than he could. What was I supposed to do?"

Soledad narrowed her eyes. "Let it go, maybe?"

"You know me better," Sassy tossed back, opening the driver's door of the Bronco. "I won, anyway."

"And he never called me again," Soledad concluded.

"If a man scares that easily," Sassy said, tossing her purse across the driver's seat into the passenger's, "he's not worth your time."

"You have a point there." Soledad's smile warmed. "I think I really do like this one."

"Then I advise you caution him against any grand declarations of food-related superiority. Unless, of course, he's secure enough in his manhood to lose to someone of my stature," she added, indicating her height limitations with a wave of her hand.

"I'll be sure to warn him." Soledad laughed. "Come on. Crank her up. Let's see if she's decided to run this afternoon."

Sassy hopped up into the high driver's seat with one foot on the running board and the other clutching the edge of the door jamb. She clambered into place, inserted the key into the ignition and gave it a twist.

The engine complained. It whined as it tried to turn over once…twice… On the third try, it caught. Sassy mashed on the accelerator until the engine responded readily. She beamed at Soledad. "Good as new."

Soledad pointed to the back of the vehicle. "There's black smoke coming out of your tailpipe."

"The filter's probably just clogged," Sassy guessed. "I'll

run her by the mechanic's shop on the way back from the hospital and see about getting it changed."

Soledad nodded, but concern still knit her brow. "Call if you don't make it."

"She'll make it," Sassy said and shut the door. She refused to let her confidence wobble, even when she shifted into Park and the engine hesitated. "Stick with me, girl," she murmured as she eased her foot off the brake. "We've been through too much together to fall apart now."

She didn't make it. The Bronco broke down three blocks from the hospital. Sassy had enough time to pull to the shoulder, coaxing the Wagon into a parallel parking space.

As she got out of the vehicle, she squatted down to see if the back tires had made it over the painted line and cursed when she saw that they hadn't. She would have to walk the last few blocks to Baldwin Memorial Hospital and could only hope she didn't return to find a double-parking ticket on her windshield.

As she lugged the paintings for the children's wing down the sidewalk, wishing she'd remembered to grab her beanie from the truck to cover her ears from the chill breeze knifing through the streets, she passed Dark Canyon Fire Station.

The bays were open, the fire engines in full view. An ambulance had been parked out front, its rear doors spread open. As she watched, a man bent low into the patient bay.

Her feet slowed as she admired the way his trim waist angled down to meet his beltline. Part of his broad upper back was visible to her, the light blue material of his Dark Canyon Rescue shirt straining against working muscles. His black pants, turned up smartly at his ankles, formed nicely to the shape of his rear.

Her head canted in admiration even as her mother, Bly's, voice wafted distantly between her ears. *Look away, Haseya. It's not nice to ogle...*

The man stretched to his full height, a cleaning towel folded in one hand. He reached out to close one of the doors, turning his head just enough for her to see the angle of his profile.

Her steps halted altogether. *What. The. Hell?*

The paramedic was no mystery man. It was Nick.

A guilty flush sank into her cheeks faster than she could spurn it. She shook her head in automatic denial as her gaze arrested on the display of his biceps flaring against the short sleeve of his left arm and something low in her belly stirred. A frisson of warmth that spread slowly in all directions as his curly hair fell across his brow in the exact same way she'd seen it do since grade school, making her reaction disproportionate. The warmth spread outward in a circle of yearning that made *no flipping sense.*

This is Nick, she thought. *Robotics club Nick. Former D&D dungeon master Nick. Six-years of brace-face Nick. Tuba-playing, double-dog-daring, sci-fi movie–obsessed Nick!*

Her partner in crime. Her ride-or-die. Her pinkie promise best friend of almost twenty years. She knew the exact date of his tonsillectomy, how many teeth he'd lost in the fourth grade, how many times he'd puked during an unfortunate field trip to the Edge of the Cedars State Park Museum.

And still, as he turned to face the street where she froze like a deer in the headlights, the heat in her face reached a fever pitch and her panties... *Dear God.* Were they... *melting*?

Never in the last twenty years had she thought of Nick Malone and her underwear in the same breath.

This is not *happening.*

As his gaze seized on her, the instinct to run hit her. She took a long step in retreat.

Then a smile sank deep into his cheeks. His teeth flashed white. The tension dissipated from his features. He slung the cleaning towel over his shoulder and braced his hands on his hips, facing her with his feet spread on the pavement. Wordlessly, he lifted his palm in greeting.

She bobbled the cardboard-wrapped frames braced against her chest. The muscles of her throat worked in an involuntary swallow. Juggling the paintings, she lifted her hand in return. When he set off in a stroll toward her, she closed her eyes for a moment, desperate to cool the burn of her cheeks. She gathered a long breath and shifted her weight, hoping he wouldn't notice their mortifying hue.

"Need some help with that?" he asked and held out his arms.

She took another step back. "No!"

He drew up short as the near shout reverberated off nearby storefronts. The corners of his mouth lowered as he hesitated, eyeing her warily. "What's wrong?"

"What do you mean 'what's wrong?'" She cursed inwardly when she heard the defensive sting in her own voice. *Calm down, Haseya. For God's sake. It's just Nick.*

Sweet-eyed Nick, his neck slick with perspiration, his shadow long over her with the sun behind him, making a white halo of light shine around his curly head.

Stop. Stop. Stop! she chastised herself, gritting her teeth together. "Nothing's wrong," she said, doing her best to modulate her tone. She made the mistake of running her eyes down his long frame, over his uniform...that trim stomach...those long, long legs. "You're working?"

His eyes narrowed slightly on her in confusion. Still, he gave a nod of affirmation. "I had a 24/72 scheduled."

Twenty-four hours on, seventy-two hours off. Her frown deepened. If she looked close enough, she could see the outline of blue capillaries under his eyes and the weariness in them. "Can you make it through a twenty-four-hour shift?"

"I don't have much choice," he said with a shrug.

"Yes, you do," she charged. "You could go home. Get some rest. Take care of yourself, maybe?"

"I'm fine, Sassy."

She shook her head. "I was hoping your trip to Dark Canyon Wilderness would get you back in touch with reality."

"Which means...?" he ventured, tilting his head.

She dropped her voice to a whisper. "You've been on the edge of burnout for weeks." When he looked away, long into the distance, the line of his mouth going firm, she went on. "I thought you getting back in touch with nature would help you see that you don't need to work yourself into the ground."

"Sassy," he said. "I said I was fine. And you know why I'm doing this."

"There are other ways to raise money for River House," she said. "Let me help you. If you won't take my money, let us organize a fundraiser like the Coltons' annual auction coming up. I could organize a fun run, a story competition, partner with local businesses. We could create a lottery, a hike, weekly trivia nights at the Sauce Spot... Hell, we could start a community skydiving event. Anything to help you and your mom through this. You've been residents of Dark Canyon your whole lives. You'd be surprised how people come together in times of need."

"I'm not a charity case," he told her, tension back in full force. "And neither is she. I don't need help. From anyone."

Why did it feel like *anyone* meant *her*? "You can't take care of your mother if you don't take care of yourself. Give your shift to someone else. I'll bring dinner over. We can watch something nerdy and you can turn in early."

His lips twitched and the ghost of humor flashed across his expression before leaving it hard and unyielding again. "Thanks. But I've got this. You need to trust me. Trust that I have everything under control."

Maybe he did. But she was afraid he was reaching the point of breaking. She'd watched him break once, after his father's death. She'd hate to have to watch it again. Her eyes burned, shocking her when she felt the familiar bite of tears against the ducts. She blinked rapidly, looking away. Anywhere but at him.

He reached up for the rag, wrapping his fingers tight around it before he tugged it off his shoulder. He wrung it between his hands. "You still want to drive to the reservation tomorrow afternoon? Check on Ava, Chay and the baby?"

She gave a scant nod. "I have to get these to the hospital."

He nodded, too. "I'll call you tomorrow at eight when I'm off shift."

He'd be too tired to talk by that point, but she agreed. "Say hi to Ryan for me," she murmured, knowing her cousin was likely on call, too.

"Will do."

She set off, telling herself not to look back. The breeze felt cool on her cheeks. It knifed through her thin denim jacket and she shivered as the fire station grew small behind her.

She was so deep in thought she didn't hear the whir of tires until the truck was practically on top of her. As it jounced over the curb behind her, she cried out, alarmed. Diving back against the front of a used bookstore, she pressed her shoulders against the wall. Springs squeaked as the truck's suspension lurched.

The front bumper flashed as it angled toward her, tires squealing as they fought for purchase. Sassy turned away, her heart pounding. The acrid stench of burned rubber stung her nostrils.

At the last second, the bumper skimmed by, a hairbreadth away. The truck bounced back over the curb, the engine revved and then it took off down the street, blowing through the red light at the turn for Baldwin Memorial.

She didn't breathe until it was out of sight. She'd dropped the paintings. They lay scattered across the concrete, their cardboard faces hiding the damage underneath. Pressing her hand to her chest, she dropped to her knees, mind reeling.

The shopkeeper came out of the bookstore, shouting her name when he recognized her. As he crouched in front of her, gripping her free hand, she watched his lips move. Whatever he said wouldn't penetrate the high-pitched terror ringing in her ears.

Her gaze fell on the sidewalk. It seized on the black stain of tire treads, marking the place she'd been seconds before.

Chapter 6

"You talk to Sassy today?" Ryan Colton asked as he pushed through the door of the break room and found Nick at a table chowing down on a quick dinner between callouts.

"Briefly," Nick answered, pinching a dumpling from the takeout container with his chopsticks. He brought it to his mouth instead of rehashing how the conversation had gone.

Ryan's incisive stare bore into him. "Before or after her near hit-and-run experience?"

The next dumpling fell back into the container with a plop. "What?"

"Truck nearly mowed her down on the sidewalk on the way to the hospital this morning," Ryan stated.

Nick cursed and reached for his cell phone. He found Sassy at the top of his contacts list and dialed, pushing away the chopsticks and the rest of the food. His stomach knotted as the line rang repeatedly in his ear, his heel tapping urgently against the floor.

"Hello?" she answered.

His free hand tightened over his knee. "You okay?" he asked without preamble.

He caught the sound of her weary sigh. "Who told you?"

"I had to hear it from Ryan. What the hell, Sassy?"

"Sorry. I meant to call you. I just started processing what happened."

He took a steadying breath and gripped his knee harder when it started to bounce. "You didn't answer me. *Are you okay*, Haseya?"

"Physically? I'm fine. I dropped the paintings, so they're a whole other story…"

"They can be replaced," he told her. "You can't."

"Yeah. I get that. I'm slowly moving past shock and into anger. It's much better than the numbness."

"Do you need someone?" he asked, lowering his voice. He never abandoned a shift, but he was sure if he called around he could find someone to cover him for a few hours so he could tend to his best friend.

"I'm okay," she said. "I'm with Fern. I think we both needed to see a familiar face."

Nick felt the muscles in his jaw tighten. He glanced at Ryan, who was still posted at the door, listening. "Heard."

"My truck broke down, so Mom said she'd pick me up," she explained. She paused. "Can I call you when I get home?"

"You know you can call me anytime you need," he assured her. It didn't matter where they'd left things this morning. Whatever arguments they'd had over the last two decades had never not been set aside in times of need.

"Thanks, Nick. I've got to go."

"Talk to you later," he said and waited until she hung up before lowering the phone. "How did you find out?" he asked Ryan.

Sassy's cousin pushed off the jamb and crossed to the table. He pulled out a chair. "Ran into Harvey after responding to an MVC an hour ago. He said the chief got called to the scene near the hospital. The report says the driver missed her by inches."

Holy shit. "Did she get a good look at the guy?"

Ryan shook his head. "It happened too fast. She didn't get the license plate number, either. Just a vague description of the vehicle. Black Ford F-150."

"That could've been anyone," Nick groaned.

"Harvey said they were pulling security footage from the bank across the street. Maybe they'll find something to identify the person behind the wheel. I'd love to know what the hell he was thinking."

It could have been an accident, Nick mused. Though, with the way women had been attacked around Dark Canyon lately...he doubted it.

"So *is* she okay?" Ryan asked, leaning back in the chair.

"She says she is," Nick said though it nagged at him whether he should believe her or not. "She's with Fern right now at Baldwin Memorial."

Ryan's hand coiled around the edge of the table at the sound of Fern's name. He'd been the first on scene at the fire that had nearly claimed Fern's life. Nick knew he visited her at the hospital as often as Sassy did, if not more. "Did you or the police find anything else out about what happened to her?" Nick asked curiously.

"Not much," Ryan said.

Nick could tell by the way the muscles in Ryan's face bunched that he was none too pleased with the lack of development in Fern's case. "Has she remembered anything new?"

"Bits and pieces," Ryan answered. "Nothing definitive. She's still in a delicate state."

Nick nodded in understanding. He frowned over his next

question. "Do you think they're related—Fern almost being burned alive and what happened to Annie Ross?"

"The police aren't saying much," Ryan told him. "Not to me. But I think they'd be foolish to overlook the possibility. Things like that don't happen in Dark Canyon."

Women didn't normally get run down in the streets, either. Nick couldn't stand the idea of Sassy getting mixed up in whatever was happening. It made the dumplings in his stomach roil.

"I need you to look out for my cousin," Ryan told him. "You spend more time with her than anyone, and I know you won't let anything happen to her on your watch."

"You can count on it."

The corner of Ryan's mouth lifted in an unconvincing smile. He'd been burning the candle at both ends lately, too, between his time on call and his visits to Fern. "She and Ava are tougher than bobcats. They had no trouble keeping up with the rest of us growing up. But after what happened to Ava, neither of them should take any chances."

Nick remembered the security alarm at Sassy's gallery and how she'd responded solo in the middle of the night. If that happened again… "She's not alone," he assured Ryan.

Ryan didn't have time to respond. The handheld radio clipped to Nick's belt squawked.

He automatically rose to his feet. "Gotta go."

"Careful out there, Malone," Ryan advised. "I have a feeling our troubles in Dark Canyon aren't over."

Sassy had come to Recovery Room 303 bearing banana nut muffins she'd found in the cafeteria downstairs and a smile she hoped her friend found convincing. Still shaken from her run-in with the black F-150, she'd sought her friend's bedside not because she wanted to rehash what had happened on the sidewalk but because she'd needed something to bring her adrenaline levels down.

She'd stopped sweating finally and felt that her pulse had returned to a normal rhythm, but whenever she thought about that grille skimming by her, trapping her between the wall of the building and certain death, it started tripping again.

She needed to stop reliving it, and she definitely didn't want to worry Fern, so she kept the details of the incident to herself and focused on the woman in the hospital bed.

Sassy had met Fern before the fire that had nearly taken her life. She'd been driving through Dark Canyon one day almost a year ago and had stopped at the gallery to look around. At the time, Zephyr had been showcasing works of female empowerment. Fern had been as captivated by them as Sassy had been. They had struck up a conversation. While she wasn't an artist, Sassy thought Fern had a keen eye for art. She'd invited her to join a series of art classes her grandmother Leolani was hosting on the reservation.

Fern had attended the classes, giving her and Sassy more of a chance to get to know one another. There weren't many people Sassy had felt comfortable showing her work to after she'd stopped painting professionally shortly after college, but she'd believed Fern when she'd complimented the work she'd completed during the classes.

After several coffee dates, Sassy had felt comfortable doing so, especially when Fern opened up a bit about her troubled childhood. Since Leolani also taught art therapy classes, Sassy had suggested Fern join them.

When she'd learned that an unidentified woman had been hospitalized after nearly being killed in a cabin fire, she'd had no idea it was Fern. Because of Fern's memory loss, it had taken some time for her to remember anything about her life, much less how she'd wound up in the cabin on the reservation with a badly broken leg. When Sassy had learned her friend was the woman who had been brutalized, she had immediately stepped in to help her cousin Ava, the psychologist on Fern's case, care for her.

Due to the ongoing investigation into Fern's near murder, she was staying at Baldwin Memorial under a fake name for protection. Tribal police were keeping the details of the fire under close wraps until they had more answers about what had led to her abduction.

Fern was still fighting memory loss and regression. But even with a badly broken leg, she was fighting to regain her strength. Other than Sassy, Ava, Ryan and her doctors, she spoke to no one.

Sassy finished off her muffin, gauging Fern's face. She had good color. Her long light brown hair had been pulled back from her face, and her hazel eyes weren't limned in near as many shadows as Sassy had seen there before. She was happy to see Fern eating and her cheeks starting to fill out again. "The Colton fundraiser's coming up," she said. "I'm heading out to the reservation tomorrow. Hopefully I can convince the artists there to contribute some pieces to the auction. In fact, I wish you were coming with me. I could use your eye."

"It's not nearly as cultivated as yours," Fern said with a wan smile. "I didn't go to art school like you did."

"Some things don't need to be taught," Sassy pointed out. "My grandmother begged me not to go to New York. She said the teachers there would try to talk me into taking me out of my work and if I came back an artist at all, I wouldn't be as authentic as I was before."

"Did your teachers talk you into that?" Fern asked, eyes round with curiosity.

Sassy lifted a shoulder. "They were critical. In some cases, overly critical." So critical, the voices in her head that had led her to quit selling her work had spoken primarily in their tones. "My grandfather says that teachers are like doctors. Their word should never take the place of natural-born instincts."

"He was married to Leolani?" Fern asked.

"The teacher," Sassy confirmed. "Yes. One of the many reasons they are no longer married or speaking to one another."

Fern peeled back the wrapper on her muffin, shaking her head. "Your family never stops being interesting."

Too interesting, at times. Especially lately on the Colton side. "I have to see him tomorrow. Maybe I can talk him into donating one of his paintings."

"He's an artist like you?" she asked.

"The most eccentric one I know," Sassy said. "He no longer sells his work. He dedicates most of his time to Indigenous rights. He took me to my first protest when I was four."

"Do you still go to protests with him?" Fern asked.

"When he's not being ornery," Sassy maintained. "So, maybe once in a blue moon."

Fern's smile lightened the contours of her face like the sun after a rainstorm. Sassy was so pleased to see it. Her friend had had little to smile about lately. "Will you go back to art therapy when you're released from the hospital?" she asked.

Fern thought about it. "I'm not sure." She seemed to gauge Sassy's reaction before she asked the next question. "Would you go with me?"

Sassy nodded. "I'd be happy to."

Fern's relief was palpable. Her smile, however, did not return. "I've been...having flashback episodes."

Sassy's back straightened against her chair. Concern struck her. "Are you okay?"

Fern bobbed a small nod. Uncertainty furrowed her brow. "I spoke to Ryan about it already. He told me to tell the investigators."

"Do you think you can?" Sassy asked.

"I want to know what happened. The truth of it. Who and why. And the images...they've been weighing on me. It's vague, but... I remember men in black masks. One was named Billy. He was the one who hurt me." She passed a soothing hand over the blanket folded neatly across her thighs. "He broke my leg to keep me from running away. That's it, really. It's enough to make the nightmares worse."

"I'm sorry," Sassy murmured. She couldn't contemplate what it must be like, wanting desperately to fill in the blanks in her memory and yet terrified of the images that filtered through. She wished there was a way she could make the process easier for Fern and had consulted Ava about it. Her cousin had simply said that companionship and constancy would go a long way toward establishing a safe bubble around Fern to cushion her from some measure of the trauma.

As if chilled, Fern drew the blankets up higher. "The investigators are coming to reinterview me tomorrow morning. Ryan offered to sit with me through it, but since he's not part of the investigative team, they would only approve Ava being at my side."

Sassy raised a brow. She dared anyone to stand between Ryan Colton and anything or anyone he deemed his responsibility. Fern fell so clearly under that umbrella, there was no hiding how he felt about her from anyone who knew him. She rearranged her feet to stand and accidentally knocked her purse over on the floor. "Oh," she remembered. "I brought you something. I've been carrying it around, meaning to give it to you." She rummaged through the contents of the cross-body bag and produced an item wrapped in bubble wrap. Standing, she passed it to Fern.

Fern cradled it between her hands. "You don't have to keep bringing me things, Sassy," she said as she unrolled it from its protective barrier.

"It's from the gallery's gift shop," Sassy excused. "And it made me think of you."

The piece fell into Fern's lap—a small wood carving of a bear. Eagle feathers were draped across its thick, furry neck.

Fern took a slow, deep inhale as she lifted it. "It's beautiful," she whispered. "Shouldn't it be part of the auction?"

"I'll replace it with other pieces," Sassy pledged. "This one's yours. Do you see the engraving on the side?"

Fern narrowed her eyes on the etching and tried to pronounce it.

"Shidziil," Sassy corrected.

"What does it mean?" Fern asked.

Sassy offered her a smile. "'I am strong.'"

Fern blinked several times, wrapping her fingers protectively around the bear. "Thank you."

Sassy picked up the purse and slung it over her shoulder, winking. "Told you it was meant for you. Tell Ava I say hey. You'll see her before I do. If you need to talk after the interview tomorrow, you know who to call."

Fern bit her lip. "I don't know what I would do without you Coltons."

Sassy beamed at her as she angled for the door. "And

you'll never need to find out. We stick around…like Gorilla Glue or Whoa Daddy sauce. There's no shaking us."

She got the desired effect of seeing Fern's smile reappear. "I'll call you tomorrow."

"I'm counting on it," Sassy said before she opened the door. "Speaking of Whoa Daddy sauce, next time I pop in, I'll stop by the Sauce Spot and pick up something messy and delicious."

"I'll ask the nurse for some Wet Ones, to be safe," Fern agreed. "Be careful out there, Sassy."

For a few precious moments, Sassy had forgotten about the truck. She kept her smile in place by sheer force of will as she waggled her fingers and left Fern's room.

He hadn't meant to swerve.

He'd nearly killed her. He could have flattened Haseya Colton against a building. And there was nothing and no one to blame but his own lack of focus. His complete and utter loss of control.

He hadn't even been following her. It had been a perfectly innocent drive up Main Street on his part when he'd seen the shine of her black hair, the swing of her perfect hips…

She'd magnetized him. He'd been fixated. So much so that the next thing, he knew his off-road tires had run up and over the curb.

She'd turned, fear eclipsing her features.

For one heart-stopping moment, he'd thought she had locked eyes with him…

It had been enough for him to get ahold of himself. He'd barely had enough time to jerk the wheel before mowing her down on the sidewalk.

His pulse racked against his eardrums. He grabbed his

shirt by the collar and wrestled it over his head. It was drenched in sweat.

He'd have to ditch the truck. No doubt she'd called the cops. He could only hope no one had seen his license plate number or written it down.

Was there a chance someone on Main Street had captured the whole thing on their store's security feed?

He cursed, tossing the shirt aside. He scrubbed his hands through his hair.

There was a reason he'd changed his name. Just as there was a reason he'd returned to Dark Canyon. He remembered the assignment, everything riding on it.

He had to finish the job. Just as he had to make certain that she hadn't recognized him.

Standing in front of the bathroom mirror, he stared at the mussed hair growing thick across his brow, at the distinctive shade of his light-toned eyes staring back at him.

He shuffled through his toiletry bag and found the electric razor he kept there. It buzzed with efficiency when he activated it. Running his hand once more through his thick hair, he leaned close to the mirror and began his work.

Chapter 7

The gunshot wound victim was one of Dark Canyon's own boys in blue after a sting operation gone wrong. Detective Abraham Hatch was a twenty-year man on the job who'd been working to disrupt a cocaine supply route. The hundreds of empty miles surrounding Dark Canyon made it an ideal place for large stash movement.

Nick and his team had arrived ten minutes after a smuggler's bullet had entered and exited through Detective Hatch's left shoulder. Even with a through-and-through track, Nick had no idea what the extent of the damage was internally. The bullet could've hit bone on its way out. His longtime emergency medical tech, Raquel Perez, ensured that Hatch was breathing freely, that his airway was secure. They put him on high-flow oxygen and worked to control the bleeding with pressure bandages and direct pressure to both the entry and exit sites.

"Any other wounds?" their lieutenant, Marshall Dilinger, asked.

Nick had already questioned Hatch and exposed his chest, cutting away his clothes to assess for additional wounds. "No."

"Get him on a backboard," Dilinger advised. "We need to get him to Baldwin Memorial. The ER and surgical staff can determine more once they examine him."

Nick and Perez worked together to strap Hatch to the backboard. Perez went through the motions of applying a cervical collar to prevent movement.

As Perez and Dilinger moved Detective Hatch to the open doors of the ambulance, Nick exchanged a glance with the officer standing by. "Officer O'Connell," Nick said with a nod, recognizing him.

"He's going to be okay?" O'Connell asked.

Nick remembered that O'Connell had married Hatch's youngest daughter, Vada, last spring and rushed to assure him, "The bullet went through. The bleeding's currently under control, but it'll be up to the surgeons to determine whether any internal damage has occurred."

O'Connell nodded grimly. At the sound of a struggle, they both looked around to see one of the smugglers, a young man with a spotty growth of stubble crawling up his cheeks, resisting the restraining hold of Hatch's partner. Red-faced, sweat clinging to the skin of his neck, he looked to be little more than a teenager.

"Bastards have been moving through here too freely under the cover of night," O'Connell muttered. "They're pouring drugs into the cities. My cousin from Moab OD'ed two months ago. Been in a damn coma ever since."

"I'm sorry to hear that," Nick said, still watching the detective struggle with the smuggler.

The detective reached back for his cuffs. The smuggler took his shot, knocking his head back into the detective's nose. The detective grunted, his grip loosening on the smuggler's arms.

The kid didn't hesitate. He leaped for the chance of escape, bolting for the wide, empty embrace of Utah's dark countryside.

Nick and O'Connell moved at the same time to intercept him. O'Connell bobbed. Nick weaved.

Together, they took the kid down in a rough tangle of limbs, Nick's arm wrapped around the kid's middle. As soon as his arm made impact with the ground beneath the smuggler, he felt his wrist torque. Hot, sharp agony went through the joint, up into his arm.

"I've got him," O'Connell announced, cuffs out and snapping into place to lock the smuggler's wrists at the small of his back.

Nick rolled away, groaning.

"Malone?" Dilinger called from the ambulance. "You thinking about trying out for the force?"

He glanced at the smuggler's seething face, or what he could see of it in the flashing lights of the emergency vehicles. "I'm happy where I am, thanks," he decided, gaining his feet.

"You'll need to ice that," O'Connell pointed out as he waited for Hatch's partner to escort the suspect to the back of a squad car.

Nick tried moving his wrist. It screamed at him to stop. "I'm good," he lied and hopped into the back of the ambulance as the siren wailed.

Perez frowned at his lame hand, already running fluids for their patient. "Can you get him on the monitor?"

Nick was already in motion. His wrist wailed, but their patient's life was on the line.

He'd think about his wrist after he, Perez and Dilinger got the detective safely to Baldwin Memorial.

Sassy didn't walk to the emergency department. She ran. The color-coded lines down the corridor pointing visitors toward the different divisions of the hospital—

red for cardiology, blue for general surgery, green for radiology—blurred, giving her tunnel vision as her boots rapped against the floor, echoing through her ears.

She tackled the double doors to the ED open and stumbled to a halt in the waiting room, surrounded by people in various stages of pain or panic.

Her purse hung from her hand by the strap, all but dragging along the blinding-white tiled floor to the registration desk, where an efficient-looking man with a topknot greeted her warmly. "Sassy Colton. What are you doing here?"

"Evander," she said between pants. She pressed a hand to her ribs and fought for breath. "Nick came through here about twenty minutes ago. I was told he'd been brought to the ED."

"Oh, they didn't bring him in, sweetie," Evander explained, toying absently with the cord of his lanyard. "He walked in all on his own and would've left, too, if his lieutenant hadn't insisted on him getting his arm looked at."

"What's wrong with it?" Sassy asked. "Do you know?"

"Gina in triage said it may be broken."

"*His arm?*" she asked, incredulous.

"Wrist, I think," Evander said thoughtfully. He splayed his long, manicured fingers over his keyboard and click-clacked the keys to life. "Let's see. It looks like he's already been seen by a doctor. He referred him to Imaging."

Sassy swiped the hair from her eyes. It was still wet from the shower she'd hopped out of when she'd received multiple phone calls from Nick's EMT partner, Raquel Perez. "Look," she said, prepared to beg if necessary. "Do you think you could get me back there to see him? I know I'm not family. I know it probably goes against protocol. But you know his situation. His mom is in a long-term care facility and his dad..."

Evander waved his hand. "Say no more, girl. I'll buzz you in."

Sassy breathed a sigh of relief. "Evander Rosenberg, I'm going to kiss you right here in front of all these people."

He winked. "Wait until I'm off duty. The other admins are threatened by my good looks and excellent people skills. They've been cruising for a good reason to get me fired."

"A drink then," Sassy offered, "at the alehouse. Friday after work?"

"Make it the Bootleg," Evander countered. "They wrap up the week with line dancing and I'm all for it."

"A drink and a dance, then," Sassy decided.

"It's a date," he returned, hitting the switch to unlock the triage station's door from the outside. "Your man's behind curtain number three."

Your man... Those words blazed across her consciousness like an ill-fated comet whizzing in the wrong direction.

Gina in triage showed her onto the floor of the ED. She ignored the smells of antiseptic and bodily fluids, counting one, two closed curtains.

The third was open to reveal an empty bed with rumpled white linens.

He'd been here, she surmised. Wondering how long he'd spent in Imaging, she sat on the edge of the abandoned sheets and worked on some deep breathing exercises.

He was okay. Nick was okay. Raquel had been too rushed on the phone to offer Sassy details on Nick's status. Admittedly, all Sassy had really heard was *Nick... hurt...hospital...*

Sassy couldn't remember if she had washed the soap out of her hair before sprinting from the shower to the closet and haphazardly throwing on enough clothes to be deemed decent.

That's a stretch, she thought, eyeing the pointy toes of her boots. She'd gotten her hands on a black maxi skirt with a slit up the thigh. From her drawer, she'd blindly chosen an overlarge '90s crewneck grandpa sweater she'd stolen from her father, complete with russet and beige pattern. It was falling off one shoulder, displaying the full strap of the black lace bralette she'd snatched from the clean clothes basket almost as an afterthought. She attempted to draw the sweater neckline back up into place. In response, it slumped over the slope of her shoulder once more and she rolled her eyes.

Some of the panic was fading. Since her Bronco was still out of commission, she'd had to knock on her neighbors' door to ask if she could borrow their minivan. They were a young couple she'd bonded with when their twin girls had painted their shared driveway with hearts, right up to Sassy's porch steps. When they had come over to apologize, she'd assured them that she thought the trail of hearts livened up the place and that the girls could come use her paints after school, if they liked.

The key fob to the minivan bit into her palm and she relaxed her grip on it. The indention in her palm told the story of the tense few minutes it had taken her to get from her neighborhood to the hospital, all the while assuming the worst. She'd thought of Ava's kidnapping, Fern's memory of her abductors, the body of Annie Ross, who had been found in Dark Canyon Wilderness, and the frickin' Ford that had nearly taken her out on the sidewalk this morning. She'd thought of the warnings that Dark Canyon wasn't the safe place many assumed it was anymore. Terror had taken a firm hold as she'd envisioned Nick locked in the cross-hairs of whoever was attempting to turn their hometown into the Upside Down from *Stranger Things*.

If she lost Nick...if *anything* happened to him...what was she supposed to do? He wasn't simply her best friend. He was often the first person she spoke to in the morning... the last person she spoke to at night...the person she spent the most time with...

They'd done life together for so long, she couldn't remember what it had been like before they'd sat down to lunch together in the cafeteria and she'd been grossed out over the egg salad sandwich his mother had packed him. She could still remember the dubious expression on his face as she'd thrown her potato chips in with the pickles, mashed them all together between bread slices and devoured hers. She'd agreed to take his carton of chocolate milk off his hands when he'd offered to trade it for the Campbell's Soup thermos filled with almond milk her mother had placed neatly inside her backpack.

His cartoon lunchbox had been their chief conversation piece before the bell had rung, signaling lunch was at an end. They'd agreed to meet back at the same table the next day. The day after that, they'd met at the playground, then raced her cousins down Dark Canyon's biggest hill on their bicycles. Nick had earned major points from the Colton boys when he pulled ahead by more than a car length.

Nerd Boy's a speed demon! Ryan had crowed while Sassy and the others whooped.

From that day, Nerd Boy and his lunchbox had been honorary members of the Colton clan.

Sassy had loved him from the moment he'd taken the injustice of drinking her mother's almond milk off her hands. In a way, she'd lost part of him after his father's death. It had taken a long time for him to recuperate physically. Emotionally and psychologically, his recovery was still taking place.

That boy at the lunch table hadn't made it out of Dark Canyon the day of the flood.

As she'd driven to the hospital tonight, she'd remembered the first time she'd seen him after his rescue. The look in his eyes hadn't been haunted. It hadn't even been sad. Instead, his eyes had looked glassy. Almost dead. The absence of light…of *Nick*, of the essence that was him… had scared her to the marrow of her bones.

He couldn't go back there again. She couldn't watch him go back there.

His wrist, she remembered Evander saying. *It's just his wrist. He can handle that. It's completely fixable.*

Even if it was broken, they would *both* handle it.

She heard the low murmur of Nick's voice and sprang to her feet. He appeared in the parting of the privacy curtain, alongside a salt-and-pepper man in a white coat and scrubs.

Sassy bit her lower lip, but it stubbornly refused to stop wobbling. He was fine. He was on his feet. An angry red scrape rode the edge of his cheekbone, and he cradled his right wrist against the center of his chest. But he was alive and well and…

"Damn it," she hissed when tears crested her eyes. She stepped forward. "Goddamn it, Nick."

He had the sense to move his wrist out of the way before she threw her arms around his neck and buried her face in his shoulder, refusing to let him see how scared she'd been.

After a moment's shock, he bracketed his uninjured arm low around the dip in her waist. He groaned. "Perez called you."

"It should've been you," she chastised. "If it'd been your

voice on the phone, I wouldn't have…" *Freaked out. Lost my mind. Jumped headlong into hysteria.*

"I'm all right," he claimed. "Really. It's not that bad." All the same, she felt his arm tighten around her. "About earlier—"

"I don't want to talk about it," she said, shaking her head firmly. She did not want to see the business end of the F-150 flashing before her eyes again.

"This is nothing," he dismissed. "My life was never in danger. You, on the other hand…"

"I'm not in pain," she pointed out. "You are. Please, can we just focus on you?"

His cheek pressed to her temple. Slowly, he took a long, cleansing breath. She felt his lungs expand then release against hers, and that affirmation of life was more soothing than any lullaby ever had been.

"So this is the wife, I take it?" the doctor drawled.

Nick stiffened. Sassy took a step back, her hands on his shoulders. She eyed the doctor. "Depends. Do you kick nonspouses out?"

"Hardly," the doctor answered.

"Good," Sassy said. She leaned toward him and lowered her voice meaningfully. "Because I could take you."

"She means well," Nick said, his voice gravelly. He cleared his throat.

"What's the prognosis?" Sassy asked, examining the wrist for herself. The skin around it was red and noticeably swollen.

"We took some pictures," the doctor explained, gesturing them both toward the bed. It felt natural for them to sit side by side, hip to hip, as the doctor toggled the monitor of the computer out of sleep mode. He clattered away at the keyboard for a moment. The mouse moved under his cupped hand. As images came onscreen, he shifted the monitor so they could more easily view Nick's X-rays.

"There doesn't appear to be a break," the doctor observed. "My guess is you've got a partially torn ligament."

"So, a sprain," Nick parsed.

The doctor's head bobbed. "Appears so."

Nick tried to wiggle his fingers and hissed at the movement. Sassy held his wrist to keep it stable, careful not to put pressure on the swollen area. "So what do we do about it?" she asked.

"We?" Nick said.

She turned to find a pained half smile desperately trying to hang on to the lower half of his face. "Someone needs to take care of you."

"Sassy, it's just a sprain."

"Will he be out of work?" she asked the doctor, smoothing over Nick's dismissal and ignoring his sigh of frustration.

"He'll need to take some time off," the doctor acknowledged.

Nick cursed. "I can't."

Sassy shook her head. "You think Dilinger is going to let you work like this?"

"I don't have a choice," he said adamantly. Strain appeared in the spots of color growing on his cheeks. "You know I don't."

She'd told him not to take tonight's shift because she'd known he needed more rest before going back to work. She'd warned him about spreading himself too thin. Even now that he was staring burnout in the face, he was still in denial. "I'll take care of everything."

"My bills are not your responsibility," he said, dark eyes boring into hers.

"But you are," she insisted, answering him cutting look for cutting look before turning back to the doctor who had watched the exchange with interest. "How long?"

"Optimistically?" he said. "Three weeks. But that's following all the protocol—using the RICE method consistently, no cheating. Also wearing a brace."

Nick cursed under his breath, his head low. She could see the flush crawling across his neck as his agitation refused to rest.

"What's the RICE method?" Sassy asked.

Nick answered from low in his throat, "Rest. Ice. Compression. Elevation."

Sassy nodded. She laid her hand across the tense line of his shoulders.

"With the right amount of physical therapy, range of motion should return the strength of your wrist gradually. Proper care will let you return to your regular activities sooner, but this too will be gradual."

"He's in pain," Sassy said. The rolling cloud of discontent practically boiled off him, reminding her again of the pain and trauma she'd watched him go through years ago. Emotional pain, physical pain…the lines blurred when they were significant. Nick had lived through enough to last a lifetime. "Is there something you can give him for it?"

"I don't want a narcotic," Nick said firmly.

"No narcotics," Sassy echoed. His mother's addiction had been rooted in opioids. In the wake of her husband's death, Margot had fallen and broken her clavicle. Her doctor had prescribed narcotics to aid with her recovery. Long after her collarbone had healed, Margot had continued to treat her emotional pain with oxycodone, going so far as to buy the pills from a street dealer when her prescriber stopped refilling the order.

Nick had never had issues with prescription drugs, but after watching his mother fall down that rabbit hole, he'd been careful not to go down the same route.

"Ibuprofen might take the edge off," the doctor suggested. "But for the next twenty-four to forty-eight hours, you'll experience the worst symptoms. I can give you a muscle relaxer to help you manage them."

"A sedative?" Nick asked dully. "Is that really necessary?"

The doctor weighed Nick's grimace, which had again taken hold of his features. "Like I said, a strict regimen of care and prevention will get you back to work sooner. The muscle relaxer won't help in the long run, but it will decrease the pain and maybe some of the swelling in the short term."

Nick closed his eyes. Sassy rubbed his shoulder, wishing she could reverse everything for him—the pain, the sprain, the fact that he was overworked, the load he carried on his shoulders every day… "We can throw them out after tomorrow," she told him. "Hell, I'll flush them down the toilet if it makes you feel better. You're staying with me anyway."

Finally, his eyes lifted to hers again, searching. "I am?"

She would've balled up her fist and punched him in the shoulder like old times if she wasn't afraid of hurting him more. "Of course you are."

"What about Riot?" he asked.

"I'm more than capable of handling you both."

Impossibly, his mirth shone through the pain. The smile that split his mouth and the light in his eyes was genuine.

Her reaction was visceral. Seismic. The softness of his eyes, the shifting lines around his mouth…they were so familiar. And yet, the fluttering in her belly and the increase in her pulse were not. Something inside her splintered and broke, opening floodgates she hadn't known were there in the first place. Need and want clashed. Awareness drew the skin at the base of her spine up tight. Goose bumps pebbled across her skin while the fluttering in her belly sank lower, turned liquid and warm. Devastating.

She'd known...damn it, she'd *always* known that Nick was a fine-ass man. She'd never been thirsty for him.

Until now.

She felt lightheaded, so she broke off eye contact and sipped at the air, reasserting herself as the doctor went on with his instructions.

This was wrong. Never...not once in the twenty years she'd known him had she caught feelings for Nick. Why now, when he needed her to take care of him and Riot and everything else? When he'd needed her in the past, she'd planted her feet and dug in. Now she felt like she was teetering on the end of a baseball bat.

She clutched her knees, digging her nails into the material of her skirt. *Get yourself together, Haseya, or get out of this man's way, because he does not* need *this right now and you love him far too much to make his burdens heavier.*

Chapter 8

"Is this a minivan?" Nick asked after he buckled himself into the passenger seat and Sassy took her place at the wheel.

"The Bronco's in the shop again," she explained. "I borrowed this from a neighbor."

He dropped the back of his head against the headrest, closing his eyes. The muscle relaxer the doc had given him was already starting to take effect. Drowsiness slunk in from the corners of his mind, but he clung stubbornly to wakefulness. He wasn't going to let Sassy carry him into her house. "Smells like stale Cheetos and soccer cleats in here."

"I think it smells nice." When he slanted her a sidelong look, she shrugged and started the engine. "Beggars can't be choosers, can they?"

She'd avoided looking him in the eye since she'd declared he and Riot were coming home with her. "You don't have to do this."

"Drive a minivan?"

"Keep me overnight," he corrected. "We're not kids anymore. I can manage on my own."

"I don't want you to just manage," she said. "I want you to get better. *You* want you to get better. The only way to get you to that point at the earliest opportunity is for me to take care of you. I'm sorry if you don't like it." She gripped the shifter to take the van out of Park, then stopped and shook her head. "Wait. Scratch that. I'm *not* sorry. You know why? Because I love you. Even if you don't know how to ask for help. Even when you're being a stubborn pain in the ass. Even when you get in your own way. If tough love's what you need, that's what I'm going to give you because, damn it, I care. I care too much to watch you suffer, and you're going to have to learn to live with that."

He struggled for the right words. He struggled to speak at all. His mouth opened, closed, gaped. She'd said a lot… so much…and yet three little words kept battering that space between his brain and his ears in a mindless echo.

…I love you… I love you… I love you…

He blinked. Made himself blink again. The buzz off the cyclobenzaprine must really be sinking in, because suddenly all he could see or focus on was the striking line of her profile. The black sheen of her hair in the dash lights. The way she bit her lip, like she did when she was nervous.

Why was she nervous? His mind refused to connect the dots for him. It was too muddled.

She exhaled sharply, her shoulders settling. "I didn't mean to lecture you."

"It's fine," he said before an awkward silence entrenched itself in the cab of the minivan.

She drove to his apartment and made him sit tight as she used her key to make entry. Minutes later, she returned with Riot on a leash and a bag of his things. "Don't worry," she said as she rolled open the door to the middle row of seats. "I packed plenty of underwear."

He closed his eyes and groaned. The last thing he needed was to imagine her touching his underwear. He felt Riot's whiskers, coarse against his elbow, and slung his uninjured arm around his neck, leaning down to kiss his snoot. "Hey, boy. Miss me?"

"I got his bed, food, toys... Anything else you two kiddos need?"

"My place isn't far from yours," he noted. "If we need anything, we can come back."

She rolled the passenger door closed before walking around to the driver's door. "Ready to go home?" she turned to ask Riot affectionately.

Home. It had always been where she was, hadn't it? As the van started rolling again, he turned his face away from hers, afraid of what might be written on it.

Sassy went through her house, Nick-proofing everything. She'd bought the place two years ago for its potential, which meant trip hazards of paint cans and drop cloths, loose trim pieces and nail guns were strewn everywhere. She made the males wait just inside the door while she rearranged everything. "It's coming along," she observed when she was done. "Don't you think?"

Nick's eyelids drooped slightly from the medication, but he couldn't hide the uncertain blip that eclipsed his face as he and Riot exchanged a look before braving the first step into her living space. "It's...something," he said.

She yanked a paint cloth off the sofa and piled it in an empty corner. "Come on. I got the crown molding up. I finished painting the kitchen and dining rooms. That was a bitch."

"Maybe because you changed your mind about the colors after you started rolling?" he ventured, peering into the dining room on the right. He stopped in his tracks, letting go of Riot's leash. "Wow."

She came to stand next to him, crossing her arms as she

admired the black-and-white chevron pattern she'd rendered there. It complemented the black trim pieces, the white tiles and the dark tabletop she'd paid way too much for at a yard sale. "I thought about curtains, but I like all the light that comes through the front window." Said window took up the entire north wall. She glanced at him. "What do you think?"

His mouth fumbled for a moment. When he finally strung words together, his voice was a stunned whisper. "Sassy. You did amazing."

She pressed her lips together to hide a wide grin. "Don't flatter me."

"When do I ever lie you?"

She narrowed her eyes. "How drunk are you right now?"

He hedged, avoiding her insightful stare.

She pursed her lips. "Sit down. Take a load off. I'll get you something to eat."

"I don't need—"

"Nick," she warned, setting his bags near the hall that led to both bedrooms. "You're on heavy medication. You need something to eat."

As he sank to a chair at the table, he lifted his ACE-wrapped hand. The RN at the hospital had kept the wrap loose to accommodate his swelling. "Do you have anything that doesn't involve a fork or spoon?"

She frowned, realizing that he had injured his dominant arm, and cursed under her breath as she walked into the adjoining kitchen. That would make his recovery that much more challenging.

She and her cousins had spent several weekends knocking out the kitchen's west wall so she could expand the space, adding an island and a pantry and room enough for more than one person to work around the stove, sink and prep areas. Not that she cooked overmuch. And not that she didn't live alone or planned on changing that.

Yet when she'd seen the place for the first time, she'd wanted the kitchen to be big enough for her whole family—not just her mother, father and grandparents but her aunts, uncles and cousins, too. She'd pictured herself hosting Thanksgivings, raising a glass to her aunts as they huddled over the stove and joining her cousins and Nick in a game of touch football in the big, sprawling backyard while her uncles sipped brewskies on the patio around the Weber.

She opened both doors of the fridge and observed her options. Takeout containers populated the space. Nick had suggested she start writing the dates of origin on top of them so she no longer had to guess how long the entrées had been residing in her fridge. Still, she made sure to sniff the contents as she took out boxes and set them on the counter. She filled a plate with crab rangoons from the Chinese place, stuffed mushrooms from that little restaurant on the corner of Fig Street that both she and Nick frequented, and chicken wings she'd snatched from the Sauce Spot for lunch that afternoon. In the junk drawer, she snagged some Wet Ones for wing-related cleanups. He still had a thing for milk, so she poured him a glass and took his meal to the table.

His head lay on his good arm on the table in a defeated posture she couldn't stand to see. "If you don't cheer up, Malone, I'm going to have to start flossing."

"Flossing?"

"Yeah, you know..." She started to execute the dance move in a flurry of arms and hips.

He raised his head, half smiling, half wincing as he watched her through the haze of sedatives and bemusement. "I'm not sure it works like that..."

"Then show me how it's done, Nick," she countered

without stopping. She threw in the Humpty because it felt right and she was determined to cheer him up.

His smile strengthened. He broke into a laugh. "You're insane."

She gave in, gripping the back of a chair to catch her breath. "Damn, I'm out of shape."

His chuckle faded away as his thoughts weighed on him again. "I forgot about my mom."

"What about your mom?" she asked, nudging his plate toward him.

"I promised to bring Riot back tomorrow. Some of the residents were in PT when I took him to River House this morning and missed out on their pet therapy session."

"What time?" she asked.

"Eight a.m."

She waved a hand. "I've got that."

"Sassy, you can't do everything."

"Nick," she countered. "Tomorrow's Saturday. The gallery doesn't open until ten. If I get tied up at River House with Riot, Soledad can open for me. It's no big deal. I can give Margot the quilt my mom made for her and take Riot to the dog park after his session to stretch his legs."

Nick sighed. "You're taking on way too much for me."

"I didn't wake up today to be meek," she declared. "What makes you think tomorrow will be any different?"

"You're incredible," he murmured, eyes softening on her as they had in the ER. "You always have been."

She swallowed when her bones began to melt and forced herself to look away so she could tear open the little packages of Wet Ones. "Be a good boy and eat your takeout."

Nick nodded at the offerings. "The best Dark Canyon has to offer."

"I thought so." He had propped his wrapped hand on the

edge of the table. She resisted the urge to trail her fingers along the back of it in a caress. "Does it still hurt?"

"It's the swelling that's driving me crazy," he admitted.

"I might have something for that," she said, backtracking into the kitchen. In the powder room beyond it, she opened the mirrored cabinet and gathered her essential oils. In a small medicine cup, she mixed an ounce of jojoba, a carrier oil that could be applied directly to the skin, with fifteen drops of ginger.

Rogue twined around her ankles, meowing irritably from the back of her throat.

Sassy glanced into the hallway and found Riot hovering, ears forward, tail milling. She let out a laugh. "He just wants to play," she told the cat. "Go. Be social."

Rogue sat on the bathmat, staring up at her with insouciant eyes as she wound her tail around her paws.

"You're going to have to get used to him," Sassy lectured. "And look at him. He's clearly harmless."

The noise Rogue made could only be classified as a growl of discontentment.

"Be nice," Sassy said, stepping around her. She went back to the dining room, pulling up a chair next to Nick's.

"What's that?" he asked, frowning at the medicine cup.

Pleased to see his plate half-empty, she answered, "Massage oil. May I?"

He nodded when she indicated removing his ACE wrap.

She did so with the utmost care. Laying his arm palm up on the tabletop, she performed gentle swipes with her thumbs across the swollen area. "Does that hurt?"

Despite a mouthful of food, his eyelids were at half-mast. "I can't really feel anything right now."

"Okay. I'm going to dab a little bit of oil near the inside of your elbow to make sure you don't have a skin reaction."

He watched as she rubbed the liquid in a small circle over his skin with the pad of her forefinger. She waited while he finished eating. When a rash didn't occur, she felt confident enough to go forward with the massage. "Hold still," she told him. "I don't want to jostle your wrist, even if you can't feel anything."

His lips twitched. "I thought I was the one with med training."

"I learned a thing or two in the House of Bly," she reminded him, referring to her artful, holistic mother. "Close your eyes. Try to relax."

"Any laxer and I'll be drooling on myself," he said but shut his eyes in easy obedience.

Careful not to put too much pressure on the injured area, she used both thumbs to sweep the oil across the swollen surface, rubbing it in generously. She didn't know if it would work, but she had to do *something* other than watch him suffer.

His chin drooped toward his chest and his respirations slowed. His shoulders lowered not in defeat but in relief. The smell of the ginger mingled with the scent of hardworking man. The musk of clean sweat and earth didn't always come from swinging a hammer. Sometimes it came in the form of a sweet-faced paramedic who didn't quit. Quitting wasn't in Nick's vocabulary. He gave one hundred percent to those around him each and every day, even if it drained him. Even if he had nothing left when he returned home.

His head came to rest on her shoulder. Though the oil had already been absorbed into his skin, she didn't stop the movement of her thumbs as she worked them down his forearm, over the heel of his hand and back up.

He groaned deep in his throat. "Feels amazing," he whispered. Then he did something that made her thumbs stop working and her heart wobble.

He turned his nose into her hair. There, he buried it and carried a long inhale deep into his lungs.

He was smelling her hair.

"You smell so good," he breathed.

Her mouth dropped. "L-like paint?"

"Mmm. And wood stain." He sniffed again, like she was in heat and they were both wolves living wild in the canyons. "And pomegranates."

His voice had dropped to a low rasp. "Oh," she said, unable to form anything more intelligible than that.

He nuzzled his nose through her hair and found the line of her throat. Then she felt his mouth against her skin and nearly lost her senses. Her blood rushed to a boil, her heart thrummed and her belly ached with what she feared was longing. "Nick…"

He stiffened. A moment later, he cursed and pulled back, lifting his head. "Goddamn it, Sassy," he said, not meeting her eye. "I'm sorry."

She saw the color in his cheeks and mustered a reassuring smile. "You're high on muscle relaxants," she said, trying desperately to make light of what he'd done…what she felt. "I think I can forgive you." Still, she carefully lifted her touch from his wrist and helped him back into his ACE wrap. "You should probably rest now."

"Right," he said, bobbing a nod, his eyes on the floor between them.

"Can you get to bed?"

"Sure." He stood slowly, using his free arm to take his weight. He took a step and tripped over the chair leg.

She made a dive, throwing herself under his shoulder

to catch him. "You good?" she wheezed. He was built like a linebacker and weighed as much.

"I told you. I got this," he declared and promptly lurched toward the wrong exit.

"You got this, all right." Slinging her arm around his waist, she propelled him toward the archway leading out into the living room. "Bedroom's this way, dungeon master."

He tilted his head toward her. "Did you just lay a D&D reference on me?"

"I did."

He whistled. His cheek rested against the top of her head. "That's hot."

"Okay, you need to stop talking," she warned, guiding him around the couch. They had to thread the needle through a freshly painted doorway. Her bedroom was to the left. She led him past the hall bathroom to the right into the guest room. "I'm mostly using it for storage until I can get all my projects completed." She made him sit on the edge of the bed. Riot hopped onto the quilt next to him, lavishing Nick with ear kisses.

If he couldn't walk to the bedroom, Sassy doubted he could take off his own pants.

Oh, boy.

"I'll be back," she said and nearly stepped on Rogue at the entrance to the bedroom. She sought Nick's overnight bag and brought it and the dog bed to the guest room. She arranged the bed for Riot, adding a blanket on top of it because the room felt chilly. As she pawed through Nick's clothes in the duffel, she took out what he would need for bed.

By this point, he had sprawled across the quilt, his arms around Riot, who was planted halfway across his chest, sniffing every inch of his uniform shirt. She wondered if this was routine for them.

"Who's my smoochie?" Nick cooed as Riot licked his chin lovingly. "Are you my smoochie-poo?"

Sassy cleared her throat. "I'm going to take off your shoes," she announced.

He lifted a hand in acknowledgment before going back to telling Riot what a good smoochie-poo he was.

She pulled each shoe off by the heel, laid them side by side against the wall. His socks joined them.

She eyed his tree-trunk thighs underneath his uniform pants and pursed her lips. *Keep your thoughts clean, Haseya*, she schooled herself before pressing one knee into the bed. She found the buckle of his belt and started to navigate it.

Nick stopped cooing. He tilted his head to see her around Riot's large one. "Whatcha doing?"

She gritted her teeth. "Undressing you."

He raised a brow. "You've never done that before."

"Nope." She finally worked the buckle loose. Next, she attacked the clasp of his pants. Then the zipper. If she found Marvel superhero tighty-whities under his duds, she was going to tease him for the rest of his life. Maybe that would boot her sudden attraction to him to the curb. Superhero undies would surely make her libido remember that Nick was her friend. Nothing more, nothing less.

Or would they? Her pulse skipped. Her mind whirled. The way he watched her... Damn it, it wasn't helping.

Ah hell. He could be wearing Sesame Street underwear and she wouldn't find him any less doable at this point, would she? Her love for Nick had been unconditional when it was platonic. Now that all her adult lady parts were seeing him in a new, inconvenient light, it wasn't going to be any different.

To put herself out of her misery, she yanked the beltline

of his pants down, careful not to take his underwear—thank the maker, he wasn't going *commando*—with them. "Lift your hips," she said when the pants didn't give.

He lifted them in a half-hearted bridge pose, laughing openly and fully when Riot rolled up his chest and landed on his face.

She managed to wrest the pants free from his hips and kept tugging until they were at his knees.

No superheroes and no kid's cartoons, she discovered. Just midnight-black boxer briefs made of some soft poly material that made her want to touch...

No touching. We are not *touching.* Even if said boxer briefs hugged attributes she hadn't known he was packing... She saw now why Nick's past girlfriends had found their sexy time with him satisfying. Why they practically glowed around him after nights well spent.

She was thinking about Nick's penis. *Nick Malone's penis.* And she was interested. Intrigued, one might say.

Her face was so flushed, she felt like she'd stuck her head inside a boiler. Perhaps it was the fires of hell warning her she'd gone too far. *Get thy mind out of the gutter while ye still can, Haseya Colton...*

"Sassy?"

She finally yanked his pant legs free and almost fell back against the wall with the effort. "Hmph?"

Nick was watching her again with soft eyes. "Thanks for this."

Don't do that. She wanted to scream it at him. Instead, she extracted his wallet, keys and phone from his pockets and arranged them on the nightstand. She caught Rogue's narrowed stare. The cat was now sitting on top of the dresser across the room, judging. "Don't mention it," she said.

"You're my lifeboat."

She was going to have to move the dog off the man to get him undressed. Neither of them were going to be happy about it. She was also going to have to get on the bed to do either of those things. Fisting her hands around his pajamas, she wished for strength over this unforeseen need to be wicked with him. *So very wicked.* "A whole boat?"

His hands paused in their caressing of Riot's coat. "That came out wrong, didn't it?"

"No," she argued, because she'd always felt the same way about him. He was the one she turned to in a storm, too. "It was sweet."

"I tried unbuttoning my shirt." He shrugged, eyes knit closed now. There was a dreamy expression on his face. Riot was already snoring soundly, his brick head nestled comfortably against Nick's shoulder. "Didn't work."

She scooted the dog over. He woke enough to whine in protest before nestling close in the warm space against Nick's side, under his arm. Sassy quickly undid the buttons of Nick's work shirt. Underneath, he wore nothing. She saw the dark arrow of hair over his tight stomach, the knots of his shoulders, his rosy half-dollar man nipples, and bit the inside of her cheek because, again, *dayum*. By the time she'd gotten him out of the shirt, she was a fermenting brew of impossible wants and needs.

He curled around Riot on top of the quilt, his hair tousled, his expression slack.

She contemplated the firm line of his back. He had dimples at the base of his spine, right above the line of his boxer briefs. How had she never noticed that before?

She wasn't going to get him on the pillow. Or under the quilt. He was down for the count, and she knew how heavy he was. She sat back on her heels, dropped her face into her hands and scrubbed, feeling tired and defeated and frustrated in more ways than she could ever say out loud to anyone. "What are you doing?" she chided herself.

Twenty years of friendship. Twenty years. Was she going to flush that all away—their whole history—because she hadn't dealt with her own needs properly of late? Because they'd gone hankering after the closest available object of her affection?

You can't have him, she told them, tracing the profile of his sleeping face with her gaze. *I can't have him. Not like that.*

She found another blanket in the closet and arranged it over his and Riot's forms. Then she turned out the lamp, gathered Rogue in her arms and left them to their repose.

Running across Haseya Colton in town had been accidental.

Driving by her house at 2:00 a.m. wasn't. He couldn't kid himself. He'd looked up her address. He'd navigated the street view of the cookie-cutter house with its shabby-looking gingerbread trim and sagging front porch on Google Maps. Before he knew it, he'd grabbed his keys and gloves and was out the door.

Her neighborhood wasn't gated, but it was pincushion quiet. The sound of dogs barking in the distance was the only thing he heard when he parked down the street from her house and shut off his engine. No light touched the windows from within. She didn't have a garage or carport, and there was no vehicle in the driveway.

If she wasn't home, where was she?

The thought that she might be warming the covers of someone else's bed made him grip the steering wheel until the leather creaked under his palms.

It wasn't his decision to get out of the nondescript rental

car he'd obtained that afternoon after the sidewalk debacle. Like jerking the truck wheel in her direction this morning or leaving his house tonight, his body went into motion. He fumbled for the pin light in his pocket, chastising himself every step of the way. What was he doing? If he walked away now, he'd stay under the radar. If he went forward, he'd get caught before he could complete the job that would set him up for life.

Finally, he'd have the security he craved—that he deserved. He hadn't gone through what he'd gone through or lost everything he had along the way to get picked up outside Haseya Colton's house by the cops.

He didn't see any activity behind the closed blinds of her neighbors' houses. The neighborhood had turned a blind eye to the street.

In his pocket, he felt the hard, cold edge of the silver-and-turquoise cuff he'd swiped off her desk. He tightened his fist around it as he walked right up to the window of her home.

There were no curtains, no blinds. He saw a dining room table, chairs and patterned black-and-white walls in the dim light from the street corner.

A single plate had been left on the table and a pair of fur-lined boots had been left haphazardly near the archway to the next room.

He felt that stir in his blood again, the one that was almost indistinguishable from lust.

Apparently, stealing from Haseya wasn't the only high he could get off on.

Moving around the side of the house, he kept his steps light and his head low. In his ski mask and black hoodie, he was a shadow within shadows.

The gate to her fenced-in backyard hung drunkenly at an angle. He kicked it with the toe of his boot.

It gave easily, issuing the only invitation he needed.

He stepped into her domain, keeping close to the house. He sidestepped a pile of construction debris—mostly demo work, from what he could tell. On the back deck, a saw had been set up with trim pieces of varying lengths scattered around it.

He eyed the back of the house, trying to decide which window would give him a clear view of her bedroom. Potentially, of her.

His body flushed with heat in the cold night, surprising in its intensity. The winter grass was sparse, and his boots squelched through mud as he crossed the steps of the deck.

His footsteps didn't make a sound on the wooden slats. He was a mountain lion stalking a sleek winter fox, cloaked by night. Sly. Unseen.

Hungry.

His heart thundered inside his head. His perception swam liquidly through the haze of his excitement.

He didn't realize he was standing at her back door until his breath fogged the glass of the half-light entrance.

He didn't realize his hand was on the knob until it turned under his hand.

Unlocked.

He heard his own sharp, ragged breathing. He hadn't planned this, any of it.

And yet…she'd left the door unlocked. Open.

For him.

He pushed the door wide. The rusted hinges gave a plaintive shriek.

The alarming bay of a dog's howl brought him up short of entering Haseya's silent abode.

Chapter 9

Nick propped his head against his uninjured hand. He felt like he was still floating on the sedative, heavy and listless.

Sassy plonked a coffee mug on the table beneath his nose.

He grunted in gratitude.

"How'd you sleep, caveman?" she asked as her hand came to rest against his shoulder.

Was what he'd done last night in her guest bed sleeping? He'd had to climb and claw his way out of it. When he'd finally managed to open his eyes, it had felt like his eyelids were doing dead lifts. He'd half expected to find himself locked inside a coffin, six feet under.

Summoning the energy to answer her inquiry, he lifted his wrapped hand in an empty gesture and winced when the pain gnawed at him. The swelling had gone down somewhat, but the discomfort wasn't going anywhere anytime soon.

"You were pretty out of it last night."

He dragged his gaze up to hers. She snatched her eyes away from his in a guilty motion that made no sense. Wetting his throat, he gripped the handle of the mug and noted the half-moon circles under her eyes. "What kept you awake?" he rasped.

She avoided looking at him again. "I don't know," she said, concentrating hard on the spoon she dragged through the coffee to mix in her go-to caramel creamer. "I just... couldn't settle."

He frowned. So not only was he burdening her with his presence, her worries over him were keeping her up at night. He scowled at the ACE wrap. *Nice going, jackass.*

"I think Riot had trouble staying asleep," Sassy pointed out. "He started going crazy around two o'clock this morning."

Nick shook his head and rubbed a hand over his face to chase the droopy feeling from the muscles there. He needed a cold shower and a sprint around the block to bring him to wakefulness. "I didn't hear him."

"Can he open doors?"

At first, the question didn't make sense. He had to chew over it for a minute before the meaning came together. "I don't think so. Why?"

"When I got to him, he was standing on the back deck," she explained. "I've never heard him bark like that before. It took me a couple minutes to convince him to come back inside."

Nick's frown deepened. "The door was open?"

She nodded. "Wide-open. If he didn't open it, then the wind must've done it?" she said in question, as if trying to riddle it out herself. A narrow divot of confusion dug between her eyebrows.

He set his teeth. "Do you not lock your door?"

She sighed at him. "Not this again."

"Sassy," he said, coming awake in increments. The incredulity helped. "After what happened at the gallery—"

"Nothing happened at the gallery. I showed you the

video feed. You agreed there was nothing in the footage to suggest anyone had been there."

The chair's legs scraped across her new floors as he pushed it back and ducked through the archway. He ran his hand along the wall to steady himself as his balance tipped slightly and righted slowly. Part of his mind was still back in her guest bed under her grandmother's quilt, wearing nothing but boxer briefs and drool on his face.

How he'd gotten there he had no idea. Had she put him to bed?

Was it her who stripped him of his shirt, slacks and shoes?

He could only hope he hadn't said something dumb as she tucked him in like a toddler.

The door still wasn't locked.

He cursed and twisted the knob. The hinges creaked noisily as he swung the door open.

At the sight of the deck, his blood froze. "Sassy."

"Look, Nick," she said as she approached. "I don't need a lecture."

He swung the door open wider, stepping aside for her to see the porch boards.

She stopped. "What the hell is that?"

"Those," he said, bringing the words up from the base of his throat, "are footprints."

She began to shake her head. Her mouth opened. He could see an explanation rising to the forefront of her mind and cut her off swiftly.

"Someone tried to break into your house last night."

"No," she said, her denial automatic. Her head shook listlessly. "Why would someone do that? There's nothing here but secondhand furniture and my artwork. No one wants that. I don't have anything that anyone would want."

He ran his gaze over her frame. She wore fuzzy leopard-print pajama pants, the garden boots she'd walked Riot in before he rose from the guest room like Dracula on the backslide of a blood binge and a loose-fitting crop top with the year 1491 on full display. It slacked over the point of one smooth, dusk-colored shoulder. Her hair was loose. It splayed over both shoulders. The ends tickled her elbows.

She was fiercely independent. She liked living alone. She was also vibrant and capable and strong. Yet he knew he could wrap his thumb and forefinger around her wrist. He knew if someone had wanted to get into her house, they could have.

He knew that if they'd wanted to catch her unawares, they could have. If it hadn't been for Riot...

Nick felt sick. His stomach roiled. He planted a hand against the doorjamb and fought a hard wave of nausea.

He spotted Riot on the floor at his feet, nose busily sniffing the threshold. He made a growling noise.

Fear dripped like ice down Nick's spine. He'd been passed out. He hadn't even heard Riot bark or Sassy investigating the disturbance. If the intruder had gotten past the dog and taken Sassy by surprise...attacked her...would Nick have slept through it?

The sick feeling doubled. He drew in an unsteady breath.

"Nick?" Sassy sounded scared now, as if despite her protests her thoughts had aligned with his.

"Call the police," he said as he traced the path of the mud-caked footprints over the porch boards, down the steps and into her yard.

Riot's appearance at River House had been canceled while Sassy and Nick dealt with the police. They took photographs of the boot prints outside her back door, fingerprinted her doorknobs and canvassed her neighbors for Ring camera footage.

None of them had it, she knew, because her neighborhood was supposed to be safe. The safest one in Dark Canyon. It was why she'd chosen the fixer-upper in the first place. When she felt like running or walking or biking, she could do so without worrying about her personal safety.

She wasn't stupid. She was a single female living alone. She slept with an aluminum baseball bat beside her bed. And normally, yes, she did lock the doors.

She'd forgotten to lock the back one after taking Riot out for a potty break before she turned in. There had been too much going through her mind. Too many what-ifs and what-to-dos and how-do-I-make-this-betters?

When she thought of someone trying to make entry into her home…a burglar…a predator…her mind automatically went into denial, because some part of her still believed that Dark Canyon was the safe place she'd grown up knowing it was.

If Riot hadn't woken her…

She shut down that train of thought as swiftly as it had come, making the turn for the reservation. "You didn't have to come with me. I'm fine."

Nick, in the passenger seat of his truck, didn't answer. There had been no answer from the mechanic when she'd called about her Bronco this morning. Nick had offered her the use of his truck when she'd told him about her afternoon plan to visit the Navajo Nation.

He'd been brooding. She pursed her lips, hating to think about his ashen face when he'd realized that someone had nearly gotten to her the night before.

She could practically hear the wheels of his mind spinning. He'd refused to take another sedative. All day, he'd sat in his pain, stewing in his thoughts.

The silence was an itch across her back. It was driving her crazy. She took a long breath, straightening in her seat. "Are you sure you're up for this? I'll be visiting at least four different houses."

"I'm sure," he grunted.

She tucked her tongue in her cheek. *Caveman*, she thought. Was this what he would do while he was off work—follow her around town, playing bodyguard, waiting to beat away the bad guys with one arm tied behind his back?

She reached for the radio dial. His preferred '80s station pumped the Talking Heads' "Burning Down the House" through the speakers. It sounded much better than his overthinking.

Tapping her fingers on top of the steering wheel, she bopped to the beat and eyed the side mirror. She got an eyeful of Riot's lolling tongue and flapping gums as he hung his head out the back window. *One of us is having fun*, she observed, unable to fight a grin.

The song changed into something slower and suggestive. Sassy stopped bopping because it made her think of man nipples and soft black boxer briefs and Nick curled up on her guest bed, happy in repose.

She hadn't thought about that…him…her reaction to him since breakfast. All the disturbingly good feelings she'd drowned in the night before had sunk to the back of her mind when she'd seen those footprints and accepted what they meant.

Unwilling to dwell on those things, she studied the terrain. "River's up," she noted.

"Mmm."

Behind her sunglasses, she rolled her eyes. She tried

again for conversation. "Must be all the snowmelt north of here. Did you notice it on your hike?"

He cleared his throat. "Closer to the canyons. Not so much on the south side."

Where he'd faced dehydration, she remembered.

When another love song started to play, he leaned over to flip the music off.

She sighed. "Nick, do we need to talk about this?"

"What?"

"You're not going to spend the next few weeks following me around everywhere, are you?"

"Maybe a little."

"Look at me," she demanded.

He turned his head. He'd left his sunglasses at the fire station and squinted against the light. A muscle in his jaw torqued as he ran his eyes across her face. The fear loosened from them, replaced by that impossible softness she'd seen last night.

She swallowed against the knot in her throat. He looked stressed, pained, worried and…scared. He was scared for her. "I'm okay," she said firmly, unable to look away. Her hand fumbled for his. "See?" She laced her fingers through his. "I'm right here. Nothing happened."

"It could have happened," he said quietly.

"But it didn't," she insisted. "I'll get new locks. I'll get a security system for the house. This won't happen again. Okay?"

"I don't know what I would've done if he'd gotten past Riot."

She didn't want to think about that. Closing off the possibilities, she faced the road again. To soothe him, she brought their joined fists to her face. She rested her cheek against the link, fighting the urge to close her eyes and sink into his strength.

She was supposed to be strong for him. It was his turn to lean on her, not the other way around.

"Do you think they're related?" he asked. "The alarm at the gallery and the break-in last night?"

"Nick, we've been over this. Nothing happened at the gallery. The alarm was a glitch."

He didn't seem convinced. Like a dog with a bone, he wasn't going to let his assumptions about what had happened that night at the gallery rest.

When it came to his own, Nick was nothing if not doggedly devoted.

He needed a distraction. Perhaps this trip to the rez was a good thing for him. "I'm stopping by Ava and Chay's house first. I want to see baby Gracie and check in with how Ava's doing."

He nodded, a fraction of his tension draining. "I haven't seen Gracie in weeks."

It had been Nick who had found her abandoned in the baby box at the fire station. He'd been as thrilled as Sassy had been when they learned that Ava and Chayton would be adopting the baby girl and starting a new life together on the reservation.

He reached across the console and turned the volume knob. The eighties' hit song made her smile across the cab at him. In answer, he turned it up to blast, and they both joined in as Freddie Mercury took them through the roller coaster highs and lows of the ballad.

She didn't let go of his hand as they crossed into Navajo territory.

Not only were Ava, Chayton and baby Gracie home, a whole Colton contingent had arrived before Sassy and Nick pulled into their driveway.

"What's going on?" Sassy asked apprehensively as Riot trotted after them into the house, drawn by the voices echoing from within.

Ava and Chayton's living room was bursting at the seams. On one couch sat Sassy's uncle Sam Colton, former mayor of Dark Canyon. Tall and lanky, he had packed himself onto the couch with the others like a sardine. Sam had lost his first wife, Kate—mother to Jacob, Mark and Noah—to cancer. Kate had been deceased for four years, and Sassy missed her dearly.

Wedged between Sam and the arm of the couch was Sassy's aunt Sherry Colton, Ava and Ryan's mother. She was married to Sam's brother, James. Sassy had envied Ava and Ryan growing up, thanks in large part to Sherry's free-spirited parenting style. They'd been able to do whatever they wanted. Though somewhat flighty at times, Sherry had stepped into Kate's shoes as the matriarch of the Colton family. Her warmth knew no bounds. She rocked slightly on the couch cushion, cooing at the baby in her arms.

Gracie, Sassy saw with a smile. Born Ella Ross, she wasn't even a year old and already she'd been through so much. The only clue to her family was the Navajo blanket she had been wrapped in before she was surrendered at the fire station. After DNA testing, it was determined that Annie Ross, the woman found dead in Dark Canyon Wilderness in January, was her mother. Chay, an officer with Navajo Tribal Affairs, had wanted her raised on the reservation. He and Ava had recently won guardianship of her. They were engaged to be married.

Chay and Ava sat hip to hip on the love seat. Sassy noted the protective hand Chayton laid across his fiancée's shoulders. They were still reeling somewhat from Ava's abduction in February. Ava visibly relaxed when she recognized

Sassy and rose to greet them. "I forgot you were coming," she said. "My parents called this morning and said to expect the whole gang. I barely had time to rustle up a meal."

"What's the occasion?" Sassy asked as she drew her cousin into a hug.

"Colton Foundation meeting," she said. "They all wanted to check in with Gracie, so they decided to kill two birds with one stone."

Sassy wrinkled her nose. "I always hated that saying."

"Me, too," Ava agreed. Her eyes widened on Nick. "You brought Nicholas!"

"I insisted on tagging along," he said, bringing her into a one-armed embrace. "Sorry. If I'd known you had a full house…"

"No trouble," Ava said with a wave of her hand. She reached down to pet Riot. "We're happy to have you. What have you done to your hand?"

"It's just a sprain," he excused.

Sassy rolled her eyes. Typical Nick, playing off his pain like it didn't exist. "So how is our newest family member?" Sassy asked, turning Ava's attention back to the baby.

"A little fussy," Ava said truthfully. "She had an ear infection earlier this week. I think she's doing better, but Chay was up with her all night again last night. We'll revisit the doctor Monday if she has another rough one."

"Are any of you sleeping?" Sassy asked.

Ava smiled. "How is any parent with a ten-month-old sleeping? We're all still settling into a family routine. It'll get better. Chay and I knew what we were doing when we adopted her."

"Bless you both for doing it," Nick said, eyeing Gracie fondly. He'd been as invested in her well-being as anyone involved in her case.

The door opened at their backs. Sassy's eyes widened as another couple walked in. "Mom? Dad?"

Richie, the baby of the Colton brothers, looked young and fit for his fifty-seven years. His dark hair had gone slightly gray and his blue eyes were the opposite of his wife's. As Dark Canyon's most trusted veterinarian, he had been caring for the town's fur babies for decades.

At his side, Bly Colton looked petite and trim, her black hair worn back, making her dark eyes look prominent in her oval face. Like Chayton, she was a member of the Navajo Nation, having grown up on the reservation. After marrying Richie, she'd reluctantly moved off Navajo land. Still, she was as dedicated to her cultural roots as she was to her family. Her handcrafted garments designed for the Navajo Nation were famous on and off the reservation for their beauty and authenticity.

Bly held Sassy close for a moment. In her characteristically quiet voice, she murmured in her daughter's ear, "We heard what happened in town yesterday."

Oh no. Between what had happened with the truck, the visit to Fern then Nick's accident, she'd forgotten to call her parents. "I'm so sorry," she scrambled to say. "You should've heard it from me..."

"We should have," Richie agreed, not waiting for his wife to release Sassy. He gathered them both in his arms for a collective hug and rested his cheek on Sassy's head. "You're all right?"

"I'm fine," Sassy said quickly. "No injuries. Just shaken a little." *A lot.* The idea of the F-150 coming at her, the sound of the tires skipping over the curb, the front bumper staring her down, took her right back to Main Street.

She thought of the police's visit to her house this morning. This wasn't the place to get into that, though she'd have to tell them both sooner or later if she didn't want them finding out from someone in her neighborhood. Dark Canyon might not be as safe as it once was, but it was still a tight-knit community, and people inevitably talked.

"We're glad you're okay," Bly said, running a hand down the surface of Sassy's hair. She pulled back and grinned warmly at Nick. "Are you looking out for her?"

"Actually—" Sassy began, but he cut her off.

"Absolutely," Nick interjected, accepting her mother's embrace. Over her shoulder, he gave Sassy a meaningful look.

He didn't want to dwell on his injury. Neither did he want to be the center of the Coltons' attention.

She sighed, because she could handle it. And she had the perfect excuse to change the subject. "I'm glad you're here. I've been meaning to ask you if you'd like to donate one of your garments to the Colton fundraiser at the gallery. Nick and I will be driving around to various artists today asking for donations."

"You're auctioning art, not clothing," Bly pointed out, bringing the folds of her colorful Másání scarf together over her chest.

"Your work *is* art, Mom," Sassy told her, not for the first time. "Please."

Bly released a breath through her nose, contemplative. "Come by the house this next week. I've been working on a storyteller skirt you may be interested in."

"It's not a custom order for someone else?"

Bly shook her head. "It's more of a personal project. If it's not something you think will be suitable for the auction, say so outright."

"No," Sassy said. "A storyteller skirt will be perfect, especially with a visionary like you behind it."

Bly pursed her lips, modest as always. "Come by and take a look," she said again.

"Okay," Sassy agreed.

Ava stared between them before blurting, "Have you thought of asking Chayton's grandmother to donate one of her crafts?"

"Yes," Sassy admitted. "It's another reason I wanted to visit you and him first. Do you think she's up for a visit?"

"I'm sure she'd love to see you," Ava asserted, "and make a donation. If you wait, I'll ride to her house with you. I think they're wrapping up the business discussions here." She nodded to Nick. "Jacob and Ryan are out back, if you'd like to say hi."

"Sure," Nick said. With a wink for Sassy, he patted his knee. "This way, boy," he said to Riot. The dog followed him to the back door, stopping to accept rubs from those assembled in the living room. Nick's progress was slow as he shook hands with Sassy's uncles and Chayton along the way.

"Do I want to know how he was injured?" Bly asked.

Sassy lifted her shoulders. "You know Nick. Always trying to be the hero, even when it's to his own detriment."

Richie cleared his throat. "Seems somebody needs to take care of him, too." This comment earned a ribbing from his wife. "What?" he asked plaintively, rubbing his side.

"We agreed we wouldn't pry," Bly stated, raising her brows, a silent entreaty for him to behave.

Sassy narrowed her eyes at the two of them. "Pry?"

Richie looked torn between the need to confess and the urgency to keep things copacetic between him and his wife. "It's nothing."

Sassy dropped her chin, giving him her best Bly stare from beneath her lashes.

He fumbled. "It's just... I was speaking to Ryan the other day and he mentioned that he thought the two of you...that Nick would...that you'd..."

If he danced around it anymore, they'd have to dress him up as a clown and enter him into the circus. "Yes?" Sassy prompted.

Ava groaned. "I think I know where he's going with this. Nick and Sassy are just friends, Uncle Richie."

"I know that," he said. "But..."

"*Oh*," Sassy realized.

"Hear me out," Richie said, accelerating his explanation now that all three women were looking at him incredulously. "Ryan thinks Nick would be perfect for you."

"*Ryan* said that?" Sassy repeated. Was her cousin in the matchmaking business? Between his firefighting hours and his frequent visits to Fern's bedside, Sassy wondered sourly where he found the time.

"It does make sense, in a way." When Sassy and Bly turned on her, Ava raised her hands. "Your personalities mesh beautifully. I can understand, though, how vital your friendship is to the two of you. You've been through a lot together..."

Bly patted Sassy's arm when she could only gape. "Don't listen to your father. He sees James and Sherry holding their grandbaby. Baby fever is catching."

"Grandbaby?" Sassy blanched.

"Richie," Bly said, studying Sassy's dumbfounded expression, "get your daughter some water. You've just scared ten years off her life."

Richie apologized profusely and went to do just that.

Sassy stared into her mother's eyes. "You think Nick and I should..."

"*I* think," Bly interrupted smoothly, "that you and Nick

are what you are and we have no right to ask for anything more of either of you."

"And Dad needs grandbabies?" Sassy asked incredulously. "*Now?*" She'd never felt the weight of being an only child like she did now.

"No," Bly answered for him. "That will come later, if you wish it. And *only* if you wish it. What I'd like first is to see you settle down." She laughed when Sassy wrinkled her nose. "You enjoy your life. I know you do. But I've been married to your father for thirty years, Haseya, and as much as I enjoyed my life on the reservation before, I can't imagine a life without a partner. I'll admit when I imagine someone for you, my mind drifts to Nicholas, because friendship is the foundation of any good marriage."

"Marriage…" Sassy needed to sit down. Fast.

"Your father shouldn't have said anything," Bly noted. "He's spooked you off the idea completely now."

Richie returned with water. Ava drew her to a chair. Sassy sat and sipped until she could feel the blood in her toes again. Next time her parents dropped a bombshell, she'd like to be prepared.

What made it worse—so much worse—was that their expectations were now mixed up with the mess in her mind that were these newfound feelings for Nick. *Unrequited* feelings. Nick didn't want her like that. He didn't want her, period.

She wished she could go back to a simpler time—seventy-two hours ago, at least—before she realized that her '80s music fiend, sci-fi movie–loving best friend wasn't just her friend. He was a man. A single man, sweet and sexy, who color coordinated his sock drawer, rescued stray canyon dogs and made her heart flutter.

She resisted the urge to drop her head between her knees.

There was no way out of this. She, Sassy Colton, had a devastating crush on Nick Malone, and it didn't appear to be going anywhere anytime soon.

Chapter 10

"It's nothing," Nick quickly explained. "Just a sprain. I'm fine, Mom. I swear."

"Are you sure?" she asked, sounding weary and strained. "Just because I'm here doesn't mean you need to hide things from me. I can handle bad news."

Nick wasn't so sure. He scrubbed the heel of his hand across his brow. "I'll have Sassy drop Riot and me off tomorrow at River House so you can see for yourself. I won't miss seeing you again like I did this morning."

"Everyone was asking where the two of you were. They all missed you."

"Well, I miss you," he said, needing her to hear and understand that just because she was there didn't mean he'd stopped thinking about her night and day.

"I miss you, too, Nicholas," she replied softly. "How is Sassy?"

Nick glanced toward the open door to the guest bedroom. He could hear rustling down the hall from hers. There was no way he could tell his mother about what had happened here last night. "She's doing okay."

"You know, I've been doing some thinking. If she wants to buy that house she was talking about—the fixer-upper—I think she should. She sounded so excited about it."

Nick froze. He was currently sitting in the fixer-upper—the one Sassy had made the leap and purchased two years ago. The smells of semifresh paint and sawdust from her months of DIY renovations didn't mix well with the sick feeling in the pit of his stomach. "Mom..."

"I could even dig into our savings—the money from your father's estate—and help her put down the down payment if it would help with the interest rate."

The room swam for a moment. Nick kicked for the surface, fighting to breathe through the tight feeling wrapped around his chest. His mother had spent that money in the grips of her addiction, so much so they'd had to sell the house they'd lived in since Nick was born. He put his head between his knees. *Goddammit. Not this. Not now.* He'd thought the therapy sessions at River House, the proximity to urgent care and his regular visits with Riot had been keeping the worst of her disease at bay.

He knew what the end game was. He knew eventually he'd lose her to dementia. But he'd thought the status quo would hold. He thought there'd be more time...

"Nicholas?"

"I'm here," he rasped. "I, uh... I'll talk to her."

"See that you do. She's practically a daughter to me. I'm happy to help. She doesn't even have to pay me back."

"I'll tell her," he promised, feeling numb. "Do you need me to bring you anything tomorrow?"

"Just yourself. And maybe some of those shortbread cookies. You know the ones?"

"I do." He cleared his throat when his voice splintered. "I love you, Mom."

"I love you, too, Nicholas."

"See you tomorrow?"

She chuckled. "I'm not going anywhere."

Something stabbed the corners of his eyes, hot, biting needles of emotion he couldn't stanch. He said goodbye and sought Riot's warmth next to him. His large snout rested on Nick's knee. He petted him, knowing his buddy needed the rest after visiting so many different people. Riot might be sociable, but spreading his love around could be wearing on him.

"Everything okay?" Sassy called from down the hall.

Nick swallowed the knot in his throat. "Fine."

"Is your mom up for a visit tomorrow?"

His hand traced unthinking circles across the top of Riot's head. "She says so."

"Good. Chayton's grandmother gave me a gift basket. She wanted me to take it to her."

"That was nice of her." Nick heard his own dull voice and bit into his cheek, trying to hold back the emotions.

"You sure you're okay?"

He sighed. *No.* "Yeah." He racked his mind for something else to talk about before he lost it. "Jacob told me his brother Mark is coming home soon."

"Yeah?"

"No one's seen him since his discharge from the Army," Nick said.

"That's right. A year ago."

Should he relay to Sassy other details her cousin Jacob, a National Parks SBI special agent, had shared with him—specifically, about a possible human trafficking ring operating in the area? He thought of the dead woman in Dark Canyon Wilderness, about Fern and baby Gracie, Ava's abduction… Glancing at the door to his room, he went through what had happened to Sassy over the last twenty-four hours…a near hit-and-run and a thwarted break-in.

He could easily believe what Jacob had told him. And

he didn't want it touching Sassy. He didn't want it anywhere near her.

A curse blew through the quiet of the hall.

He frowned at the door. "Are *you* okay?"

A pause. Then, "No."

He rose to his feet. "What's wrong?"

"It's nothing. I just… The zipper's stuck."

His feet planted in the thick carpet at the threshold of his room. She'd said something about changing when they'd returned home from the reservation. For her meeting with artists, many of whom she represented, she'd dressed in a flowing yellow maxi skirt with a purple chunky knit sweater over the top. She'd completed the look with a floppy wide-brimmed hat. By the end of the day, she'd managed to collect nearly a dozen pieces for the silent auction and had looked good doing it.

Nick knew how important the Colton fundraiser was to her. She wasn't comfortable with the idea of generational wealth and enjoyed employing her family's holdings to bring attention to the Indigenous and/or female artists she'd dedicated her life to championing. The money for the auction would filter back into the community, and the buzz the fundraiser would bring to Zephyr Gallery would benefit the artists she exhibited on a regular basis.

She grunted, clearly frustrated. He planted his hand against the wall, measuring the steps between his room and hers. "Need help?"

"Um…"

He waited. She'd been practically monosyllabic toward him after the visit to Ava and Chay's place. As much as he'd loved watching her interact with the artists on the rez, he'd wondered over the clear verbal distancing. The quiet return journey to Dark Canyon had been markedly different than the ride away from it this morning, with their hands clasped and the radio at full blast.

"Yes," came her hesitant reply.

He crossed the distance to her partially open door, parting it the rest of the way. Across the room, she stood before a full-length mirror. The chunky knit sweater puddled around her bare feet. Her hat lay upside down on the bed with Rogue's large bottom overflowing the hollow bowl in its center. The cat flicked her tail irritably and narrowed her eyes on Nick as he froze in the doorway.

The sweater had been hiding the fact that the skirt was actually a dress—a sunny yellow sleeveless number that complemented the perfection of her warm copper skin.

His thoughts eddied, mind upending rapidly and emptying. The zipper was caught near the line of her waist. He could track the small round knobs of her spine. She held the bodice of the dress in place with her hands, eyeing him over one shoulder. When she shrugged, the movement of one wing-shaped shoulder blade made his mouth dry completely.

"I can't get it over my hips like this *or* over my head," she pointed out, gesturing helplessly, "and I'm afraid to rip the back, because I just bought this dress last week and paid way too much for it."

"It's nice," he said lamely, toes rooted to the floor.

She pivoted enough to get an angle on what was happening at the base of her spine in the mirror...enough for him to see that she'd shed the dress's straps and the front of her shoulders and collarbone were bare, too.

His brain fried. It was the only excuse for the bolt of need that lit through him with all the devastation and intensity of a Saturn V rocket on the verge of implosion.

"The zipper's teeth are caught in the fabric," she noted. "Could you try prying it loose without tearing it?"

He spread his fingers on both hands apart and ignored the jarring protest from his injured one. Suddenly, they felt ungainly. He didn't know what to do with them any more than he had when he'd hit his first growth spurt in junior high. Giving himself a good pep talk, he moved to her as she turned back to the mirror, gathering her long black tresses against the left curve of her slender neck.

Concentrate, Malone, he coached, tilting his head to get a better look at the culprit. The zipper had indeed tried to eat the dress's yellow linen. "Hold still," he said when she shifted on her feet.

The words came out rough, and she stilled. He saw gooseflesh pebbling across the surface of her back and closed his eyes. She was so beautiful. It wasn't news to him. He'd realized it in eighth grade after he'd invited her to his house. They'd shut themselves in his room to work on a joint science fair project. He'd had the ideas. She'd had the artistic flair to make it come together in an attention-getting fashion the judges couldn't possibly ignore. As they'd hunched over the trifold poster board on his floor, it had struck him. *She* had struck him—the way her smile dug into one corner of her mouth, the way she tucked her hair behind the shell of one ear, the slightly wide set of her eyes and the effervescent laughter that always lurked there, waiting to bring someone a smile.

She was the most perfect human being he'd ever seen or imagined. With his comic book collection and his penchant for sci-fi, he'd imagined a lot.

His attraction had had him in a bind. He'd been dumbfounded, disillusioned and scared out of his gourd of her ever finding out.

Because he couldn't lose her. In those days, her laughter...it had been vital for him, pulling him out of the quicksand of memories of his last camping trip with his father. Her sunny smiles and ready humor had been the rope he'd used to escape the maws of depression, hand over hand. She'd made breathing—existing—easier.

He didn't know what he would have done or how he would have survived those years if Sassy Colton hadn't decided he was worthy of being her best friend. He'd have protected her with his life. That hadn't changed.

Protect her...protect this...this incredible, life-affirming cord that keeps us together. That keeps me *together. At all costs.*

Nick made himself open his eyes and take hold of the fabric and zipper. It took him a full minute—hell, maybe *a year*?—to loosen one from the other without shredding the delicate linen overlay of the dress. Sixty seconds of smelling the rosewater heart notes of her shampoo and the natural fragrance exclusive to her. The scent of her soap had changed in twenty years, but those subtle, warring tones of sweet honey and warm musk hadn't.

He took a long step back when the zipper was free. "I didn't rip it," he said, moving away from her. Fresh air. He needed fresh air and distance.

"You're a lifesaver." Her laugh tripped through the room, a high-pitched bell. She aimed her heartbreaker smile over her shoulder at him. "Thanks."

He shoved his uninjured hand into his pocket and balled it into a fist. "I'm going to step outside," he said.

"Everything okay?" she asked as he roved determinedly in the direction of the door. "You didn't hurt yourself?"

"No," he assured her. "Just... I need a walk before dark."

"I can go with you."

He had to bear down to keep from barking *I'm fine* at her. It wasn't her fault his entire body had rebelled against his better judgment. "I'd like to leave Riot here," he said instead. "Can you keep an ear out for him? He's resting and I don't want to wake him."

"You know I will."

He did know. His heart chugged against his sternum in awareness as he lingered at the door. "Just so you know... I'm not going to take any more muscle relaxers."

"But—"

"I need you to listen," he added quickly. "I can't go down that road again. Not after what happened last night."

"I doubt whoever tried to break in will come back for a second run."

"You don't know that," he said. When he finally got up the courage to meet her gaze again, he saw that truth hit home. "You don't know what this person is capable of. It could have been random and, in that case, yeah, the bastard's long gone. Or it could have been targeted. Someone almost ran you over yesterday. The incidents could very well be linked."

Her brow knitted. "Who would come after me like that? There's no reason—"

"No one in their right mind would hurt you, Sassy," he said, keeping his voice soft. It was true. She was the most compassionate, incredible person he knew. "But we can't assume whoever tried to break in last night *is* in their right mind."

Her throat moved on a swallow.

He wished he didn't have to deliver hard truths. For a stolen moment, he thought of ways to make the apprehension on her face disappear. It would be easy...so easy to cross the room to her again and...

He shut down that train of thought before it went off the rails, meeting Rogue's unbroken stare. The cat dropped her chin and glared like she knew exactly what he was thinking.

He stepped back, out into the hall. Away. "I won't be long."

This time, Sassy didn't dream of the sun on her face. The warmth came from another source altogether. Another body.

He wasn't just warm. He was hot, his skin damp against hers.

There was nothing between them. Nothing dividing them or holding them back.

Her blood raced. She felt like molten wax. Instead of fleeing the flame, however, she was melting toward it.

His body fit to hers, pieces finding each other, fitting seamlessly…like they'd done this dozens of times before. He moved, rocked, against her. She rocked, moving with him, coming apart in slow, steady increments.

She wasn't afraid of the free fall. Not when he was there to catch her.

She wasn't afraid to fall at all.

She came awake all too quickly, gasping for air. Rogue yowled in alarm, running for cover as she sat up. In the light from the parted door of the attached bathroom, she saw herself in the mirror, a wild woman with drenched skin, mussed hair, eyes alive and gleaming, the sheets a tangle around her hips.

The alarm clanged against her eardrums, and she swiped a hand out for her nightstand, desperate to bring the racket to a halt. She jabbed at the screen until the noise stopped. Breathing hard, she stared at the images on her phone until they started to make sense.

It was the grayscale feed from the back of the gallery.

She groaned, realizing that the security system had tripped again. "You've *got* to be kidding me." This was the final straw. She was going to call the security company and chew someone out until they figured out why it kept waking her in the middle of the night...

A flash of white charged across the screen, too fast for her eyes to track. She fumbled the phone, her already racing heart tripping in her ears. The languid remnants of lust fell away fast as terror took hold.

Something was outside the gallery. Something big.

Or...someone.

She swung her legs over the side of the bed, frustrated by the state of her sticky clothes. "This is ridiculous, Haseya," she lectured herself as she shrugged out of the damp tank top and shimmied out of her pajamas. Quickly, she grabbed a change of clothes off the dresser where she'd folded them but hadn't yet tucked them into the appropriate drawers. Layering a loose boho blouse underneath a pair of paint-specked overalls, she shoved her feet into her garden boots, ran her hands through the unkempt reams of her hair and stomped out of the bedroom. Rogue followed in a stealth belly glide across the carpet, chasing the loose, frayed cuffs of the overalls.

Moonlight streamed through the windows and transoms of her living room, illuminating the still, dark figure in front of the back door.

Sassy let out an errant scream.

Everything happened at once. The silhouette at the door jumped, yelped and barked, cowering from the door and racing behind the couch, where blankets thrashed, someone shouted and stood. Before Sassy could clap her hand over her heart to stop it from leaping out of her mouth, Rogue joined the fray, releasing a terrified screech and bolting toward the thrashing, blanketed shape. Claws rent fabric as she climbed a leg, a torso, a face into the hair of the figure before leaping for freedom and retreating into the darkness of the kitchen.

Sassy had the sense to flip the light switch, spotlighting the scene. When she saw Nick emerge from the blankets, her jaw dropped. Rogue had left scratches across his cheek, neck and naked chest. What came out of her mouth wasn't exactly as she'd intended, but all the same, she shrieked, "What are you doing *here*?"

He eyed her through a web of pain and incredulity. "What do you mean, what am I doing here? We said goodnight not three hours ago."

"I meant..." *Oh, no.* The scratches pebbled with blood. They were deeper than she'd thought. She waved wildly at the couch. "I gave you a bed. What are you doing sleeping out here?"

"I *couldn't* sleep," he said, hissing as he fingered the slice across his pectoral. "Riot kept sniffing at the door."

Sassy eyed the back door warily. She thought of the darting shape in the camera view of the security feed at the gallery and held up the phone clenched in her hand. "I'm sorry. The alarm tripped at the gallery again and I—"

"What?" he asked, dropping the blanket at his waist to reveal the gym shorts he was sleeping in. They hugged his hips as he closed the gap between them.

Her body was still tingly. She was still warm in places. Too warm. And she could remember every detail of the guilty dream she'd been having of him and them and... He looked good kissed by moonlight.

Riot nosed against her knee and whimpered. She reached down to pet him, glad to divert her attention on someone...

anywhere but Nick's marble slab of a chest. There was definition there. He wasn't a gym rat, so it wasn't overdone. But he looked trim and fit and strong and she was...thirsty.

Water. She'd drink a big glass of water.

"Did you see anything?" he asked, toggling the image to replay the footage from the last ten minutes.

"No." She thought of the quick, white flash of movement and swallowed. "Yes. Maybe."

"Where'd you put my truck keys?" he asked.

"Why?"

"I'm going to check it out," he said, taking her phone with him to the guest room.

She made the mistake of following him. By the time she raced through the door after him, he was down to his boxer briefs. She swiftly turned away, hissing through her teeth as her thighs clenched. Gritting her teeth, she said his name.

"Yeah?" he asked distractedly.

"You can't drive. The doctor hasn't cleared you yet."

"He thinks I'm on muscle relaxers. I'm not."

"You're down to one hand. Can you really drive with one—"

"Yes."

Dear God, he was stubborn. She heard the rasp of a zipper and revolved slowly on the spot. His jeans were on, thank goodness. The panels of his red-and-blue-plaid shirt hung parted over his torso. When he began to rush past her, she stepped into his path.

He drew a sharp breath, fighting exasperation. "I'm going, Sassy. Someone needs to check it out. It's either going to be me or I call the cops again. Take your pick."

Silently, she tugged the two halves of his shirt together. Leaving the top button undone, she threaded the others through their corresponding holes, trying not to notice how warm the line of his torso was or the fact that he was breathing heavily…just as he had moments ago in her dream…

Banishing visions of skin, she finished buttoning him and stepped back. "You can't go out in the cold like that," she told him.

His shoulders lowered. "Thank you," he said softly.

"We'll both go," she decided.

He hesitated for a moment before glancing down at Riot. "He can watch the house."

"I have one condition."

"What's that?" he asked as he pocketed his wallet.

She raised a stern brow. "*I'm* driving."

Chapter 11

Nick found Sassy in the office upstairs above the gallery, her eyes glued to the open screen of her laptop on the desk. She looked harried, her hair a haphazard bun on top of her head. He hated how pale she looked. He recognized weariness in the slump of her shoulders and nerves in the way she pulled at her lower lip, just as she'd done when they were teens facing finals at the end of the school year.

He knocked on the doorjamb to alert her to his presence. When her head snatched in his direction, he said, "I swept the lower floor."

"Did you see anything out of place?" she asked.

"No," he said. "Everything, down to the storeroom, was neat as a pin."

"Soledad's a wonder," she murmured with a faint smile.

He stepped into the room. "What are you looking at?"

She hesitated for a moment before turning the screen to face him.

The security feed from the back door. She'd frozen it on an image. He looked at the time stamp. "This is from half an hour ago."

"This is what woke me up," she admitted. She hit the space bar on the keyboard, and the image started moving in real time. "I've frozen it several times. Whatever it is moves so fast, I can't get a screen grab."

"Do you mind if I try?" he asked.

She hit the back button until the feed milled backward to a minute before the disturbance took place.

Nick leaned over her until the stray hairs of her topknot brushed against his cheek and tapped the space bar with his thumb.

They waited. One minute and fourteen seconds crept by before the white figure darted across the feed again, making Sassy jump.

Nick quickly hit the space bar, trying to freeze the frame with the shape somewhere in the middle. She was right. It was too fast.

He laid his hand on her shoulder to steady her nerves and his own. He didn't like this. The truck. The house. The gallery. What next?

"The back door wasn't breached," she said as she picked at one cuticle with a nail.

"It could have been and whoever this was covered his tracks well."

"We don't know it's a him," she pointed out. "We don't even know if it's a person. It looks like a big white blob to me." She snorted, trying to make light of the situation. "Should we call Area 51—tell them they have an escapee?"

She liked to lighten the mood in tense situations. That was her MO. He loved her for it.

Slowly, he let his hand fall from her shoulder. His nerves were on edge. Hers were buzzing just beneath the surface. He had to think clearly or he would let his emotions make his decisions for him.

She released a sigh, all traces of mirth lost to the gravity of the situation. "I don't want the police here."

"Why not?"

"The fundraiser is in two weeks," she stated. "I've nearly

finished curating all the pieces we need for the auction. It's not just Zephyr's reputation riding on this. It's the Colton Foundation. Not to mention the artists themselves. The gallery can't afford any bad press or suspicion."

Conflicted, he felt the knots of his jaw tense, watching her profile as she ran through the footage again. "Do you trust me?" he asked quietly.

Her eyes swung to his, wide and fathomless. He watched her pupils dilate as her gaze raced across his face. "Of course I do."

He tilted his chin at the screen. "Do you trust me to handle this?"

She narrowed her eyes. "How?"

"I need your answer."

She looked back at the computer, frowning at the unidentifiable shape. Shaking her head, she said, "I don't want you to do anything that's going to get you hurt."

"I won't."

Glancing back up at him, she searched his eyes until he felt his toes curl inside his shoes. "Promise?" she whispered.

He resisted the urge to run his fingertips across her cheek just to feel the softness of her. "Promise."

She gave a nod. "Okay," she said with some reluctance.

Relieved, he let the rough framework of a plan solidify into place. He had work to do and two weeks to do it.

"Full disclosure?" she asked.

He drew his attention back to her unerringly. "Of course."

She bobbed her head in a decisive motion before pulling the middle drawer of her desk open. From its depths, she took something out, wrapping her hand around it tightly.

"The first time the alarm pinged, I found this at the back door."

When she held it out, he opened his palm so she could drop the metal object into it. He frowned at the silver rod. "What is it?"

"I believe it's a bar rod for a style of bolo tie. The kind cowboys sometimes wear. If you turn it over, you can see a longhorn skull brand."

He flipped it over and angled the rod toward the light. "What does it mean?"

She lifted a shoulder. "Maybe it's a maker's mark. A signature. But I don't recognize it. I've been asking around discreetly among local jewelers, but no one's been able to identify it. Even if someone did, I doubt we could trace it back to its owner based solely on that."

He thought about it. "You mind if I keep this?"

"What good will it do?"

"You never know."

She eyed the piece for a moment before she looked away. "Take it."

"Thanks." He closed his fingers around the rod and tucked it into the pocket of his jeans. "Is it okay if I show someone else this footage?"

Her head low, she picked at her cuticle again. "You will let me know if it leads to anything?"

Unable to stop himself, he dropped to one knee next to her chair until she lifted her chin and looked at him again. He took the hand of the cuticle she couldn't seem to stop maligning and gave it a small squeeze. "What do you take me for, Haseya?"

She rolled her eyes at the sound of her real name. "Why does everyone have to keep calling me that?"

Because it's extraordinary, like you. She'd shown him

every part of who she was. She'd trusted him with each. Haseya. Sassy. All the versions of her she showed the world and all the ones she tucked away for self-preservation purposes. "Tell you what," he said, "I'll never call you Haseya again."

Her lips twitched, and he saw the miracle of her sunny disposition peering through the gnarl of fear and worry the last few days had wrought. "If..." she prompted, sensing that he wasn't finished.

He turned his lips up into a smile. "If you give me back my truck keys."

The laugh burst out of her, surprising them both. Groaning, she stuffed one hand into the pocket of her overalls and pulled out the fob. Before he could take it, she held out her pinkie finger. "Pinkie swear you'll use it wisely," she warned, brows raised.

Even without makeup, she was stunning. Did she know how stunning she was? His heart leapfrogged over the next few beats and he fought to keep the smile in place. He would protect her, defend her...and he would figure out what was lurking outside her door, come hell, high water or heartbreak. Extending his pinkie, he linked it with hers. "I pinkie swear."

The next morning, Nick caved and let Sassy take his truck keys once more to drive to the auto shop after she dropped him and Riot off at River House. As she parked on the curb in front of the elegant facade of the long-term care facility, she rolled down her window. "Aw. Look, Riot. Your fan club awaits."

Nick stared in surprise at the welcome party on the benches and rocking chairs lining the porch. Among them was his mother, waving as soon as she saw them, and her friend, the surly-faced Mr. Kincaid, Sassy's favorite octogenarian. "Watch out for that one," she cautioned.

"Why?" Nick asked, swinging the passenger door open to step out. Riot tapped happy paws against the floor of the backseat in anticipation of his owner unleashing him on the River House residents.

"He's my boyfriend." Sassy winked when Nick's jaw dropped. "Don't make him jealous. He's feisty."

"Should I tell him we're not together?"

Her teasing smile fled. Running her tongue over her teeth behind her lips, she frowned at herself. That *was* their truth. Why did it bother her? "Nah," she said, trying to sound nonchalant. "Let him think I'm playing the field. Keep him guessing."

Nick chuckled as he dropped to the ground, closed his door and opened Riot's. He gripped his leash. "Out you go," he said, grunting as he caught Riot's middle before he could superman to the ground.

She caught his grimace as the save tweaked his wrist. "Meet you for lunch?"

"At the brewery, right?"

"I'm tired of burgers," she contemplated. "How about Jessamine's?"

"Sounds good," he decided, wrapping Riot's leash around his good hand. "Good luck at the auto shop."

"Bye, boys," she called. "Make good choices!"

Nick shut the door, but not before she caught his rueful grin. Sassy tooted the horn, waving at those on the porch, and eased the truck away from the curb.

She could've walked to Bucket of Bolts Auto Tune, the shop owned by Sal Spalding who'd sold her the Bronco back in high school. But she was wary. It would be a while before sidewalks were her friend again, even if the near hit-and-run had been an isolated incident.

After what she'd seen on the security feed last night, she didn't know what to think anymore. Worse, her imagination was getting the better of her. She hadn't been able to fall asleep once she and Nick had returned to the house last night.

Perhaps that was a good thing. She couldn't afford any more wet dreams with the subject of her current fantasies and his lovable pooch couch surfing to ensure she was safe inside her own house.

It took seconds for her to pull into Sal's parking lot. She could see the Bronco in one of the open bays of the shop. The sight of it raised off the ground on the hydraulic lift made her anticipation falter.

Sal's message this morning, she'd assumed, had been good. Why then was her baby still jacked up on stilts?

She blew through the door of Sal's. The shop was empty, an unfortunate result of competing against the chain auto shops popping up on every corner.

The grizzly-bearded man with tattoos winding around his muscled arms came through the door to the garage, wiping his hands on a shop rag. He took one look at her and sighed. "Sassy."

"Sal," she greeted, then launched right into it. "I'm not taking my girl home today, am I?"

Pity webbed across his rough-hewn features. His mouth pulled low as he gestured to the waiting area. "You'd better sit down."

Chapter 12

"Terminal?" Soledad gawped at Sassy. "What does that mean?"

"The engine's shot," Sassy muttered, picking at the contents of the platter Jessamine Baker had placed in front of her. The country-fried steak she'd ordered tasted like ash in her mouth despite Jessamine's talents in the kitchen. "Sal says he's replaced every part twice over. It needs a rebuild, and after buying the house two years ago and the reno, I'm not sure it would be wise to drop more cash on my princess when this could happen again in a year or two."

"I'm so sorry," Soledad commiserated. "I know how much you love her."

"She got me to New York and back," Sassy said ruefully. "The first time a boy kissed me, he racked his nuts on the center console trying to get to me."

"You're not eating," Jessamine said with a tsk as she returned to the table to refill their glasses of iced tea. "My cookin' not good enough for you girls anymore?"

"No one's saying that," Sassy said, spooning up a large forkful of Brussels sprouts. She made yummy noises to combat Jessamine's puckered expression.

Soledad followed suit, sipping creamy chicken noodle soup out of the Oh My Heck mug it had been served in.

Her thin black eyebrows rose to her hairline and her hand came to her mouth when she realized that it was still steaming. With a thumbs-up, she offered a stilted, closed-mouth smile to the hovering chef.

Jessamine lifted her chin. "You two aren't leaving without dessert. I got Jell-O salad today."

As she moved to the next table, Soledad groaned. "The last time I ate dessert here, I gained five pounds."

"Mmm," Sassy said with a nod. "Her Jell-O salad is frickin' dangerous." From the outside, the established hole in the wall looked more like a refurbished trailer than an eatery. When Dark Canyon's beautification committee had come after Jessamine and her husband, Joe—both of whom ran the place with just a handful of staff—they'd added a wraparound porch and a small cupid's fountain out front.

Nick and Sassy had a running bet on bare-as-a-bumpkin Cupid's real reasons for being there. Sassy thought the fountain was a polite way for Jessamine and Joe to show their asses to the committee. Nick had odds on it being a misguided attempt to class up the place.

Cupid's chipped nose and stained basin looked like something they'd picked up from a yard sale rather than a garden center. He fit right in, though, with the potato sack–lined ceiling, the scarred wood floors so soft in places walking over them felt sketchy as hell if you were paying attention and the chicken and egg salt and pepper shakers on each table.

If the city council ever decided to shut down Jessamine's based on appearance, they'd find Sassy and a good many others at the front of the picket line.

She spooned mac and cheese and made herself eat it. If comfort food wasn't going to get her through this, what would?

The door opened with a tinkle of bells, and Nick breezed through, Riot's leash in hand.

"Boy," Jessamine called from across the dining room, "you can't bring that dog in here."

Nick crouched behind him, using his hands to perk Riot's ears at a jaunty angle. "But, Miss Jezzie, look! He's *starving*."

On cue, Riot lifted one paw off the floor in a plaintive pose.

"You're one horse away from a dog and pony show." Tossing her checkered kitchen towel over one shoulder, Jessamine turned toward the swinging kitchen door. "I'll turn my back this visit. Next time, he eats on the porch like the rest of the barnyard animals."

"Yes, ma'am," Nick said, dropping into the chair next to Sassy that she'd already kicked out for him. "After twenty-seven years, she still scares the hell out of me. Why do we keep coming back?"

"Jell-O salad," Sassy said around a bite from her honey biscuit. She counted off others on her fingers. "Sweet corn. Fried peaches in honey. Funeral potatoes. Homemade fry sauce…"

"Oh yeah," he said dreamily. Coming to his senses, he nodded to Soledad. "How're you today?"

"Great," Soledad replied. "Lunch is on me. Sassy's letting me go early today so I can meet my friend Fletcher. We're going dancing tonight."

"Boyfriend," Sassy stage-whispered behind her hand.

Nick grinned at Soledad. "Has he passed Sassy's inspection?"

"Not yet," Soledad admitted measuredly.

"She likes this one too much to expose him to my scrutiny," Sassy pointed out.

"I really like him," Soledad explained. "He's an artist from Moab making a fresh start here in Dark Canyon. He likes the slower pace."

"Those pieces of his you showed me were promising," Sassy noted, handing Nick her fork so he could finish off her greens. She pinched off a corner of the biscuit, checked the kitchen door to make sure Jessamine was out of sight and passed Riot the bite under the table. "He works with metal."

"Huh." Nick's brow creased as he finished off the Brussels sprouts. "Interesting."

Was it? Sassy studied him for subtext, but he reached for her iced tea.

A hand flew out of nowhere to swat his away.

"Ow!" Nick cried out.

Jessamine set a fresh glass in front of him. "Margot taught you better than to reach across the table. Drink your own."

"Thank you?" he ventured as she filled it.

"Stop eating Sassy's food and tell me what you want," she charged.

He didn't have to look at the menu board to know what she offered. Quickly, he rattled off, "Wild game chili with French fries and fry sauce on the side."

"And the whelp?" she asked, pointing a finger at Riot, who cowered so far under the tablecloth only his snoot was visible. "What'll he have? Can't have those doleful eyes tempting my customers to pass good food on to him."

"Turkey meatballs, no sauce?" Nick said, leaning out of reach in case she swatted him again.

"Hmph," Jessamine said before turning her back.

"Christ and all the latter-day saints," Nick muttered, watching warily as she stomped back to the kitchen. He rubbed Riot's protruding nose in comfort. "Is she going to poison my food?"

"I'd still eat it," Sassy opined, downing more mac and cheese.

"Where are you two going tonight?" Nick asked Soledad.

Was he interested in Sassy's executive assistant? Envy fired along her neurons, making her drop gooey Monterey jack cheese into her lap. She picked up a napkin and swiped furiously at the stain on her favorite pair of bell bottoms. Soledad was as much her friend as Nick. Sassy would *not* be jealous. Carefully, she asked him, "Are you wanting to go dancing tonight, too?"

He turned his attention away from Soledad and combed his gaze across the sweetheart neckline of Sassy's bubble-sleeved blouse. "Maybe."

Her heart rolled belly up like a puppy looking for caresses. She swallowed.

He looked away.

Soledad looked from him back to Sassy then reached for her iced tea, eyes round. "Um… I think Fletcher wanted to try line dancing at the Bootleg."

"Sounds fun." Nick nudged Sassy's shoulder with his own. "You like line dancing."

Why are you being weird? She curbed the urge to hiss it at him. "When it's called for."

Soledad considered the two of them. "So…should we double?"

"Double?" Nick asked, confused.

"Double date," Soledad clarified.

Nick's lips parted. "Double date," he parroted like he'd never heard the phrase before.

Sassy leaned toward him, lowering her voice to drop

the words in his ear. "It's like regular dating but with two couples instead of one."

He snorted. "I know what double dating is."

Sassy raised her hands. "Sorry. You looked clueless there for a second. Has it really been that long for you?"

A muscle twitched along his jaw. "All right," he said. "Count us in."

"What?" Sassy felt all the blood drain to her toes.

"Are you not up for this?" he asked her.

It sounded like a challenge. The gleam in his eye told her it was a challenge. *What are you up to, Nicholas?* she wondered. "Sure," she shot back. "Why not? Let's double date." It felt strange coming out of her mouth.

So wonderfully strange. The possibilities careened around her head. Her and Nick. Nick and her. Dancing the night away at the Bootleg before going back to her place and…

Her face heated fast. Riot let out a startled, muffled bark when she pushed her chair back from the table abruptly. "Don't mind me," she said when both Nick and Soledad looked up. She rose, grabbing her purse. "I'm going to see a man about a horse." With that, she retreated to the ladies'…hopefully before either of them noticed that she was blushing furiously.

Nick felt underdressed next to Sassy. Damn, but she knew how to dress for the occasion. He'd nearly swallowed his tongue when she'd emerged from her room in the tasseled suede off-the-shoulder dress that displayed the smooth line of her shoulders and clavicle to perfection. She'd completed the look with vintage brown boots.

He quelled the need to run his thumb in a circle over the

sweet round knob of her knee. To wrap his fingers around it and tickle the sensitive skin of the crease.

He chanced a glance at her now as he drove to the Bootleg. Her gaze was tuned to the passenger window, watching the lights of Dark Canyon pass. Her hair tumbled down from her brown felt hat. He had trouble distinguishing her profile from its shadow. He knew, however, that her lips were painted fire-engine red. She'd curled her hair so it tumbled over her shoulders in waves.

Shifting in the driver's seat, he hoped to direct the flow of blood away from his groin. His jeans felt tight. What had he been thinking, daring Sassy to go on a double date with him? He'd never known her to shy away from a challenge. She usually went all out like she had tonight. Now Nick was in a heap of trouble. He cleared his throat. "What did Sal say about the Bronco?"

She fiddled with the strap of her purse, her chin low. "It's not good, Nick. I don't think she's going to make it."

"Why do you say that?"

"She needs a complete engine rebuild," Sassy told him. "Since I bought her off him in high school, Sal has replaced nearly every individual part under her hood at some point or another. Not to mention that parts are harder and harder to come by because she's an older model. I just don't know how much more money I can spend on her. Not with the way things are going right now." Before he could ask, she raised her hand to stop him. "Financially, I'm stable. The gallery's doing well and my artists are thriving. But with the house note and the renovations…" She sighed. "I don't know. If this keeps up, I won't be able to keep the Bronco in belts and lug nuts, much less valves, crankshafts and manifolds. I guess I have to face the fact that she's older, she isn't environmentally efficient, her gas mileage is a nightmare and she's always going to have issues."

He considered the situation, sensing that she needed to mull it over. "Are you going to sell? Busted engine or not, she's worth something. You don't have any payments on her. If you sell, it's all profit and you could use the money to buy something more economical."

"That route does make the most sense." A small smile flirted with the edges of her mouth. It was thin, but the light in her eyes shined through, hitting him somewhere near the solar plexus. "But it's hard giving up on something so special."

Sassy wasn't in the business of giving up on things. Neither was he. Riot. His mother. His life in Dark Canyon even when his dreams of traveling the world and professional hiking hadn't panned out. Sassy. What they had together. Like a compass, she had always drawn him back to Dark Canyon.

"I get that," he whispered.

"I knew you would," she said, the smile wavering.

At the neon sign for the Bootleg, he used one hand to turn the wheel, steering the truck into the packed parking lot of the red barn turned honky-tonk. He found a space and squeezed his Dodge cheek to jowl between a banged-up Chevy and a Jeep Grand Cherokee. As he stepped down to the ground, careful not to ding his door on the rusted Chevy's passenger mirror, he scanned the lot, trying to clock the vehicles that matched the description of the F-150 that had tried to take Sassy's life. He reached into his pocket and found the bar rod she'd given him. It felt cool to his touch.

Was there a chance this metalsmith Soledad was dating may have been the one who'd dropped it? If so, did he drop it outside the gallery door on a visit to his girlfriend? Or could he have dropped it at another time—at night, perhaps, when he was trying to avoid the cameras? The gallery housed several pieces that were worth upward of five grand or more. With the auction closing in, Zephyr's storeroom would be stocked with exclusive pieces that would fetch a pretty penny for someone who knew what they were looking for.

That storeroom was right inside the back door, the one Nick suspected had been breached not once but twice.

Who better to know what was inside than someone close to either Sassy or Soledad? Since Nick knew the bulk of Sassy's close friends and every member of her family, he figured Soledad's associates were the best place to start.

She'd mentioned her boyfriend was new to Dark Canyon. How did the timing of his arrival align with the first alleged break-in?

Sassy met Nick at the front bumper of his truck, hitching the strap of her purse over her shoulder. "Ready?"

He gazed at her. She made boho Western chic look good. Once they were through the door of the Bootleg, every head would unerringly turn in her direction. Men would line up out the door to buy Haseya Colton a drink or ask her to dance. A few would try to cop a feel and she'd handle them like a boss.

Nick would bet that none of them would see the sheen of sadness lurking beneath the dazzling smile. He clutched her arm through the tassels of her dress and tugged. "Come here."

She fell into his embrace like she was starving for it. When he felt her arms link across his spine, he pulled her hat away, dropped his cheek to the top of her head and tightened his hold. She responded by burying her face in the fabric of the denim shirt he'd struggled to button so she wouldn't have to dress him like a kid again.

He felt her fisting his shirt between her hands above his beltline and swayed her gently from side to side. "I'm sorry," he breathed into her hair.

"I'm *not* going to cry," she said through gritted teeth.

"Later," he told her. "We'll grab a pint of ice cream and stream your favorite movie. You can cry then. I won't judge."

She breathed a laugh into his lapel. "You never do." Tugging away, she raised her fingertips to her lower eyelids to ensure they were dry and her makeup was still in place. "It's stupid to cry over something so material."

The Bronco wasn't material. She'd gone places and done all the things she'd dreamed of doing. Her gas-guzzling chariot had gotten her there. "Whatever you decide to do, I'm here for it. You want to sell? I'll find a buyer. You need a new car? We'll haggle with a dealer. You decide to say screw it and drop what's left of your savings on a new engine? I'll support you."

"You've got way more important things to worry about."

"Not true," he said, slinging his arm around her shoulders and guiding her toward the din of voices raised over crashing country music. "You know, once we walk in here, I'm going to have to fight for a place at your side." He set her hat back on her head, angling it just so. "So do me one thing."

She swung her dark gaze to his, tipping her chin to see him from under the brim. "What's that?"

He couldn't help it. Letting his touch brush across the ridge of her cheek, he followed the angle of her jaw down to meet her chin. His thumb circled the point. He dropped it when her eyes rounded and her steps slowed, forcing him to match his pace to hers. "Save me a dance?"

She blinked at him, lashes thick and heavy as she searched his expression. Then she smiled in a way that reminded him of daybreak in Dark Canyon Wilderness. Glancing down, she extended her pinkie. "Promise."

Chapter 13

A sea of hats greeted them inside the Bootleg, along with an upbeat blast of a country western two-step. On the busy dance floor, boots slapped in time to the Electric Slide. Spectators clapped and offered appreciative whistles and catcalls. Under the glassy eyes of mounted game and chandeliers made of crisscrossed antlers, weekend revelers drank and mingled.

"There she is," Sassy announced after spotting Soledad waving furiously through the crowd to get her and Nick's attention. "She's already grabbed us a table."

"All right," Nick said, angling his body toward Sassy. In the crush around them, his hands went to her waist, and she tried not to shiver at his touch or forced proximity. "The line at the bar's nothing to laugh at, so I'll grab us a couple of beers and meet you over there."

"Good luck," she said before they parted ways. She needed some space. His touch still scalded her cheek, and she caught herself lifting her hand to cup it. She focused instead on fighting her way through the shoulder-to-shoulder crush. A few friendly locals stopped her to exchange greetings. Someone unseen tapped her south of the belt. Wisely, whoever it was ran before she could dislocate his digits.

Evander veered into her path, his standard top knot undone so that his hair flowed down to the shoulders of his rhinestone-studded western-style shirt. "Want me to claw his eyes out for you?"

She beamed. "You caught me. I was holding out for a hero."

"Oh, girl, please," Evander said with a roll of his eyes. "Your hero's at the bar."

She didn't look for Nick even if she wanted to.

"You still owe me a line dance," Evander pointed out.

"Come find me later," she invited, winking.

"I'll hold you to that," Evander replied.

By the time she reached Soledad, she was nearly out of breath. "Wow," she called, greeting her friend with a hug. "My dance card's already full."

"Girl, you look like a million doubloons," Soledad said, holding Sassy's arms wide for inspection. "That dress is fantastic. Where'd you get it?"

"A friend of my mom's made it," Sassy said.

"Give us a twirl," Soledad said, raising their clasped hands over Sassy's head. "You know you want to."

Sassy laughed, suspecting that her friend had arrived early and was already three beers deep. She indulged her, spinning so that the dress's tassels billowed in a festive circle around her. Wolf whistles flew in her direction, along with an indecent offer she ignored, stepping up to the hightop table Soledad had snagged for their party. Empty bottles stood like scattered soldiers across the surface. "I saw that dress in the window at Wagon Wheel," she said, pointing to Soledad's pretty ruffled floor-length number. "I'm glad I didn't get it. Looks much better on you."

Soledad looked around indicatively. "I'm not the one everybody's eyeballing tonight."

Sassy waved a hand. "Half of them are too drunk for

sense." The room smelled of beer and bad decision-making. The floor was already sticky, and peanut shells crunched underneath her boots. It was also a touch too warm since the place was filled to capacity. As an eating and drinking establishment, the Bootleg was far more questionable than Jessamine's down the road. Yet it had its charms. "Nick went to order drinks."

"Fletcher, too," Soledad pointed out. "I can't wait for you to meet him."

Sassy smirked. "Tell the truth."

Soledad let out a breath. "Okay. I'm nervous. Just... promise to go gentle on him. He's... Well, he's different."

"In what way?" Sassy asked, curious about the mysterious man who clearly had her unflappable executive assistant so smitten.

"He's kind of soft-spoken."

"He's *shy*?" Sassy asked with a catty grin.

"More reserved. Not city at all. Though he is more cultured and refined than..." She rolled her eyes toward the clutch of man-boys in too-tight jeans ogling them from the next table. "Well, *them*."

"So what're the odds of him scaring easily?"

Soledad calculated them silently then gave her a nervous glance. "Fifty-fifty. Things between us are still a little new. But, Sassy, I *really* like him."

"I can see that." Sassy wanted to be happy for her. However, Soledad's effusiveness amplified Sassy's knee-jerk tendencies toward caution. If this guy broke her friend's heart, she was going to have to pay to fix her Bronco just so she could run him over with proper mud tires.

"Oh, here he is now," Soledad hissed. She beamed, waving through the bystanders.

Sassy's first impression of Fletcher was that he was

tall—tall enough to play in the NBA. *Does Soledad have to climb him just to get to first base?* she wondered wryly as Soledad bounced up and greeted him with a kiss he had to bend nearly halfway over to receive. His hair was shaved close to the scalp, and, oddly enough, he wore a suit minus the tie with the first button of his shirt undone, perhaps to combat the formality of his outfit choice in the decidedly informal environment.

When he stood up straight again and met Sassy's gaze, she received a jolt. His eyes were icepick blue, piercing enough to be disconcerting yet fascinating. He might be a city boy, but he had a Nordic vibe going on. And if Sassy wasn't mistaken…he looked a touch familiar. In the time it took him to reach the table and set his and Soledad's new drinks down, Sassy tried to chase the déjà vu to its source.

It eluded her. If she'd seen him before, he'd certainly have been hard to forget.

"Sassy Colton," Soledad presented, "meet Fletcher Ryder."

"Fletcher," she acknowledged, holding out her hand.

He hesitated minutely, just long enough for Sassy to pick up on the wariness lurking underneath the Thor, God of Thunder, thing he had going for him, sans hair.

"I don't bite," she assured him. Glancing sidelong at Soledad, she grinned and added, "Much."

Soledad laughed. One corner of Fletcher's mouth tipped up before he grasped her hand and held it without shaking it. His grip was anything but soft, however. She could feel the calluses on his fingers and palms. A metalworker, she mused, who didn't bother with gloves in spite of his spit and polish. She could see why Soledad would be drawn to him. The man was an enigma.

"Nice to finally meet you," he said.

"He speaks," Sassy said, then winked to soften the blow

of her teasing. He hadn't let go of her hand. "Soledad says you're from Moab."

"Yes," he said. He seemed to realize he hadn't let go of her and released her hand suddenly, taking a step back.

When he said nothing more, she rubbed her lips together before asking, "And this is your first time in Dark Canyon?"

"It is," he answered succinctly. Soledad linked her arm around his waist, drawing him closer to her. He seemed to soften, draping a long arm around her in return.

"I showed her some photos of your pieces," Soledad told him. "I hope you don't mind. She doesn't just run Zephyr. She's a visual arts agent."

He seemed unsure what to say for a moment. "I don't mind," he said to Soledad in an undertone before forcing his attention back to Sassy. "There's enough artists in a small town like Dark Canyon for representation?"

"You'd be surprised how many the community of Dark Canyon has fostered through the years," Sassy pointed out. "But I don't just represent local crafts folk. A lot of my artists are from the Navajo Nation. Others are as far away as Provo. I represent female and Indigenous artists."

He shook his head, a shade of amusement touching his expression. "I'm neither Navajo nor a woman."

"No, but the pieces Soledad showed me piqued my interest."

His wide brows shot up. He stared blankly at her for a handful of seconds. "Did they?"

She nodded. "Soledad and I have an auction coming up. A charity fundraiser to raise money for the Colton Foundation. I'll need to acquire at least five more pieces to round out the collection for bidding. I could include one of your sculptures. If it does well at the auction, we could discuss an exhibition. Unless you're promised to another gallery."

"N-no," he stammered. To see such a large man flummoxed was almost endearing. Soledad thought so, too. She smiled softly and placed a hand on his arm, running her nails up his sleeve and back down. "I've, uh, never had a showing," he admitted.

"A virgin?" Sassy wondered if he'd picked up metalwork more recently. The caliber of his sculpting skills and his calluses said otherwise. *Indeed, an enigma.*

"I guess you could say that," he said. He thought for a moment, then blew out a breath and settled on, "I *don't* know what to say, actually."

"Think about it," Sassy invited. "Soledad can give you my work number, if you like."

He glanced at his girlfriend, who nodded encouragement. A silly smile worked over him, transforming him into someone less stilted, more relaxed and natural. Even the line of his back softened toward her. They were ridiculously cute together. Sassy couldn't help but grin along with them.

Nick materialized out of the crowd, double-fisting draft beer. "For you," he said, passing one off to Sassy. He reached into his back pocket. "As are these."

She took the handful of napkins. Some felt damp. Others were stained with substances she preferred not to identify. "What's this?"

"Numbers," he said, setting his cup on the table. "A dozen of them."

Soledad hummed. "Which of these do you think belongs to the future Mrs. Malone?"

"We should choose one at random," Sassy decided.

"A bridal lottery!" Soledad exclaimed. "Yes!"

"It's a nice thought," Nick drawled, "but they aren't for me."

"No?" Sassy studied each group of digits. A few had names: *Tate. Carter. Andres. Morgan...* "Oh."

Smirking, Nick took a sip then crossed his arms over the table and leaned over them. "So which is going to be the future Mr. Colton?"

"Ha-ha," Sassy quipped, gathering the napkins up quickly before he could snatch one. She used them to wipe up water rings.

Nick clicked his tongue and gave a small shake of his head. "Sassy Colton, crushing the hopes and dreams of young cowboys since 1998." He noticed the stranger at the table and extended a hand. "You must be Fletcher."

Fletcher shook. "And you are?"

"This is Nick," Soledad told him. "He and Sassy... Well, they take care of each other in a sweet and platonic kind of way."

Sassy rolled her eyes at the description, even if it was true. "He's my bestie."

"I didn't know men and women could be besties," Fletcher pointed out, bemused. "When you two date, don't your significant others feel threatened?"

"If they don't trust us to begin with, what's the point of a relationship?" Nick asked.

Fletcher glanced at Soledad. "You don't have any male besties. Do you?"

Soledad sighed dreamily. "Not like Nick."

Nick chuckled. "Aw, Sole. You're making me blush."

Soledad laughed and touched his arm, and heat staked itself out inside Sassy, blooding her cheeks. She was blushing again, too. Furiously, just as she had at Jessamine's.

From the bar, the clatter of a cowbell caused everyone to look around. "Bottoms up!" the bartenders shouted in unison.

Sassy automatically grabbed her cup. Nick and Soledad did the same. Before Soledad could explain to Fletcher what was going on, Nick and Sassy had already lifted their cups to their mouths and were gulping the draft beer down. Sassy wanted to gag on the foamy head. Out of the corner of her eye, however, she saw that Nick was ahead of her, half his beer gone. She buckled down and gulped faster, not coming up for air until the cup was empty.

Both their cups kissed the tabletop at the same time, and they both gasped for breath and joined the cheering of the participants around them. Soledad finished moments later, with Fletcher coming in fourth. Sassy applauded them both. Whatever she'd felt seconds ago had been a filthy, ugly emotion she never wanted to feel toward either Nick or Soledad again.

So what if they flirted? Sassy flirted with men around Nick all the time. He was more subtle about picking up women, and the idea had never bothered her before.

It was all harmless fun, anyway, the normal pattern of conversation whenever they saw people they were acquainted with in public. Sassy hated that she could for one second be jealous of Soledad. She hated how much she'd wanted to pick up her glass and throw the beer in Soledad's face. "I think I need another," she decided.

"I told TJ to bring a pitcher round soon," Nick told her.

"Is the whole thing just for me?" she asked, hoping he would miss the lingering lashes of color across her cheeks. Or at least chalk them up to alcohol consumption.

Not that she couldn't drink him under a table...

He bumped his shoulder into hers in answer. "So, Fletcher, what kind of metal art do you do?"

"Uh, sculpture, mostly," he answered.

"Any jewelry?" Nick probed.

Fletcher shook his head. "Not really, no."

"Are you in the market, Nick?" Soledad asked curiously.

"Maybe," Nick said in all seriousness.

Sassy narrowed her eyes and started tearing a napkin into teeny, tiny pieces. Again, what was he up to? Fletcher must be wondering the same thing, because he looked a bit uncomfortable. Sassy jumped into the exchange. "Did you train with anyone?"

"No. I guess you could say I'm self-taught," he asserted.

"Wow," Sassy said, impressed.

"Soledad tells me you're an artist, too?" Fletcher asked.

"I was," she asserted. "At one time."

"What happened?" he asked. "If you don't mind me asking."

"Not at all," she assured him. "I was awarded a grant that helped pay for the art school of my choice in New York."

He raised his brows. "That's fortunate."

"For a kid from Utah, it felt like winning the Powerball."

"What was your preferred medium?"

"I was a painter," she told him.

Nick leaned in. "You're still a painter, Sassy. You just don't sell your work."

She glanced at him. Him handing her easy wins in his leather-smooth voice wasn't going to help her eradicate this heat she felt for him.

"Why don't you sell your paintings?" Fletcher asked.

"My work never made much of an impact," Sassy explained. "Not like others'."

"So you just gave it up? Just like that?"

Sassy couldn't tell if the question was more surprised or judgmental. Neither could Nick, apparently, because his shoulder nudged into hers again and stayed there, supportive. She didn't move away. "I don't see it that way. I'm still passionate about art, and I love working with artists. I love seeing their faces when they sell something they put their whole soul into. It's that lightning-in-a-bottle feeling, the same one I felt when I painted years ago. I lost that feeling as an artist. But that doesn't mean I don't still feel it for others who deserve it, especially those from marginalized communities. Giving up professional painting never felt like selling out. Not when it felt like I'd found what I was meant to do with my life."

"Hmm," Fletcher said contemplatively. "You do still paint, like Nick says?"

"Sometimes," she admitted. "For myself. Art and creative release can be a private endeavor, too."

"Mine's been a private endeavor for years," Fletcher said, "but not by choice."

"Sometimes life leads you in a different direction than you expected," Nick said. "You wind up exactly where you were meant to be all along."

"True," Soledad agreed with a nod.

Sassy wanted to lay her head on his arm and close her eyes in thanks. He turned his head, met her eyes. Something in his glimmered. He understood her implicitly.

Inside her, a lock broke open, unleashing messy torrents of emotion. Stunned, she looked away, blinking rapidly as her eyes stung and the back of her throat tightened. She felt it across the bridge of her nose. The particles of her being sought him with an intensity she felt from head to toe. She wanted this man and this man only. He was all she needed, all she'd ever needed. She just hadn't realized it.

Soledad bounced in her seat. "Ooh, I love this song!" She whirled on Fletcher. "Dance with me, mi amor?"

Fletcher took her hand and helped her up. "We'll be back," Soledad called before they disappeared amid the raucous patrons.

Nick waited until they were well out of earshot before he said, "I don't trust a man who wears a suit to a honky-tonk."

"Maybe he's trying to make a good impression," Sassy surmised.

"What kind of starving artist wears a Rolex and Italian shoes?" Nick challenged.

Sassy lifted a shoulder. "Maybe his family funds his ambitions? Mine would have, had I been willing to accept their help."

"You didn't see it," Nick said, "but during that whole conversation, he was looking at you when he should've been looking at her."

She rounded on him. "What?"

"It's true," Nick said. "I didn't like it. Not one bit."

The cowbell rang again, but she couldn't look away or join the hooting and hollering as everybody's favorite drinking anthem cued up and those around them linked arms and began to sway as one. Her chest felt taut and her throat began to close. "Nick."

"Yeah?"

She fought for a decent breath and couldn't quite fill her lungs all the way. They hurt, all of a sudden. "Do you have feelings for Soledad?"

His jaw loosened. "Why...why would you ask me that?"

"Oh, God." She dropped her temple to her palm and shook her head. "How did I miss this? How long has it been going on?"

He grasped her shoulder. "Sassy, I'm not into Soledad."

"It's okay," she said without looking up. "You don't have to hide it from me."

"I'm not hiding anything." He stopped, cursed before continuing. "Not about her."

"Then why're you giving Fletcher the third degree?" she asked. "Why did you agree to come tonight? We've never double dated before. I know there's some ulterior reason we're here with them."

"It's this guy," Nick explained. "I don't like him."

"Why not?"

"I don't know. The fancy watch. The overpriced cologne. It's all fake."

"I think you're being a little unreasonable," Sassy opined.

"The guy made you uncomfortable, too. Admit it!"

They were practically yelling at each other. She glanced around, aware of the looks they were drawing from bystanders who were trying to sing along. "I don't know what to think other than that you've been acting strangely. Are we here to check up on Fletcher or are we here because…"

"Because what, Sassy?" he asked.

"Because you *wanted* to go on a double date with me?" she finished, throwing it out there.

Again, he only looked at her, staring blankly.

She took a steadying breath. "Look. The other night… after you took the muscle relaxer, you…you kissed me."

He stilled. "No, I didn't."

"Yes, you did," she insisted.

"That's not possible," he said, shaking his head emphatically.

"Why?" she demanded. They were definitely louder than the singing. "Because I'm not sexy enough or I'm not desirable at all to you?"

She might as well have kneed him between the legs. He paled and his mouth worked as he fought for a response.

"You kissed me, Nick!" she accused.

"Maybe you *imagined* I kissed you. Or misinterpreted something. Because I have never—I *would* never—"

"Do you know what women hate most?" she hissed, mad as a cobra. "Being told that a man's clear and present actions are all in her head!" Her chair fell over in her harried attempt to get as far away from the table as possible.

"Sassy, wait!"

She yanked her purse over her shoulder and elbowed a path through the happy throng to get to the closest exit, ignoring the lyrics being shouted around her.

"Sassy!"

She picked up the pace. Someone grunted as she stepped on his instep. His arms flailed and he fell into the person behind him. A woman shrieked. Shouting that had nothing to do with joy or merriment commenced. The sound of a fist connecting with a face and a cry of pain eclipsed the next lines of the song.

She found the side door at last and barreled out into the night. She drank the cool night air, ignoring the way her breath hitched. Wrapping her arms around herself, she looked toward the road. Should she walk home? Call an Uber? Call Ryan or her parents to come pick her up?

The door opened at her back, spilling noise and light into the graveled side lot. She spun with a frown to find Nick.

He was breathing heavily. A little wild-eyed, he jerked his thumb over his shoulder and said, "I almost got my head taken off back there."

"You think I *imagined* it?" she asked, bewildered. Before she knew what her feet were doing, she charged him. Planting her hands on his chest, she pushed him back against the closed door. "Hold still."

As she planted her boots between his and her torso slid into the warmth of his own, he drew in a sharp breath and raised his hands. "What are you doing?"

"Oh, I'm sorry," she drawled. "Does this look like a pass to you? Maybe *you're* imagining things."

His jaw flexed and his eyes darkened. "You've made your point, Sassy."

She lifted herself to her tiptoes, ignoring the fact that her face was on fire and she was still short of breath. "Imagine this," she invited, turning her nose into the collar of his shirt. She let the tip of her nose brush against the skin of his throat. It was hot—like a branding iron. His scent drenched her. She missed a breath entirely and bit her lip to stop a whimper from escaping.

A shiver coursed through him. She felt it sink into her as she parted her mouth, letting her breath whisper across the heat of his skin. Then, emboldened, she closed her lips over the spot, kissing him just as he had kissed her. The feelings coursing through her demanded it. They needed the taste of him…a subtle clash of soap and salt.

A soft, plaintive noise escaped her. She opened her mouth, suckled.

Air hissed between his teeth.

Her hands spread through the hair on the back of his head, bringing it down so that she could nibble a titillating line up to his jaw.

His warm palm spread across her cheek, gentle as it maneuvered her back a step.

It took a moment for him to solidify before her. She'd gotten lost in him—the heat of him, his smell, his taste…

His pupils had dilated and the look in his eyes was a straight whiskey shot of…

Hunger.

It didn't take much for him to reverse their positions, him crowding her into the door. The hand on her cheek caressed her, his thumb sweeping across her skin as he studied her eyes, her brow, her mouth… Her heart pounded between them. She wondered it didn't beat through her chest wall as he took his time considering her and the inches that separated his mouth from hers, stretching the moment out until anticipation whistled between them at a frequency only dogs could hear.

Then he closed the distance and his eyes held hers as he kissed her—*really* kissed her—for the first time.

Chapter 14

So he'd lost his mind. That was his only excuse for pushing Sassy against the wall of the Bootleg and pressing his mouth to hers like it belonged there.

Now things between were stilted. Messed up. Awkward as hell.

Nick was furious with himself. Why couldn't he have just let her win the argument? Why couldn't he have laughed off that sexy nibbling thing she'd done on his neck and said, *Okay. Okay. You've made your point.* Then at least they wouldn't have driven home in silence after he practically frickin' devoured her. After he pressed his body into hers so she could see...so she could feel what her lips, tongue and teeth did to him.

Now she knew. And now *he knew* how she felt against him. Soft and curvy, sensual and sweet.

He'd found hell. He'd practically leaped there with his own handbasket and presented himself at the gates. *'Sup. My name's Nick. I just kissed my best friend, the most beautiful woman in the world, and effectively ruined my entire life. Bring on the whips and chains.*

He'd thought...he'd actually thought for one mindblowing moment that she'd wanted him—that for the first time his ill-advised feelings for her weren't unrequited.

He'd thought that for the first time he wouldn't have to hide his body's reaction to her—the one he'd been choking down for years out of fear and respect.

The truth had sunk in real fast when she'd said nothing to him packing his clothes, grabbing Riot and announcing their departure from her house.

As he approached Zephyr Gallery three days later, his feet slowed. They'd been no calls, no texts, nothing between them.

It was the longest they'd ever gone without talking.

He looked down at the items he'd brought along, hoping they would be enough to get him through the door. Normally, Sassy couldn't turn down a free lunch.

Things were far from normal, thanks to him, but he had to try. He needed to get back in her good graces, because life without her sucked.

He swung the door to the gallery open before his second thoughts got the better of him and nearly ran into Fletcher.

The man drew up short at the sight of him. "Hey," he said. "It's Nick, isn't it?"

Nick nodded stiffly. The guy had all the wrong vibes. That was something he hadn't changed his mind about since the Bootleg. "What are you doing here?"

Fletcher jerked a thumb over his shoulder. "I was just dropping off the piece Sassy asked for. For the Colton auction?"

Nick lifted his chin in understanding. "So you're going through with it?"

Fletcher jerked a shoulder. "Why not, if it helps me get through the door? An exhibition at Zephyr Gallery isn't anything to sniff at. I'm grateful Sassy's even considering my work for her space."

"Right," Nick said. "I hope it works out for you."

Fletcher smiled thinly. "Thanks. I guess I'll see you at the fundraiser?"

Nick nodded. "I'll see you." He waited until Fletcher made his getaway, following his departure through the glass. He'd left the suit at home this time, at least. Instead, he was wearing dark-washed jeans and Jordans that probably went for five hundred dollars on eBay. Was that a peacoat he was wearing? It was black and double-breasted. Nick wondered how much it had set him back, too.

Fletcher came to a stop on the driver's side of a parallel-parked Stingray. The car wasn't at all subtle. Nick watched until Fletcher had driven off before going to find Sassy.

Soledad waved from her position in the main showroom, where she was leading a customer around the current exhibit. He lifted his hand silently then nodded toward the floating staircase up to the second floor.

She nodded before turning her attention back to the customer.

He took the stairs slowly, practicing what he wanted to say in his head. *I'm sorry. You have no idea how sorry I am. It was a misstep, a fluke, and it will never happen again. Can we just forget it ever happened and go back to the way things were? I miss you. I miss you so goddamn much, Sassy.*

He would get on his knees. He'd grovel, if necessary. Anything to erase the last few days.

He found her behind her desk, wearing the reading glasses she rarely let anyone see. She tapped a pen on the desk as she read through the paperwork in front of her.

Nick tried swallowing past the lump in his throat and gave up before rapping his knuckles against the jamb.

Her eyes lifted from the papers. Behind the glasses,

her dark eyes looked overlarge. They widened at the sight of him.

He waited for the smile that normally followed. *No dice.*

Lifting the brown paper bag in his hand, he said, "Sacrificed a chicken for you."

She only stared. The pen had ceased its tapping. Her guarded expression remained unchanged.

Nerves beat wings around his stomach. He lowered the bag. "Or, Tony did this morning. Now you get to reap the benefits."

She glanced from him to the greasy bag and back. Finally, she leaned back in her chair, setting the pen down on top of the papers. "I'll take it."

He almost bounded across the space to her desk, setting the bag down on the edge. "I grabbed extra Whoa Daddy sauce for you."

"Thank you," she said quietly, watching him unroll the bag and take out the Styrofoam-encased offerings. It wasn't until he tugged a bottle of Diet Coke from his jacket pocket, though, that a smile touched the corners of her mouth.

He set it down amid the impromptu feast. "I've got napkins here," he said, pulling them out of his other pocket.

"Nick."

"Did I forget anything?" he asked, studying the tableau carefully to be sure she wouldn't need anything else.

"Nick," she said again.

He met her gaze. She'd taken off her glasses. They dangled from one hand, much like his chances. He pulled in a bracing breath. "Yeah?"

"Sit down," she invited. "Eat with me. There's enough for both of us."

He stuffed his hands into his pockets and shook his head. "Nah. I'm good. They fed me at River House this morning."

She hesitated, then tugged one of the Styrofoam takeout containers closer to her. "How's your mom?"

"She's walking now that the weather's warmer, just around the park. Mr. Kincaid and an attendant go with her once a day."

"He *is* sweet on her."

"I'm not sure she's noticed," Nick considered. He wasn't sure how much his mother was aware of. She'd seemed frazzled this morning, convinced that she'd lost her purse.

She'd stopped keeping a purse when she'd moved into River House and Nick took over her financials.

Worst of all, she'd asked for her pills. Nick had checked with Ms. Porter to be sure his mother had received her medication that morning. She had, which meant she'd either forgotten or she'd been looking for the prescription pain meds she'd become dependent on after his father's death.

It had broken Nick's heart a little more, watching her search for something that wasn't there.

"You don't have to go," she murmured, dripping Whoa Daddy sauce on her wings from a spoon.

He frowned. "Sure about that?"

She nodded slowly. "Stay."

He drew up a seat. For a while, he just watched her eat with his elbows braced on his knees and his hands laced between them.

She'd skipped breakfast. He could tell by the way she scarfed. Soon, there was little left but bones, a quarter cup of coleslaw and some balled-up napkins. She downed the Diet Coke and wiped her face. "I guess we need to talk about the other night, huh?" she asked finally.

"If you're up to it," he replied.

She closed the Styrofoam containers one by one. "I don't like not speaking to you."

"I don't like it, either," he admitted.

"I need you, Nick," she said, her gaze colliding with his. She looked a little tired, as if she hadn't slept any more than he had over the last few days.

"I need you, too," he asserted.

At once, they both said, "I'm sorry."

She frowned. "Wait. Why're you apologizing?"

He fumbled, confused. "I was going to ask you the same question."

"I kissed you," she reminded him.

"No," he argued, "I kissed *you*."

Her eyes narrowed. "So...you're not mad at me?"

He laughed nervously. "I thought you were angry at me."

She shook her head. "None of this would have happened if I hadn't pushed you up against the side of a building and..."

The blood sank swiftly to his groin at the memory of what she had done to him. He shifted in his seat, crossing his ankle over his knee. "I took it a step further. Way further than I should have."

Spots of color appeared in her cheeks. He saw it licking the surface of her neck and fought a groan at the sight. She remembered, too.

Sassy cleared her throat, looking down at the empty containers. "I've been trying to get up the courage to tell you that I'd like to start over. Forget the whole thing happened."

He breathed a sigh of relief, coming to the edge of his chair. "I want the same thing."

Her expression was almost plaintive as she scanned him again. "It didn't mean anything. Right?"

"Absolutely right," he said, nodding vigorously. It was a blatant lie, but he'd agree to *anything* to make things right between them again.

"Okay," she said. "I guess that's settled."

He beamed stupidly at her for a moment. Then he reached into his pocket. "You left this at the Bootleg."

She stared at the offering in his hand. "You found this where?"

"The Bootleg," he repeated. "It was on the table when I went back in to pay for the pitcher. Right where you were sitting."

She didn't reach for the silver-and-turquoise cuff. She looked like she'd seen a ghost. Small lines dug between her brows as she shook her head. "That's not possible," she breathed.

"Why not?" he asked. "I thought it looked familiar. Is it Soledad's?"

"It's mine," she clarified. "I just thought I left it here on my desk a week ago. It's been missing for days. How did it wind up on our table at the Bootleg?"

"You weren't wearing it?" Nick asked. He chastised himself when her eyes lit with indignation. Of course she hadn't been wearing it. If he'd been paying attention to anything other than her tasseled dress and her red-painted mouth, he'd have known that. "Sorry. I'm just trying to make sense of this. You say it went missing from your desk?"

"I thought so," she said with a nod.

"How does its absence correspond with the security alarms?" he asked.

She thought about it. "I noticed it missing the day after the first alert. Soledad and I combed every inch of this room to find it. We came up empty."

"Okay," Nick considered.

"Oh, God," Sassy groaned. "What if you were right this whole time and someone *did* break in to the gallery? But that doesn't make sense, either. Why would they leave all the priceless art on the walls along with everything of value in the gift shop…leave my computer here on my desk, even, and take the single piece of jewelry I left here that afternoon?"

It didn't make sense. Unless this whole thing was far more personal than either of them had bargained for. "I've been talking to some friends of mine," Nick said. "They work in security. They suggest we install more security measures around the gallery."

"How much will I have to pay to get it installed?" she asked measuredly. "I'm still car shopping, so my budget won't stretch far."

"I told you," he reiterated, "they're friends."

"You can't expect me to believe they'll do all this work for free."

"They will if you're willing to advertise the name of their security firm on the entry door," he said.

"Nick," she breathed. "That's far too generous."

"The owner has a sister. She's a small business owner, too. He knows how difficult it can be to juggle the books and the cost of security. His wife also happens to love Zephyr Gallery."

"Tell me who she is and I'll make sure to discount every piece she walks out the door with." She let out a disbelieving laugh. "This is unbelievable."

"Don't worry about any intrusion or conflicts between the security installation and prep for the fundraiser," he added quickly. "They can come in after hours and work on the new system. It shouldn't take more than a couple hours to install. I'll oversee everything, if it makes you feel better."

"It might." She smiled fully. "Thank you, Nick. I owe you."

"That's not how this works," he argued. He placed a

business card on her desk next to the silver cuff she had yet to touch. "I talked to Theo at the Dodge lot. This is his cell number. He'll talk to you about financing a new or used vehicle. You've got the credit to secure a loan. He'll cut you a good deal."

She picked up the card, read the numbers, and shook her head. "You did all this while believing I was mad at you?"

"I haven't forgotten what I promised," he told her.

"No," she said, running the card between her first and middle finger. "You've never broken a promise to me. Ever."

He tried not to watch the movement. "Are we good?"

She bobbed her chin in a nod. "We're good."

He wanted to hug her. Would it be wrong to do so? Had what had transpired at the Bootleg certified that casual affection between them would forever be misconstrued? He tapped his knee before standing. "I'll see myself out."

He made it to the door before she said his name.

She had risen to her feet as well. He noticed her hands clenched on the edge of the desk. She seemed to hesitate, as if struggling for the right thing to say. At last, she settled for, "Thank you for lunch and…everything else. I do owe you. I don't care if you disagree."

He snorted a laugh, though it made him sad to think that that was their relationship now. Trading favors to keep the scales balanced. "I'll call you when I talk to the security firm," he said in answer. He eyed the cuff on the edge of her desk. She still hadn't touched it. "Let me know if you need anything else in the meantime." Without waiting for her reply, he turned away and took the stairs down two at a time.

"I appreciate you both taking the time to discuss this," Nick said as he eased onto Chayton's couch. He'd driven straight from Zephyr Gallery to the reservation for the pre-arranged meeting. Ava had gone to the hospital to check in with Fern while her mother babysat Gracie. Nick knew how close Ava and Sassy were. He didn't want word of this getting back to her. Not yet. "I know you're busy, so I'll get right to the point." He glanced at Jacob. "Did you find any information on Ryder?"

Jacob sat forward over his knees, elbows braced on his thighs. He clasped his hands between them. "I looked into him. He appears to be clean. But there was something weird about his background." He lifted a hand to Chay. "I brought it to Chay to see if he'd draw the same conclusion."

Chay picked up the discussion. "Ryder's background is incomplete."

Nick frowned. "I thought you could do a complete background check."

"I can," Jacob confirmed. "But if someone's living under an alias, law enforcement sees only what they want us to see on paper."

Chay nodded agreement. "Fletcher Ryder's paper trail began three years ago."

"Before that," Jacob continued, "nothing."

"You're saying the guy Soledad's dating is operating under a false ID?" Nick asked.

"More than likely," Chay agreed.

"Which means he's hiding who he really is?" Nick ventured. "Why would he do that?"

"Could be he's hiding out from someone," Jacob noted. "Maybe he witnessed something he wasn't supposed to. Maybe he owes money to the wrong people. Creditors, loan sharks, gambling debts, etc."

"Or," Chay cut in, "he's got a record he doesn't want anyone to know about."

"How do we find out?" Nick asked, his head spinning with possibilities.

"Before we get into that," Chay said, "why don't you tell us what your interest in this person is?"

"Does this have anything to do with the attempted break-in at Sassy's?" Jacob asked. "Or the near hit-and-run involving her on Main Street?"

"I'm not certain exactly," Nick said. "But here's what I do know. On two separate occasions, the security alarm for the back door of Zephyr Gallery has tripped in the middle of the night. The first night, the security footage shows nothing. On the second, there's movement, but it's hard to decipher what or who is there. Sassy noticed that a silver bracelet she left on her desk was missing from the gallery the day after the first alert. The bracelet reappeared at our table at the Bootleg a few days ago."

"Could she have been wearing it that night?" Jacob asked.

Nick shook his head. "She wasn't wearing jewelry that night."

"Let me guess," Chay said. "You saw Fletcher Ryder there that night."

"He was sitting at the same table," Nick revealed. "Soledad, too."

"Is there a chance she may have witnessed him placing the bracelet on the table?" Jacob asked.

"I haven't asked," Nick said with trepidation. "From what I can tell, the relationship between them is new, but she's happy with him."

"Are they intimate?" Jacob asked.

"Why?"

"Because if he's got access to her house, more than likely

he has access to her key to the gallery," Chay pointed out. "I assume you've checked for signs of a break-in?"

"The night of the second alert, yes," Nick answered. "There weren't any."

"Which means if he's gaining entry into the gallery without breaking and entering, he's got opportunity and means," Chay concluded.

"There's another issue that complicates this further," Nick pointed out. "Sassy added one of his art pieces to the charity auction catalog. If it does well during the Colton fundraiser, she's offered him a chance to display his work at Zephyr."

"So she doesn't suspect him," Jacob guessed.

"I don't think so," Nick said.

Chay narrowed his eyes. "I'm surprised you haven't told her. You two are tight."

The wave of uncertainty and guilt warred with his determination to see this through. He knew in his bones that Sassy wasn't safe. He'd realized belatedly after moving out that he'd left her alone. He had spent several sleepless nights wondering if he should stop by and check to make sure her doors were locked and that no one was lurking about.

He had a duty to keep her safe. His gut told him that the near hit-and-run and the break-ins at both Zephyr and her house had to be related. He couldn't even conceive of the events being part of some wild coincidence.

Maybe he should have informed her of his theory that Fletcher Ryder was involved. Though she did have a lot on her mind with the renovation, the Bronco and the fundraiser. Not to mention what he had allowed to happen at the Bootleg.

He buried the recollection, digging his fingers into his

knees. "I'll tell her in due time. But I need evidence if I'm going to accuse a man of theft."

"How do you plan on getting it?" Jacob asked.

"I made a call to a friend at a security firm," Nick replied. "He's going to install a new security system at Zephyr to curtail any more break-ins. They're also going to place hidden cameras on the gallery floor, the gift shop, the storeroom and outside Sassy's office."

"Does she know this?" Jacob asked.

"She knows about the security system," Nick noted. "Not the hidden cameras."

"Don't you think she should?" Jacob pressed. "It's her building."

"We'll be lucky if whoever's doing this doesn't catch on to the new security measures and decide to cut his losses where the gallery is concerned," Nick explained. "If she starts acting differently or changes her pattern of behavior because she knows what's going on, it'll double the chances of letting this asswipe off the hook."

Chay's frown deepened. "You'll need to at least contact police to make sure the surveillance is all aboveboard."

"That's the next step," Nick said. "I was hoping one or both of you could use your contacts in the Dark Canyon Police Department to help."

Jacob nodded slowly. "I can talk to Dad, too. See if he can't use his political influence to get the ball rolling before the fundraiser. If Ryder is responsible and his piece does well at the auction, he'll have his foot further through the door of Zephyr Gallery."

"And more time alone with Sassy," Chay said. "If he's the one trying to get into her house, this is personal."

Nick's gut twisted. "I know," he said with a swallow.

"He's potentially violent as well, if he's the one behind what happened on Main Street," Jacob expounded.

The situation felt volatile. The instability of the house of cards Nick was building to keep Sassy safe made him want to hold his breath. "Do you think the detectives at DCPD will set up a sting?"

"Ryder will be there the night of the fundraiser, correct?" Chay asked.

Nick nodded. "All of Sassy's artists will be."

"He'll likely make a move then," Chay concluded, looking to Jacob in question.

"It's probable," Jacob said. "I'll talk to Dad this afternoon and call you when we have a meeting set up with the chief of police."

"Please ask your father not to mention anything to Sassy's parents," Nick requested. "I know the family's close, but if this is going to work, we need as few people to know about this as possible."

"What if we request that police send a patrol car to sit outside her house?" Jacob asked. "That'll give us some peace of mind about her home safety."

"That's something you can tell her," Chay said.

Nick nodded in agreement. "I'll sleep better knowing she's okay there alone."

"We all will," Jacob said. "You've done some good investigative work here, Nick. The chief's going to ask you to join his investigative unit once your wrist's healed."

Nick circled his wrapped wrist with his good hand. Even the dregs of pain had started to ebb. He would start physical therapy exercises soon to get his strength back up. His return to work couldn't come soon enough with bills piling up. "I like where I'm at," he claimed. He missed making a difference in people's lives every day.

Would he have been able to deduce what was going on with the gallery and Ryder's possible involvement if he hadn't been on sick leave? Maybe spraining his wrist had been a good thing in disguise.

Chapter 15

"I'm sure you have many other things to focus on other than me," Margot said as she sat before the vanity mirror in her room at River House. "Your auction's tonight."

Sassy tutted, running her fingers through the ends of Margot's fine silver hair. "Why would I throw over my very first client?"

Margot released a fluted chuckle, her features transforming. "You only wanted to be a cosmetologist for one summer."

"And you were the only one brave enough to volunteer to be my guinea pig," Sassy remembered fondly. She set aside her shears and placed her hands on Margot's delicate shoulders. "How did I do? Not too short?"

"It's perfect," Margot said, reaching up to lay her hand over Sassy's. "Thank you, sweetheart."

Sassy set the shears in her purse, lifting Rogue—who she'd again sneaked into River House—off Margot's lap so that she could remove the nylon cape. She shook it out once, letting the loose silver tendrils litter the floor. "I'm sure Mr. Kincaid will agree."

"Mr. Kincaid?" Margot shook her head as she rose from the stool in front of the mirror. "Sassy, how you do carry on."

"I was talking to Ms. Porter," Sassy noted, folding the

cape and setting it aside so she could pick up the broom and dustpan. "Word is Mr. Kincaid can foxtrot like there's no tomorrow."

Margot cackled so hard she crumpled to the edge of her bed with its lace-trimmed coverlet and held her stomach. Knuckling the tears from the corners of her eyes, she struggled for breath. "Oh, dear. I haven't laughed like this since…"

Sassy's broom paused midswipe as Margot struggled to remember. Quickly, she resumed. "That just means Rogue and I don't visit enough."

Margot lifted her hands so the cat could pad across her lap and settle there again. Sassy smiled as Margot caressed Rogue's curled-up form. Rogue might be salty as hell, but she knew a thing or two about timing and compassion.

As soon as she disposed of the hair in the dustbin, she took a seat next to Margot. "You want to be my date to the fundraiser tonight?"

Margot pursed her lips but couldn't hide the amused flash behind her eyes. "Really, Sassy."

"I'm serious," Sassy said. "Nick's going to be there. So are my mom and dad. The whole Colton clan. I'll find you a dress and some cute shoes to wear. You can drink fizzy water, eat canapés and bid on my dime."

"There's no sneaking out of here," Margot said measuredly.

"If I can sneak Rogue in, I can sneak you out. Do you think Nick used to get himself out the second-floor window of his room?"

Another chuckle surfaced. She patted Sassy's arm. "You go on. You and Nick will have a marvelous time without me."

Sassy tilted her head. "You know, one of these days I'm

going to convince you to join my shenanigans. It worked on him."

"Indeed," Margot agreed. "You worked your charms on my son before anyone else had a chance. For him...there's only ever been you, hasn't there?"

Sassy stilled. "You act like I ruined him for all others."

Margot eyed her beadily in response.

Sassy felt her smile flee. "I... I never intended..."

"Perhaps not," Margot said. "But it wasn't long after that first conversation in the lunch room that I knew I'd lost him to another. A mother always knows, Sassy."

That breathless feeling she'd been trying to forget wound its way around Sassy. She wanted to apologize...to ask what exactly Margot really meant. She wanted to know long Nick had...what? Loved her?

No. Not since grade school. Margot must be mistaken.

A knock clattered against the door, and they both looked up as Nick entered the room. He raised his brows when he found the two of them seated hip to hip. "Plotting against me, I see."

"We were doing no such thing," Margot said as she rose to greet him.

Nick wrapped his mother in a warm hug, his cheek resting against the side of her head. When he opened his eyes and looked at Sassy, she made a silent gesture toward her hair, widening her eyes in indication. He placed his hands on Margot's arms, moving her back a step. "Wow. You look amazing. Did you get a haircut?"

Margot touched the ends of her tresses. "Sassy just cut it. Doesn't she do a fantastic job?"

"She does," Nick acknowledged. He looked to Sassy again and mouthed, "Thank you."

She bowed her head slightly in answer, gathering Rogue into her arms.

"Do you have a date for tonight's fundraiser?" Margot asked him.

"No," he said. "I'm going stag."

"Well, I think you should take Sassy," Margot told him.

Sassy looked up, startled. "Me?"

"Yes," Margot said, nodding vigorously. "You just asked me to be your date. I assume that means you don't already have one."

"Of course it does," Sassy replied. Margot cut her off before she could continue.

"It's settled then. Nick will go with you."

Nick met Sassy's gaze, as unsure as she was. They both knew neither of them was capable of refusing Margot anything. Even so, they'd kept a studied distance from one another physically ever since they'd kissed at the Bootleg. He hadn't so much as let his arm brush against hers in passing. She'd stopped all manner of touching, down to punching him on the shoulder when she was right and he was wrong.

It hadn't silenced the weird vibes between them, but they were down to a dull roar, so maybe the status quo was working.

Tonight's auction was a black-tie affair. If they behaved as badly as they had on a casual date night at the Bootleg, Sassy hated to imagine what the expectations for tonight would be.

Okay, so she didn't exactly hate it. In fact…she could easily imagine bringing the night to a conclusion by grabbing Nick by his tie and—

She forced herself out of the reverie. By the look on Nick's face, he too knew that this path led to danger. Still, the words that surfaced from him said something decidedly different. "I'd love to if she'll have me."

Margot looked to Sassy expectantly.

Sassy took a bracing breath before she forced a smile and nodded. "Count me in."

"It's settled then," Margot said, bringing her hands together and beaming at both of them. "Before you go, Sassy, I have something I wanted you to see."

"Oh?" Sassy followed her to the small storage closet attached to the room. Margot rummaged around for a moment before revealing an item wrapped in a vibrant silk scarf.

Margot held it as if it might shatter, handing it carefully to Sassy. "I thought you might consider it for tonight's auction."

Intrigued, Sassy unwrapped the scarf from around it, recognizing the shape and weight of a canvas. When the silk slid away, she froze.

The painting was small—a simple eight-by-ten. The subject stood in the center of a vast, empty red-sand desert, facing the wind. Her hair and ceremonial dress billowed out behind her. Little by little, her sleek black mane and skirt were being carried off by the breath of air in the form of scarlet petals.

Sassy found her own initials scrawled across the bottom corner.

Margot's voice dropped to a murmur. "It was a gift you gave me for Mother's Day after...after Lincoln died."

Sassy raised her gaze to Margot's and found her eyes swimming every bit as much as Sassy feared hers were. "I remember," she said hoarsely.

Margot nodded. "It meant the world to me."

"Then why are you giving it back?" Sassy asked.

"Because others should see it," Margot told her. "I've

selfishly held on to it all these years, even though I knew it belonged to the world."

"I painted this for you." The woman in the painting was Margot against the world. Against the odds. Fate might try to break her down, but she stood tall regardless. "It's yours."

When Sassy tried to transfer it back to Margot's arms, the woman closed Sassy's fingers around the edges. "I want you to hang it in your gallery. I want you to tell people that you made this. This is your work. No one else's. You don't have to sell it to the highest bidder. But it should be known. It should be seen. It's worthy of that, and so are you."

Words of gratitude were locked tight in Sassy's throat. She struggled against tears as she wrapped her arms around the canvas, hugged it to her chest and nodded. Stepping forward, she touched her lips to Margot's cheek.

Margot ran a hand over her braid in answer. "Take something for yourselves tonight. Both of you. Promise me?"

Sassy nodded, still unable to speak.

Nick's whisper touched her ear, making her skin tingle. "Should we pinkie swear on it?"

A breathless laugh escaped her. Unable to turn toward him with her emotions rippling across the surface like this, she gave her answer. "Yes."

Zephyr Gallery practically glittered. Between flutes of gold champagne, shimmering gowns and the Chihuly-inspired chandelier consisting of hundreds of translucent spiral glass horns, the Colton Foundation fundraiser was proving to be the classiest event on Dark Canyon's social calendar. The chandelier was one of many pieces up for grabs tonight. Its starting bid was the highest on the auction floor.

Nick watched the bidders file in. Tension sank into his

body slowly but surely as a crowd packed the space. Catering attendants circulated, passing out drinks and tiny bites of stuffed mushroom or smoked salmon. From his position on the floating stairs, he could track each person. He could also see the closed door to the storeroom.

He clocked Ryder the moment he entered the space, dressed in a bespoke three-piece suit. Cuff links flashed at his wrists. He wore a diamond stud in his left ear.

Everything about the man was a lie. According to his dossier, he had no other employment outside of his fledgling metalworks business. Not officially. Sassy's theory that his family supported his artistic ambitions hadn't panned out. He had no family to speak of. He wouldn't, living under an alias as he was.

The detective he'd worked with at DCPD had used his resources to try to uncover Ryder's real identity. Whoever he'd paid to help him change his name had been skillful. Nick was no closer to finding out who he really was or what he was hiding.

Soledad, decked out in a shining strapless silver number, met Ryder halfway across the gallery floor, offering him a glass of bubbly and an auction catalog. As he wrapped his fingers over hers on the stem, he used it to pull her closer and lay his lips over hers.

Nick raised a brow. *Bold move for a shy guy*, he noted. Ryder hadn't exactly appeared comfortable with public displays of affection at the Bootleg. What was rallying his confidence tonight?

A face from the crowd tilted up toward his. The detective, Rick Finbar, from the local PD, acknowledging Ryder's entrance. Nick gave him a slight nod. He sought another form belonging to the executive of the security firm, Todd Olsen, who had brought his art-loving wife, Kelly, to the event. His windswept hair hid an earpiece that allowed him to communicate with the guys in the security van outside, monitoring the scene with cameras they'd hidden during the installation of the new security system.

If Ryder made a move toward the storeroom, they would alert Olsen, who would cue Detective Finbar and his team.

The Coltons were out in force. He heard the pealing laugh of Sherry on the arm of her husband, James. Gathered around them were their children, Ryan and Ava, with Chayton close by. Nick spotted the Colton patriarch, Sam Colton. He'd surprised a good many people by bringing Susan Baylor, introducing her as his girlfriend. Nick wasn't sure how his sons Jacob and Noah felt about the arrangement. The two had been watching the couple warily throughout the night.

Sassy's parents were in attendance, too. The faceless mannequin garbed in the elaborate Navajo ceremonial dress her mother, Bly, had sewn for the occasion stood directly underneath the blown-glass chandelier, a showstopper in its own right. Bly was drawing admiring looks, too, dressed in one of her own designs, a dress of stunning blue with shining metal buttons. Her ornate turquoise necklace dripped over her bodice. She touched it often as she hovered near the mannequin, answering questions from bidders in her calm, informative way.

"It's going well, I think."

Nick turned on the stairs. He did a double take.

He hadn't seen Sassy since she'd ducked up the stairs before the doors opened to change into her evening garb.

Speaking of showstoppers, Nick thought dimly as he took her in. She left him speechless.

Bly had supplied her with another one of her designs. This one screamed for attention, with a bright yellow velvet bodice lined with metal studs down both sleeves and along both edges of the collar. They marched across the bodice in a symmetrical pattern. Four quatrefoils of turquoise dripped in a line from her throat and nearly reached the line of her wide belt. Its gold discs stood out in relief, crowned by beads of turquoise. It snatched her waist. Beneath, the fall of her vivid skirt tumbled to the stairs with a sheer lace overlay in red-orange. The underlay was yellow like the bodice and looked as soft as satin. Twisted tassels of red, white and black draped over each hip, and her mohawk dragon braid and large beaded earrings crowned the look.

She was a desert marigold. Nick thought of the woman in the painting—her painting—standing strong against the erosion of nature and life's elements.

His heart wasn't his own. It felt outside his body, yet every part of him rang with its hard, insistent knells. She was always the most beautiful woman in the room, but tonight she eclipsed everything—the guests, the artwork, the spiral chandelier.

Nick knew in that moment with absolute certainty that he was doomed. He'd never find anyone who would make him feel this way. There was no one else on Earth like Sassy. He *wanted* no one else.

And he needed her like his next breath.

She touched the top of the three-dimensional braid. "Is it too much?"

"No." The answer leaped out of his mouth, unbidden. He felt unharnessed. His mind had fled the paddock. It bolted freely from one thought to the next, all circling her in that magnificent dress. He said the first word he could reach for. The first word that made any sense at all, the Navajo greeting she'd taught him at the lunch table that first day they'd shared a meal. "Yá'át'ééh."

Her expression softened. He thought he saw her eyes dilate, darkening to delicious umber. "Aoo' yá'át'ééh," she replied in a silken voice that arrowed straight to his restraint. She came down the steps farther, stopping on the tread above his. On the hand rail, their hands rested centimeters apart. His skin hummed for the silken texture of hers.

Her gaze followed the line of his shoulders. She reached up to brush something from his dinner jacket, a smile tugging at the corner of her cherry-red mouth. "Riot hair," she indicated.

"Ah." He lifted his chin, watching her down the long line of his nose as he drew the fragrance of nighttime roses into his lungs and held it there. "You're a picture," he said, trying to do her justice. She was the subject of a painting who had walked out of the canvas to wreak havoc on him. If he touched her sleeve, would the velvet soften under his fingers? Or would she vanish like a midnight pumpkin?

She pressed her lips together and raised a brow, avoiding his eye. "Looks like a date. Talks like a date. Margot would be proud."

"Did you hang it?" he asked, voice caught in a reverent near whisper.

She nodded. "For now, it's in my office. When the auction's over, I'll find a place for it in the gallery."

"Good," he said. "She's right, you know. It deserves to be seen."

She fussed with his tie, still avoiding his unerring gaze. "You look like the cover of *GQ*."

The urge to kiss her brought him up to his toes. She stilled. He reined himself back by the skin of his teeth. *Bite the bit, Nerd Boy*, he told himself firmly. All of Dark Canyon was in the space below. Her mother, father, aunts, uncles, cousins, clients…and he'd sworn he would never lay his lips on hers again. There might never be another woman in the world for him, but he dared not cross the line again for fear of losing her completely.

She bent slightly at the waist, just enough to break the barrier between them.

His breath hitched as her lips grazed his cheek.

When she pulled away, she wiped the lipstick from his cheek. Then she took his hand and said, "Wanna be my arm candy?"

He didn't think. He just grinned. "As you wish."

Chapter 16

"Have you seen Fletcher?" Soledad asked, going up on her toes to search the attendees. "I want to congratulate him."

According to the description placard next to the sculpture, Fletcher's horse-head piece had been forged from spare horseshoes. Though Sassy knew exactly how heavy the sculpture was, it looked weightless. Its wavy mane floated back as if the horse was in midflight. Fletcher had left the head and the eyes hollow, too, giving it a diaphanous look. The silver gleamed under the accent lighting above its pedestal.

A Sold sticker had been placed on the placard. The horse had fetched a remarkable four-figure sum.

"I haven't seen him, no," Sassy said, glancing around. The fundraiser was winding down. Members of Sassy's family were helping to pack and move pieces that could be transferred easily to recipients' vehicles. She'd been so busy speaking to artists and winners, she hadn't thought to look for the gallery's newest artisan. "I'd like to speak with him, too, before he leaves."

"Sassy," Sherry said, arms opened wide as she approached. "This fundraiser was a runaway success. You did fantastic."

"Thank you, Aunt Sherry," Sassy replied, accepting the embrace. "But I can't take all the credit. You've met my executive assistant, Soledad Yazzie. Without her, this wouldn't have been possible."

"Ms. Yazzie," Sherry said, shaking Soledad's small hand vigorously. "You and my niece are the dream team."

"Thank you, Mrs. Colton," Soledad returned. "The dream is working here. I wouldn't trade it for anything."

Sassy exchanged a smile with her. Soledad definitely needed a raise. Without her wrangling Sassy's march of ideas into something functional, this auction never would've gotten off the ground in the first place. She was the yin to Sassy's yang and a consummate professional to boot.

"We're proud of you," Sassy's father said, coming up behind her.

She turned into him, resting her head on his shoulder. "Thanks, Dad."

He touched an affectionate kiss to her temple. "My girls stole the show tonight," he said, plucking at her sleeve.

"This is all Mom," Sassy noted, spreading her arms wide. "Where is she, by the way?"

"With the winner of her design," Richie explained. "She wanted to make sure they understood the washing instructions and protocol for ceremonial use."

"Ah," Sassy said knowingly.

Nick rushed toward them, urgency written on his face. "Out of the way!"

The storeroom door banged open behind her, hitting the wall with a resounding thud. Guests who had lingered shrieked as a figure darted through the opening, running pell-mell for the exit.

"Fletcher!" Soledad cried out in surprise.

He didn't acknowledge her. Instead, he barreled straight for Sassy, face flushed, sweat pearling at his temples.

"Sassy, down!" Nick called, making a dive for her.

She didn't have time to react. Fletcher came at her like a heat-seeking missile. He shoved her roughly out of his way.

The force sent her colliding into the pedestal and the horse's head balanced on top of it. She tumbled to the floor with it, unable to get her arms in front of her to catch her fall.

The floor didn't cushion her. She turned her head in time to avoid driving her face into the marble tiles. The ball joint beneath her cheek absorbed the blow, the impact singing into her teeth.

People screamed. There were shouts of "Police!" "Freeze!" and "On the ground!" Boots slapped against the tiles in a cascade of running footfalls.

Someone cupped her head between their hands. "Sassy," Nick said, kneeling over her.

"I'm okay," she claimed.

"Are you sure?" he asked, helping her to a sitting position. Worry clouded his tawny lion irises.

She nodded. "Yeah." Uniformed officers filed through. Their radios squawked as they parted what was left of the bystanders. Sassy gawked as two policemen led a struggling man in a dark hoodie and jeans from the storeroom. "What is going on?" she asked.

"We got him."

Sassy whirled to find a DCPD detective with a badge hanging from his neck. She had seen him mixing with the partygoers, yet he'd lost his jacket and tie and the light in his eyes was grim. "Who?" she asked numbly.

"A drug dealer by the name of Rodrigo Kenton," the detective explained. "He was wanted in connection with the shooting of our own Detective Hatch during an undercover operation two weeks ago."

The same shooting Nick and his team had been responding to when he sprained his wrist? "What's he doing here?" she wondered out loud, cradling her jaw.

"Someone left a pretty large cocaine drop for him in the crates in your storeroom," the detective told her.

"What?" she exclaimed. "Who?" It clicked slowly. Fletcher running out the storeroom. Fletcher barreling into her, sending her, the pedestal and the horse's head crashing to the floor. A commotion, a distraction, to aid in his escape. Sassy's gaze flew to Soledad, who was shaking her head listlessly.

"No," she said, going an alarming shade of white. "No. No, no, no... Fletcher... He wouldn't do something like that..."

"I'm sorry, Miss," the detective said, moderating his tone to soften the blow. "We have the exchange on surveillance video, thanks in large part to Mr. Malone, who helped install hidden cameras throughout the place."

Sassy revolved toward Nick. His mouth fumbled open on an explanation. It quickly fled, apparently, because his lips seamed shut and a guilty expression took hold as he confronted her questioning stare.

"This is true?" Sassy asked in an undertone. "You rigged the gallery with hidden cameras?"

His Adam's apple bobbed. "I gave the security firm permission to install them." He hesitated before adding, "And I oversaw the installation. I coordinated with the firm and Detective Finbar here to set up the sting on Ryder."

Soledad let out an involuntary sob. Sassy reached for her, bracing her arm around her waist, because she looked seconds away from crumbling. "How could you possibly know he was setting up a cocaine drop?"

"I wasn't sure what he was doing," Nick enumerated. "But I did suspect it was him who tried to break into the gallery."

"How?" Sassy demanded to know.

"The bracelet," he said. "You said it went missing from your office the day after your first security alert. The one you checked out alone. I told you it reappeared that night at the Bootleg at our table. There was no sign of forced entry at the gallery. I checked when we investigated the second security alert, which led me to believe that the thief had a key." He seemed hardly able to bring himself to look Soledad in the face, but he made himself do so. "I'm sorry, Sole. He probably lifted the key from your purse."

"Did he ever spend the night at your residence?" Detective Finbar asked.

Tears ran in rivulets down Soledad's face. They dripped off her chin. Her eyes were huge, almost glassy as she nodded.

"He could have taken the keys while you were sleeping," Finbar went on, "and made a copy so he could case the gallery as much as he needed to before the drop. Tonight's fundraiser gave him the perfect opportunity to do so. While the auction was taking place here on the gallery floor, Ryder made entry into the storeroom, disengaging the locked security door along the back alley. That was how Kenton made entry. He would've exited through the back if we hadn't had officers on standby. Once Ryder saw them take down his partner, he made a run for it through the gallery and escaped onto the street."

"He wasn't caught?" Nick asked incredulously.

"We're conducting a search. We'll bring him in," Finbar

said in all confidence. He cleared his throat. "Ms. Yazzie, would you mind coming to the station? We'd like to ask you some questions about your connection to Fletcher Ryder."

"Must she?" Sherry asked, bracketing Soledad between her and Sassy in a protective hold. "She's clearly distressed. I think it's best she have a lie down."

"You shouldn't go home, Soledad," Nick said. When everyone turned to frown at him, he added quickly, "If Ryder's running, he could likely drop in on her place instead of his own. If he wants to get out of Dark Canyon, he'll need supplies. We don't know what he's capable of."

"Fletcher would never hurt me," Soledad said brokenly. She looked to Sassy. "He wouldn't."

Sassy struggled to nod, rubbing her shoulder. Soledad was clearly in denial. "I know. But you can stay with me. You shouldn't be alone right now."

Soledad blinked at her, unable to stem the flow of tears. Her breath hitched. "I didn't know, Sassy. I swear. I can't believe he would do any of these things. If it's true, though, and he did… I promise I knew nothing of it. I would never hurt you or the gallery—"

Sassy ended the tumble of watery words by pulling Soledad into a hug. "I know," she murmured. "It's okay. Everything's going to be okay."

Soledad's sobs escalated until she was a shuddering mess in Sassy's arms.

"Here, dear," Bly said, turning Soledad to her. She dried her face on a handkerchief. "Let's get you to the car. You can come home with me until Sassy's done here. Okay?"

Soledad nodded, letting herself be led out between Sassy's mother and father. Richie paused, leaning into Sassy to whisper, "Do you need me here? I'll stay if you do."

Sassy shook her head, knotting her arms across her

chest. She dug her fingertips into the muscles of her upper arms. "I've got it."

"You're sure?" When she nodded affirmation, he pressed his brow to hers. "Call us if you need *anything*."

"Thanks, Dad," she muttered and watched her parents and Soledad go. The police had escorted everyone out. A few lingered, like Chay, Jacob, several officers—and Nick.

Nick. Her jaw tightened. She winced when the movement tweaked her bruised cheek. He'd done this...all of this without her knowledge.

They were supposed to be starting over, making a fresh go at their friendship.

Had it all just been an attempt to set up the sting on Fletcher? She thought of the meal he'd brought her, the apologies he'd made, the promises...

She closed her eyes, knowing he was watching, waiting for her to speak. React. Anything.

She couldn't bring herself to look at him. Not when her emotions were all over the place.

"Are you sure you're all right?" he asked quietly.

She didn't need to answer. She chose to address the hovering Detective Finbar instead. "I assume the gallery's under investigation now."

"I'm afraid so," Finbar said. "It's just routine until we can rule out the possibility that this was an inside job."

"I told you," Nick bit off. "Sassy and Soledad were unaware of what was happening at their back door."

"Like I said," Finbar said, "we're required to follow through with our investigative efforts. If Ms. Colton and Ms. Yazzie are clean, it won't take long to rule them out as accomplices."

Sassy mashed her fingers into the space between her

eyes. A headache was starting to make tracks there. "Am I under arrest, Detective?" she drawled.

"No, ma'am," Finbar stated. "But your cooperation will be noted in my report."

She inhaled deeply, wishing she could paper over this entire nightmare. The night had been such a success for Zephyr. How had it all fallen apart so completely? "Do what you have to do," she said, hearing the finality in her voice.

"Thank you, Ms. Colton," Finbar said. "I'll be in touch."

Nick waited for him to walk away before he touched her, his palm spreading warm across the base of her spine. "They were supposed to catch him. This was all supposed to be over after tonight."

"How?" she asked.

"How what?"

"How could you do this?" she hissed. Shaking her head, she fought for grace that wasn't there. The horse's head stared at her from empty eyes on the floor. She shook her head again. "How could you lie to me about what you were doing in the gallery with Olsen Security?"

"I didn't lie," he argued. "They did install a new security system. A better one."

"And the hidden cameras?" she asked. "Are spy gadgets part of the standard security package or did they throw those in for free?"

He balked. "I—"

"A lie by omission is still a lie," she reminded him. "Twenty years of friendship haven't taught you that?" Before he could think of a reply, she stepped into him, asserting herself in the space between them. "You've been planning this for God knows how long and you didn't breathe a word of it. Not one word. Is that what this—" she gestured from him to her and back "—has come to?

You lying and sneaking around and planning to catch drug dealers in my wheelhouse without me any the wiser?"

"I told you," he said, fixed and finite in the face of her fury. "I told you, Sassy, that I was going to protect you."

"At the expense of our relationship?" she challenged, her voice escalating to ring off the walls.

"You two need a ref?" Jacob asked as he and Chayton edged closer.

"We're fine," Nick said, his voice maddeningly calm and even. He didn't break the stare down between him and Sassy. "If you or Soledad had known about tonight, you might have inadvertently tipped Ryder off."

"Oh, so she and I were the liabilities in all this?" Sassy asked, unable to stay quiet. "We were both blindsided by what just happened, but she is shattered. The least you could have done was soften the blow by being honest about *something*."

"I did what I thought was best," he said, shoulders straight, unrepentant. "For you, Soledad and Zephyr."

"It wasn't your call to make," she tossed back. "Do you have any idea what this investigation will do to us? Soledad will have to stand for questioning. I guarantee she's humiliated already. I won't escape unscathed, either. They may not find anything in the surveillance footage or on the books, but this won't put Zephyr in a good light. There is such a thing as bad press. That doesn't simply affect the bottom line, Nick. It affects every single one of my artists. Everyone associated with Zephyr will feel the repercussions in some way."

"He tried to break into your house!" Nick said, finally losing his cool. "What was I supposed to do?"

"You don't know it was him outside my house that night," she pushed back.

"Tell me you don't believe it was him," he challenged. "Tell me you don't believe Fletcher was the one who tried to kill you on Main Street."

"You're not a detective," she told him. "You were the first person I turned to when I needed someone. You were the first person I could call when anything went wrong. After this, how am I supposed to trust you ever again?"

"I'm still here," he said, reaching for her hands. When she pulled back, he looked stricken. "It's me, Sassy. I've always been here for you. Even when you went to New York, I waited for you to come back. I *knew* you would come back."

She swallowed this new knowledge. "Maybe. But I can't stand for your hero complex to get in the way anymore."

"My what?"

"You always have to be the hero, the one who sweeps in and saves the day. You think you're the only one who can fix things when they're broken and to hell with anyone who gets in your way."

"That's not true!"

Tonight felt like a betrayal. Worse, it felt like the ending of something. That rush of feelings she'd felt when she'd accepted Margot's wishes that they would go to the fundraiser as a couple. That this was maybe a real date and they could start over as more than just friends.

He'd been reckless. She'd been foolish. Now they'd both face the consequences.

Glancing around the gallery, she noted the investigation already in progress, the forensic team, the photographers crowded inside the storeroom. She avoided the curious looks sent her way. The catering staff needed help navigating the cleanup with the police in house. If she was going to answer Detective Finbar's probing questions, she would do so tonight. She'd need to give him access to her computer and files, every business transaction she had on record, if she was going to clear the name of her business anytime soon.

She glanced at her cousin and Chay. "Thanks for staying. But I can handle things from here."

"Are you sure?" Jacob asked. "I don't mind staying longer."

"I'm a big girl," she reminded him and softened the words with a thin smile. "Go home. I'm sure Noah and Uncle Sam are going to have questions." She looked to Chay. "Ava, too."

"What would you like us to tell them?" Chay asked, hands deep in his pockets.

"The truth," she said. "I have nothing to hide."

"Of course you don't," Jacob said, gathering her in against his side. "Don't hesitate to call if you need us. It was a good night."

She nodded, feeling bereft on the back of the fundraiser's success. "Maybe this won't impact the family foundation negatively."

"Let Dad, Uncle James, Sherry and your parents worry about that," Jacob advised. "I'm sure everyone will come through just fine, especially once the police collar Ryder."

Chay nodded, offering Sassy a commiserating embrace. "Call me, too, if you need to, anytime."

She made a face. "You have a baby at home."

"I want to help, Sassy," he insisted. "Ava would want me to as well."

"Thanks, Chay." He raised his hand in a final goodbye as they both made their way toward the door. She tensed, feeling Nick at her back. "You should go, too."

"I'll stay as long as you have to."

"Let me rephrase," she said, biting the words off one at a time. "I *want* you to go."

"Don't do this, Sassy. I'm not going to leave you in the middle of this mess."

"Then you shouldn't have made it," she stated, tired. All of a sudden, she was so tired. She wanted to slide to the bottom step of the staircase and curl in on herself. "Go. Please."

He waited several seconds, as if expecting her to change her mind. Then he sighed. "I really did think I was doing the right thing."

"Think different," she suggested. "Good night, Nick."

He didn't respond before winding around her to the exit. Maybe because her "good night" sounded all too terribly like "goodbye."

Chapter 17

Sassy balanced the level on top of the painting. The bubble centered between the lines, ensuring her that she had hung it straight. Soledad had surprised her by ordering a plaque for it.

Woman v World
Artist: Haseya Colton
Oil on canvas
Donated by Margot Malone

She'd never imagined one of her own works hanging in Zephyr Gallery, but she'd made a promise to Margot. Climbing the ladder underneath the canned light, she angled it so that it spotlighted the canvas, then stepped down to check the display from every angle.

Satisfied, she took a step back and simply stared.

She'd hung it halfway up the stairs. The significance of that spot wasn't lost on her. This was the place she had first encountered Nick the night of the auction.

Pressing the heel of her hand over the ache beneath her breastbone, she scrubbed, wishing she could erase it. She wished she could forget that night had ever happened. It had been four days, and though Detective Finbar and his team had cleared Soledad of any wrongdoing, Sassy and the gallery were still under investigation.

Worse, Fletcher Ryder remained at large. Someone matching his description had been spotted at a gas station several miles past the border into Colorado, driving what appeared to be a black F-150.

He hadn't returned to Soledad's residence, as officials had projected. He hadn't dared. The patrol car they'd stationed outside her home in Dark Canyon had moved on. She was no longer under police protection...or scrutiny, as Sassy had suspected the close watch on her friend to actually be.

The success of the auction had been eclipsed by newspapers and local news stations reporting on the apprehension of the dealer who had shot Detective Hatch earlier in the month and speculation about his partner, Ryder's, whereabouts. Fletcher's double life in the cocaine business had quieted the mystery around how he was able to afford his expensive watch, Italian shoes and suits.

However, it was difficult for Sassy to conflate the Big C supplier with the reserved man who had been dating one of her closest friends. Soledad's bewilderment and heartbreak doubled down on the conundrum.

I don't understand. How could I have been so wrong about him? she had asked Sassy after returning to work the previous morning.

Sassy had had no answers for her, and every word of consolation had felt insufficient to what Fletcher had left them. Gallery traffic was down, and they both knew it wouldn't pick up again until after Sassy was cleared of all wrongdoing. In the meantime, she'd been on the phone with her artists on and off the rez, assuring them that all was well. Some had asked if the gallery would close.

The mere thought of Zephyr closing its doors staked fear in her heart. No matter how many assurances she'd extended over the past forty-eight hours, something inside her niggled with doubt.

Could Zephyr survive this? Could Sassy's reputation as an agent weather the fallout of the sting Nick had orchestrated?

Sassy turned away from the painting, closing up the ladder and hauling it back down the stairs to the storeroom.

Soledad looked up from the crate she had been in the process of breaking down for lack of anything more to do. They had both taken care of their daily tasks. Without walk-ins, they were spinning their wheels trying to fill business hours. "Have you heard from Finbar?"

Sassy pressed her back against the wall and slid down to a crouch, checking her watch. "No, and I don't expect to before the end of the day. He seems content to drag this investigation out as long as possible."

Soledad's eyes brimmed with regret. "I'm sorry. This is all my fault."

"Don't," Sassy said sternly. She shook her head to get her point across. "I told you. You are not to blame for any of this."

"I thought he was a stand-up guy," Soledad said plaintively.

"Because he conned you into thinking so," Sassy pointed out. "You wouldn't invite anyone into your life that would do something like this." Soledad wouldn't have fallen for a man who would do such a thing, either. Fletcher must be exceptionally skilled at this level of subterfuge if he'd fooled a good woman into thinking he was everything she was looking for in life.

Soledad retracted the blade on her box cutter, frowning.

"I keep wondering if any of it was real. Did he seek me out in order to make this deal happen or was my connection to the gallery just too convenient to pass up?" She went from a crouch to a sitting position on the floor and dropped her head into her hands. "Ugh. I'm pathetic, aren't I?"

Sassy placed her hand on her shoulder. "I don't see it that way." Though she had no further answers for Soledad. Until Fletcher was caught...*if* he ever was...they wouldn't know anything about his motives.

Had it really been him outside her house that night Riot had alerted her to a stranger's presence? Was the F-150 he'd supposedly been spotted driving across state lines the same one that had tried to mow her down on Main Street?

If he'd needed her gallery for a drop-off location for his buyer, why would he have targeted her personally prior to the Colton fundraiser? If he'd been caught doing either, wouldn't that have tipped police off in regard to his hidden life?

Her cell phone rang from her back pocket. Soledad stilled. Sassy unconsciously held her breath, drawing the device out.

On the screen was the snapshot she'd taken of Nick, grinning during his birthday dinner at the Sauce Spot with Whoa Daddy sauce all over his hands and lips.

Sassy hadn't spoken to him since the night of the auction. She still felt too raw where he was concerned. Ending the call before it could begin, she stuffed the phone back into her pocket.

Soledad visibly deflated.

"You should go home," Sassy told her. "I can close."

"Are you sure?" Soledad asked.

Sassy nodded. "Stop by Jessamine's. She keeps trying

to send food home with me. I'm running out of room in my fridge."

"I could use one of her pep talks," Soledad admitted.

"She likes you better, so she'll go gentle on you," Sassy pointed out, helping Soledad to her feet.

Soledad paused. "Next time Nick calls, you should answer."

"Why?" Sassy asked, covering her shock with a dry laugh.

"Because," Soledad said, "you two are peanut butter and jelly."

"What happens when Peanut Butter messes up?" Sassy asked. "Is Jelly just supposed to close her eyes and keep truckin'?"

"No," Soledad reasoned, "but think about it. Peanut Butter wasn't the one masquerading as Nutella on a stick."

Sassy couldn't manage to keep a straight face. "Peanut Butter would never."

"And how many times has Peanut Butter messed up in the last twenty years?" Soledad asked.

"Did he have to mess up *this* badly?" Sassy asked, wincing.

"So he was due for a screwup," Soledad explained. "Even Jif was recalled a few years ago. At least Nick didn't give you salmonella."

Sassy couldn't hold back a laugh any longer. "Is it weird that this conversation is making me hungry?"

"Could you be craving… Peanut Butter?"

"Clever girl," Sassy drawled. "I'll see you tomorrow."

"Call me if you hear anything," Soledad returned, growing serious again.

"Same goes."

It took Sassy ten minutes to find her car parallel parked across from the gallery. She'd finally broken down and bought a new one—a spiffy Durango with Bluetooth and a sunroof.

Not that she knew precisely how to work said sunroof. She was still learning to finagle the Bluetooth.

Normally, she'd call Peanut Butter for these things, but she was determined to figure it out for herself. She'd spent the last two decades depending far too much on a man who was neither father, brother, uncle or cousin.

Nobody needed to know she'd raged out the first time she'd tried linking her phone to the car's smart system. Or that the rage session had been followed closely by a crying jag. She'd eventually dusted herself off and decoded the problem.

It didn't matter that she missed him. She was still steaming over what he'd done. But she thought of him when she went to lunch or when she sat on the couch at night with no text notifications to distract her from Rogue's Grumpy Cat impressions. She'd broken down twice and watched her favorite movie alone with a pint of ice cream.

She started the car. Instantly, the local '80s station hit her with a blast of the eighties' ballad they had sung along to in his truck on the way to the Navajo Nation not that long ago.

"Goddamn it," she muttered. She switched to Bluetooth and kicked off her favorite righteous-woman playlist. Because the weather was unseasonably warm and Dark Canyon had had a break in the rain clouds that had been hanging around lately, she rolled down the driver's window and let the breeze buffet her as she drove home. When she caught herself wondering if she had any peanut butter in her pantry, she cranked the tunes and belted the lyrics.

She'd stick to her plan of thirty minutes of wall Pilates followed by a hot shower and a plateful of Jessamine's pity food. She'd google Detective Finbar, print off a copy of his headshot, pin it up and practice using her new pneumatic drill on his face.

Bonus points if she could find Fletcher Ryder's driver's license photo on the web. She also needed to try her hand at the Skil saw a friend in construction had cautiously let her borrow.

Dusk was coming on fast by the time she pulled into her driveway. She waved to her neighbors, who were busy tilling flower beds while their girls played tag in their front yard.

She was still singing as she entered the silence of her home. Rogue failed to greet her at the door as she usually did. Sassy set her purse down on the kitchen bar, peeking into the laundry room to make sure she hadn't accidentally shut her inside before she'd left this morning. The door was open and the cat food bowl was empty. "Rogue?" Sassy called, shedding her blazer.

Her phone rang. She lifted it from her pocket.

Nick again.

She thought about what Soledad had said. She thought about Jif and eighties' ballads and the fact that she missed him.

She didn't have to forget what happened. But she could open the lines of communication. Had she really planned on never talking to him again?

In what world could she and Nick not coexist together in some manner?

Determined to remain guarded, she thumbed the green toggle on the screen and raised the device to her ear. "Hello?"

There was a pause. Then, "You actually answered."

The ache behind her breastbone flared again. She

crouched to check for Rogue underneath the dining room table. "It would seem so."

"Listen, Sassy, I need to talk to you. Not like this. Not over the phone. Are you free tonight?"

"I don't know," she hedged, going down on her hands and knees to look under the couch. "I don't know if I'm ready."

She could hear him expel a breath. "You answered the phone. That's a good sign."

She sat back on her haunches, seeing no sign of her cat. Frowning, she planted one hand on the coffee table to help herself up.

A breeze whispered across the side of her face, turning her attention to the back door.

Her body locked in place. The door was slightly ajar. The muddy tracks across the deck had crossed onto her hardwood floors, their tread unfamiliar as they trekked to the hall leading to her bedroom.

The skin at the back of her neck prickled with alarm. A chill skated through her, thorough enough to strike the marrow of her bones.

She didn't dare breathe. There were no outgoing prints.

"Sassy?" Nick said in her ear. "Are you there?"

She cupped her hand around the phone's receiver. "I think... I think someone might be in the house," she whispered. Her pulse beat her eardrums like a wrecking ball.

"*What?*" he hissed back. "What do you mean?"

"The back door's open," she reported. "And there are tracks, like before. Only these come all the way in..."

"Okay," he said, seeming to get a grip on himself. "Okay, I need you to get the hell out of there. Now. I'm dialing the police right now..."

She felt the urge to run. Hide. Cower.

But this was her house. Her own.

When Nick pressed her to answer him, she muted him, slowly placing the phone back in her pocket with the call still in progress. She found her cordless nail gun under the sawhorses near the archway leading to the bedrooms and picked it up, hoping a charge remained on the battery.

The light in the bedroom was off. She could see the tender blue strokes of dusk painting the walls of her room. She shed the heels she'd worn to work, allowing her toes to sink into the thick, sullied carpet of the hall, steps silent. Tiptoeing to the door, she pressed her back to the wall, out of sight.

A voice crept out of the darkness. "Hello, Haseya."

Her blood went cold. It was him. She took a bracing breath before stepping into plain view, framed by the threshold.

Fletcher sat on the edge of her bed. The sight of him perched there on the sheets she'd forgotten to smooth this morning turned her stomach. Signs of strain were apparent on his face, especially under his eyes, where fatigue had painted pink crescents. His eyes themselves seemed sunken. The weight of his wide shoulders had folded forward. He didn't look up from the floor between his booted feet.

It was strange seeing him in a wrinkled black T-shirt and jeans. He'd been stripped of his polish, his importance.

The worst thing, though, was the long hunting knife he held in his right hand. As she watched, he fed it through his left hand. The blade came away wet with blood.

Sassy bit the inside of her lip, struggling to remain calm. "You don't look so hot, Ryder."

He continued to stare fixedly at the carpet. "I had to come back," he said dully.

"Not on my account, I hope," Sassy replied, shifting her

weight from one foot to the other. The nail gun hung heavy in her grip at her side.

At last, he did look up. The emptiness in his gaze sank through her like a stone. "I came back for you."

Her mouth dried. Determined not to let her voice shake, she countered, "No offense, but I could've done without the reunion."

He straightened his long body to standing, the effort drawing the motion out gradually. He fisted his hand around the knife wound. Blood ran down his arm to his elbow in rivulets. She saw it between his fingers. It dripped to the floor, soaking into her carpet.

It was on the bed.

Was all that blood from what he'd done to himself…or from what he'd done to Rogue? Was that why Sassy couldn't find her? Her mind raced, blind panic threatening to overrule the cool voice of reason that told her to watch and wait for him to make a move.

"I came back for you," he said again, taking a step toward her.

She fought not to back up a step. "Don't come any closer," she warned.

He didn't seem to hear her, moving to the halfway point between them. "You don't remember me, do you?"

She narrowed her eyes on him, recalling the vague sense of familiarity she'd felt upon meeting him for the first time. "What don't I remember, Fletcher?" she asked, hoping the sound of his name would ignite a flicker of life in those eerie, dead eyes.

"My name's not Fletcher," he claimed. "It's Weston Childress. Does that ring a bell with you, Haseya?"

It didn't. Not even a little bit. She remained silent, unsure how to proceed. She had to keep him talking to allow

Nick enough time to alert the authorities, for Nick to get here. His name was on a loop through her mind. *Nick. Nick, I need you...*

The movement of Fletcher... Weston's mouth sharpened her focus. She zeroed in on his grim smirk, the first show of emotion she'd seen from him. It wasn't pretty. She almost wished he'd go back to his dead-eyed stare. "Okay, your name's Weston. Now tell me what you did to my cat."

"First, you listen. I guess it's easy to forget the kid from Moab that you screwed over ten years ago."

"What are you talking about?" she demanded.

"We were once competitors," he revealed. "The two most promising art students Utah had seen in a long time. That grant you won that sent you to art school in New York? It was supposed to be mine."

"Who says?"

"You might want to hold on to any more smart-ass remarks," he advised. "I'm feeling a mite stabby."

She eyed the blood still dripping from his closed hand. "I noticed. You want to put some pressure on that? Some iodine? Your blade could be rusty."

"Shut up," he said without raising his voice. She'd have rather he yelled it at her. His calm was unnerving. "The executors who awarded you the college grant promised it to me. They made me believe I had it in the bag. And I needed it. While you were enjoying high school, I was nursing my mother through lymphoma."

She pressed her lips together, careful with her words now. "I'm sorry."

"No, you're not," he said, cracking another unfeeling grin. "Her name was Letta Childress. She gave me her name after my piece of shit father took off while she was still pregnant with me. It was her and me against the world for years until cancer decided it was going to take everything from us. Her treatment costs were exponential. She couldn't get insurance with a preexisting condition. She managed to get Medicaid, but it wouldn't pay for the clinical trial that might have been more effective than the chemo that broke her body down piece by piece until there was so little of her left, she couldn't work. She damn sure couldn't take care of me. I took on the role of caretaker. I tried dropping out of high school, but she wouldn't let me. She said I had a future. She said my art would make me a household name, that it would take me places—places she'd never had a chance to see because life kept its boot on her neck. She said I would be in museums, that I'd make enough off my work to provide for both of us, cancer bills be damned."

Sassy knew this story didn't have a happy ending, for Letta Childress or her son. "What happened?"

"I didn't have money for art school, obviously," he continued. "What little money we had saved went into her treatment. But with the grant, I'd be well on my way to making all my mother's dreams come true. She was there that night they awarded it to you, wearing her head scarf to hide her missing hair. She was emaciated, barely strong enough to walk, but she wanted to be there when they called my name. When you took the stage in my place, I thought the heartbreak would kill her."

The words *I'm sorry* surfaced once more. She couldn't say them. There was nothing she could say to make up for the struggle between a mother and son she'd had no understanding of at the time. Her compassion for both of them, however, battled her fear. She looked at the knife again.

If he could cut himself, what would he be willing to do to her?

A tattoo on his wrist caught her eye. She'd never seen it.

He'd always been buttoned up before. The longhorn skull stared at her out of empty eye sockets. It was a dead ringer for the artist's mark she'd found on the bar rod outside the gallery.

The empty eyes of his horse's head sculpture bubbled to the forefront of her mind, too. How had she not noticed the correlation between the two?

Wariness prickled along her spine. *Come on, Nick.* "I take it you didn't get to go to art school."

"Despite having earned it, no. That was you, wasn't it, gallivanting off to New York in my place? And why do you think they chose you, Haseya?"

She frowned. "Because I earned it, too."

He shook his head. "They gave you that grant because you have Navajo blood running through your veins."

"No. They gave it to me because they thought my paintings were as good as your sculptures."

"You're deluded," he laughed. "The state of Utah wanted to send an Indigenous girl off into the big wide world with a generous grant because it made them look good. Because it made them feel good about all the opportunities the Utah Territory and the US Army stripped the tribes of all those years ago. They didn't send you to New York based on merit. They sent you because your ancestors were oppressed and they felt bad about it."

"You're the one who's deluded," she shot back. "I worked my ass off for the recognition, just like you did."

"No," he said firmly. She saw the flash of his teeth, though he was no longer grinning at her. "You don't know what I went through, what *she* went through, to get the executors to sit up and pay attention, only for our money to be stolen away by some ridiculous small-town girl nobody had ever heard of. When that grant didn't come through, ask me what I did to keep us off the streets."

"Did it have something to do with cocaine?" she ventured.

"I became a small-time drug dealer on the streets of Moab," he confirmed. "I sold cocaine, pills, whatever I could get my hands on. Whatever paid the bills. Whatever kept my mother comfortable. And you know what? She went into remission. Her hair started growing back. She began to put weight back on. I saw her smile again. Heard her laugh. She went back to work because she wanted to start putting money aside for art school again. Despite everything, she never gave up on me. Then the cancer came back for her."

Sassy automatically went back on her heels when he advanced a step. The strain on her wrist from holding the weighted nail gun made her grit her teeth. *Keep him talking.* "That's terrible."

"The only way for her to get better was to undergo a bone marrow transplant," he continued. "To pay for the procedure, I got careless. I got caught," he said, the words speeding into one another. His emotions were starting to take over. His eyes were wet. "After I was locked up, she went forward with the transplant. There were complications. Her body rejected the donor cells, and she died. I did everything I could to be released when she told me she'd found a match and the doctors had scheduled the procedure. I begged everyone I knew to vouch for me so that I could see her for a few moments, just a few moments, before they put her under. I even wrote to the executors of the grant. They claimed not to remember who I was. They lied again to make themselves look better. I wasn't allowed to say goodbye to my own mother."

Oh, God. "I'm sorry for that."

"Are you?" he scrutinized. "Sorry? Because you had a charmed life. You had the right ancestry, the right angle, the right grant, the right opportunities, and you still took it all for granted. You gave it all up, didn't you—painting, art school? Which proves you were never an artist to begin with."

"Is that why you chose the gallery for the cocaine drop?" she asked. "Out of revenge?"

"I made some powerful friends in the drug trade. They got me out of prison. They helped me get out of Moab and leave Weston Childress behind. To repay them, I had to set up a fresh drop zone. What better place than here out in the boonies? If that two-bit dealer hadn't shot that undercover cop, they wouldn't have put half the effort into stopping me."

"You're wrong," she told him. "Remember my friend Nick?"

"What about him?"

"He put it together," she explained. "He knew you weren't being entirely truthful about who you were and what you were doing in Dark Canyon. It was a mistake leaving my bracelet on the table at the Bootleg. By that point, he was already on to you. He's the reason the police were there the night of the auction."

He sniffed. "Did your family keep the money they earned from my sculpture?"

"No," she said, feeling at last that justice had been done somewhere. "The funds are being donated to Detective Hatch's family to help pay for his recovery from the gunshot wound."

His eyes glimmered with malice. "Was that Nick's idea, too?"

Sassy couldn't help it. She smiled. "No. It was Soledad's."

His eyes flared with something like pain.

She snorted. "You don't expect me to believe you actually had feelings for her."

"I'm not heartless," he claimed. His gaze flickered over her torso, her hips... "To tell you the truth, she reminds me of a far less negligent version of you. Dark hair. Dark eyes. Same height and build. It wasn't hard imagining you underneath me when I was on top of her."

She swallowed the bile rising up her throat. Her hand tightened around the handle of the gun. Was he close enough for the nails to make it past the skin? To stop him?

"She should be running your gallery," he told her. "Like me, she had it rough growing up. No rich, Goody Two-shoes family to help her along in life."

"Was it my rich family," she wondered, "or my ancestry? I'm having trouble keeping up with your excuses."

"It's not an excuse."

"Why did you come back to Dark Canyon? That was you in Colorado driving the black Ford. Why risk going to jail to return here?"

"I told you. You're coming with me."

"Why?" she snapped.

"You haven't repaid your debt to me, Haseya," he said. She could see through his calm, his cynicism, to the madness underneath. It lurked there with tentacles ready to drag her under. He raised the knife and stalked over the carpet between them...into the nail gun's range.

She raised it, aimed at the center of his chest, pressed the trigger...

Nothing happened. The battery was dead. He kept coming.

No. She would not be dragged out of this house against her will. He did not get to decide how her part in this ended.

She danced back at the first swipe of the hunting knife, then swung the nail gun—all ten pounds of it—at his face.

Chapter 18

Nick pulled up to Sassy's house to find a squad car already there, lights flashing. Her neighbors stood outside in a cluster, each one holding a little girl. "What's happening?" he asked, getting out of his truck. Riot barked incessantly from the passenger's seat, but Nick left the windows rolled down slightly and closed the driver's door.

"Not sure," the man said. "The officer told us not to approach the house."

"I hope everything's okay," the woman added, concerned.

The wail of an ambulance preceded the van as it rolled to a stop on the curb. Perez and Dilinger jumped out. "Nick!" Perez called. "Dispatch said someone's down inside the house. Is Sassy okay?"

Nick didn't stop to answer. With the sounds of Riot's panicked barking chasing him, he hurdled a hedge and charged the open front door. "Sassy?" he called.

The tracks were easy to find. He followed them from the living room down the hallway to the master bedroom, urgency and anxiety pent up inside him. *Someone's down*, Perez had said.

Someone.

He entered the room to find Officer O'Connell crouched

next to a body. For a second, Nick's heart racked his ribs painfully. Then he blinked, scanning the figure with more clarity. Ryder.

Ryder was down. Blood marred the whole right side of his face. A blood-tinged knife lay next to his form along with a cordless nail gun.

Nick's gaze lingered on the knife. "What happened here?"

O'Connell blew out a breath. "She pegged him with the nail gun. The bleeding's slowed, but the man's out cold."

Perez rushed in after Nick, crowding him against the wall. "Is he breathing?" she asked.

Dilinger joined the fray, but Nick had already tuned them out. He'd found the trail of blood across the floor to Sassy's bed.

His breath backed up in his lungs. There was blood in her sheets. It was wet and vibrant, red and fresh. Fresh blood on Sassy's bed…

"Where is she?" he heaved, whirling on O'Connell.

He pointed to the cracked door of the walk-in closet. "I couldn't get her to come out."

Nick passed through the door and found Sassy sitting against the wall, her knees high, her arms full of Maine coon.

Her wild eyes swung to him, glazed with shock. "Nick?"

"You're all right," he blurted, bracing his hand against the wall when his knees softened in relief.

"He tossed her in the hamper and closed the lid," she cried. "Who *does* that?"

Nick crossed to her, planted his back against the wall and slid down to the floor, giving in to his own weakness. He fought the urge to drop his head between his knees and breathe until visions of her hurt or dead faded like smoke on the wind.

"She must've attacked him when he broke in through the back door. She knew a predator when she saw one," Sassy went on, stroking Rogue under the chin. The cat clung to her, too, as if she was as afraid to let go as her owner was. "I wasn't that smart."

Her voice broke on the last word. He watched her lower lip tremble and gathered her into his arms, against his chest. "You took care of it. You took care of him." The only one who wouldn't come out of this unscathed was Ryder.

Christ, she'd nearly staved the guy's skull in.

"He shouldn't have come in my house," she muttered against his sternum, head tucked beneath his chin. "He should've thought twice before coming into our town."

"Damn right he should have," he breathed into her hair, closing his eyes and absorbing the fact that she was whole. She'd come through. He reached down, cupping her face in his hands. He studied it, giving her a thorough scan. "Are you good?"

Her eyes were still wild, but the glimmer in them was certain. "He didn't touch me."

He sighed, dropping his brow to meet hers. There was so much he needed to say to her. He pulled her to him once more and didn't let go.

The Coltons arrived in droves. First Ryan, having heard the news from dispatch. Then her parents. Ava and Chay pulled in shortly after. Then Jacob. Detective Finbar proved an unwelcome addition to the party, earning an especially chilly reception from Bly and Richie. While Nick and Jacob tried to prevent him from taking Sassy's statement before morning, she insisted on giving it anyway. Nick paced outside the door of the guest bedroom where Finbar had closed himself in with her and O'Connell.

When the officers emerged, Finbar was grim-faced. Nick peered into the room, spotted Sassy sitting on the edge of the bed, her head in her hands. He shoved past the detective to see to her. Finbar caught him by the elbow, bringing him to a halt. "She may need a moment."

Nick shoved off his grip. "If you had any compassion for her, you'd end this investigation into her and Zephyr before tomorrow."

Finbar lowered his gaze. "I'll see what I can do," he stated.

Perez sent updates on Ryder's condition, but Nick reported none of them to Sassy. Her mother and Ava had already stripped the bed in her room, yet when Sassy caught them taking the sheets to the laundry room, she shook her head. She bundled the heap into her arms, comforter and all, and walked to the front door to toss them in the trash outside. No one stopped her.

Eventually, she wound up on the couch with Riot's head on her lap and Rogue wrapped around her shoulders like a mink stole. She listlessly petted the dog's head and began to answer Jacob and Chay's questions about what had happened. The story came out fast—a stream of consciousness that played through the events from beginning to end and left everyone silent. Richie looked shell-shocked. Bly pressed her hand to her chest, speechless. Ava paled significantly. She hugged Sassy. "I hate that this happened to you," she murmured. "I hate it so much."

Bly lowered to the couch beside her daughter and wrapped both her and Ava in her arms.

They all offered to stay, spend the night, anything to prevent Sassy from being alone. She refused each suggestion, promising that she would be fine for the night. When Richie and Bly insisted, she said, "This is my home. If it's going to continue to be my home, I need to reclaim my space. Please understand."

They balked, but at last agreed to go home. Nick doubted either of them would sleep. Bly would definitely sit up long past midnight, waiting for the phone to ring so she could rush to Sassy's side.

As Nick walked them out, he let the front door swing closed at his back and said, "I won't let her be alone. Not tonight."

Bly nodded while Richie shoved his hands in his pockets, lowered his head and remained silent. They were both stricken by the events of the evening. She placed her hand on Nick's shoulder. "If she's going to let anyone in, it's you. Please call if she needs us."

"I'll bring ice cream," Richie offered. "Tell her...whatever she needs."

Nick nodded. "I'll make sure she knows it."

"We need her to be okay," Bly told him. "She's not okay. Not right now. That's why I don't want her to be alone."

"She won't be," he swore.

Bly patted his cheek gently. "Bless you, Nick," she said before she walked Richie to the car, her arm curved over the slumped line of his shoulders.

Nick entered the house once more, locking the door behind him. Everyone else had already gone. He found Rogue on the couch, half-buried beneath the blanket Ava had draped across Sassy's lap. She meowed in Nick's direction. He scratched her between the ears. Relieved when she didn't take a swipe at him as she usually did, he asked, "Where's your mama?"

He heard whining from the hallway to the bedrooms

and decided to investigate. No sooner had he turned the corner than he danced back to keep from getting hit by the full-length mirror that had been leaning against the wall of Sassy's room. "What the…"

"Coming through," Sassy said as she hauled it to the guest room.

Riot was close on her heels, his brow wrinkled in concern. He looked to Nick for clarification. Nick gave him a half shrug. Scratching the hair on the back of his head, he crossed to the door of the guest bedroom. "You need a hand with that or—"

She nearly ran into him in her rush to get through the door and back down the hall to her bedroom. "You can help me haul out this carpet."

Perplexed, he followed her into the larger bedroom and balked when he caught her trying to tear up the carpet from the base in the corner where the mirror had been. "Sassy," he said cautiously. "Why are you doing this?"

"I have to get it out of here," she said, yanking. Seams tore; the carpet ripped.

His gaze landed on the blood spots that led from the bed to the door. He closed his eyes, because he knew exactly what was in her mind. She needed to purge the encounter with Ryder from this room before she could even contemplate sleeping in here again.

The problem was that no matter what she did, there would be no forgetting. She could demo the entire house again. Still, the memories would remain.

"Sassy," he murmured. When she didn't stop yanking the carpet from the nail strips, he crossed the room to her. He closed his hand around her arm. She pulled away. He didn't release her, keeping his grip gentle. "Sassy," he said again.

"It has to go," she insisted. "It all has to go."

"It will," he told her. "I'll help you. I'll help you repaint, refloor, refinish everything. But not tonight."

"I don't want this to be here tomorrow."

"You need to take a beat," he said. "A night, maybe two. You can come home with me and Riot so you don't have to see this in the morning."

"I can't leave Rogue."

"Rogue can come, too," he insisted. "Come home with me, Sassy. Let me take care of you."

She shook her head in a listless motion. "This is *my* house."

The quiet strength of her was loud inside his head. Would she ever know how proud he was of her for the way she'd handled Ryder? And terrified of what would have happened had she been someone…anyone else. "After what you did today, there's no one who doubts that."

Her throat moved on a swallow. "Nick, did I kill him?"

"No," he answered. "Though a big part of me wishes you had."

She gave a little nod, then whispered, "You were right. You were right about him…about *everything*."

"Not everything," he admitted. "I should've found a better way to prove he was lying about who he really was. I shouldn't have used your fundraiser or the gallery to catch him in the act."

She shook her head again, mute this time.

He traced the line of her cheek with his thumb. "Look, if you don't want to leave home, I'll stay here with you."

Her glassy eyes swung to his, searching. "When we spoke earlier," she said, "I told you I wasn't ready to talk."

He remembered, and it crushed him. "I can't leave you alone."

She blinked. "I never said that I wanted to be alone. In fact, I don't ever want you to leave me alone again."

He drew her to him. "Come here."

She let him take her in his arms. Strong woman that she was, she wrapped her arms around his neck and let him carry her from the room. He kicked the door closed. "Tell me what you need. I'll do anything to make this right."

"You already have." She dropped her head back until their gazes locked. "Now take me to bed."

His steps faltered.

Her eyes flashed, heat and emotion building behind them. "You heard me."

Images lit his brain in a lightning storm of possibilities. He tried shutting them down, but they remained, fixed and vivid. "That is far from what you need right now."

"You asked me," she reminded him. "What I want... what I need... It's you."

Her fingers were in his hair, her nails teasing his scalp. He struggled to speak beyond his muscles tensing, his temperature rising and his jeans growing tighter. The promise in her eyes silenced every well-intentioned thought. It muted the sharp pain in his wrist from carrying her. "Sassy," he said, latching onto her name. It was the only thing he knew. The only star in his sky. "I need you to be honest with the both of us here..."

"This is the most honest I've been with myself in weeks," she revealed. Her lips cruised across his jawline, enticing, bringing his blood up to a boil. "What about you, Nick?" She closed her mouth around the lobe of his ear and released it slowly, grazing it with her teeth. "Stay or go?"

Chapter 19

One night. Just give me one night. The silent plea was all she had. Nick had been right. She couldn't be alone. Not tonight.

She wanted one night with him. One night to forget. One night to discover. One night to silence all the questions she'd been asking herself lately about what could have been if either of them had been brave or foolish enough to cross the line.

She still didn't know if this was brave or if it was completely and utterly stupid, but in Nick's arms, she couldn't think about tomorrow. She was blind to the consequences when every fiber of her being was saying *yes*.

He set her on the bed, their positions reversed from the night this had all started, the night he'd been loopy on muscle relaxers and she'd realized that her attraction to him had taken off. Her feelings for him had always been larger than life. Yet that night, she'd seen him through new eyes.

He looked down at her now with heat stirring in his gaze. Her thighs quaked as he reached for the snap of his jeans.

She quickly mirrored the motion, in a hurry to know him in all the ways she didn't already. Wriggling out of the loose-legged coffee-hued trousers, she kicked them over the edge of the bed.

His stare went to the vee between her legs, covered only by the lacy swath of her black panties. No sooner had his jeans hit the floor and he'd wrestled his shirt over his head than he gripped her underneath her knees and dragged her to the edge of the bed.

She wanted the silk shell she'd worn underneath her blazer gone. It rode halfway up her belly, but he went down on one knee. Then two, draping one of her legs over each of his shoulders. She gripped the quilt squares. "Oh, God, Nick."

The tip of his nose brushed the seam of her through the thin panties. She arched toward him, desire a furnace at her core. He breathed on her and she nearly came out of her skin.

"I've dreamed about this," he groaned, need a fervent bar across his brow. "How you'd look… How you'd sound… How you'd taste…"

She dropped her head back to the bed as he spread kisses over the insides of her thighs. He could find out if he'd just…

His lips closed over her, the dampness of his mouth easily penetrating the lace and lighting her up. As he suckled, she arched up to meet him. Every pulse of his tongue, she answered until his hands cupped the underside of her hips in support. The barrier of lace drove her to madness. Impatient, her fingertips sank beneath the waistband to bring herself further up to climax.

He made a noise of dissent, pulling her hand free, replacing it with his own.

As soon as his touch lit across her clit, he set her on a collision course with climax. He groaned against the lace, the noise vibrating across the bundle of nerves his fingers worked with precision, and she was helpless in the face of free fall. She dug her heels into his shoulder blades and screamed in abandonment.

By the time she came down, he was braced on hands and knees above her. His chest rose and fell in quick succession, as if he'd run a marathon. She saw the flush of color on both sides of his neck and reached up to trace it as she rasped, "I've...never come that fast before."

His dark eyes glimmered with excitement. "Get used to it." Then he kissed her, going down on his elbows to give her mouth the same amount of devotion. She lost herself in the kiss, in his hands as they crept beneath the silk shell to coax the skin of her ribs, her breasts. He circled her nipples. Her hips arrowed up to meet his. She felt him, ready and hard—so hard, her desire sharpened. "Undress me," she demanded.

"Not yet," he groaned into her mouth, as lost in the kiss as she was.

She ran her nails up his ribs then down, thrilled when gooseflesh pebbled under her roaming touch. "I want to know you."

He sipped at her lower lip like he was sampling a dessert wine and he couldn't part with just one taste. "You know me," he replied. "Better than anyone."

Would he make her spell it out? "I've dreamed of this, too. How you would feel. How *we'd* feel together."

He seemed to lose his breath, touching his brow to her temple. "Sassy," he breathed.

"Let me feel you," she pleaded, wrapping her legs around his waist. She touched her heels to the base of his firm buttocks and spread her knees, bringing her core up to meet him. "Please, Nick."

He cursed.

"What is it?" she asked.

"I'm sorry," he said, bracing himself on his elbows once more. "I don't… I didn't plan this, and I just realized I don't have protection."

She nearly wept. "Neither do I."

"God dammit," he groaned into her hair.

Her thoughts exactly. And yet… "I've been on the pill since I was seventeen."

"I know," he said. "I just figured you'd feel more comfortable if I wore a condom."

She smiled. That was Nick, always thinking about her comfort first. She raised herself on her elbows to reach his lips with her own, rewarding him with a lingering lip lock. "I haven't been with anyone since my last checkup. I'm clean."

That ardent bar between his brows was back. "Same here."

"Then what's stopping you?"

His fingers worked at the waistband of her panties, coaxing them down her hips to her knees. She struggled until she was free of them, then fought with the shell. No sooner had the air kissed the tips of her breasts than his mouth found them. With her arms still caught in the shell above her head, she arched her back to meet the promise of wet heat. Her heart fluttered beneath his ministrations as he dug his knees into the quilt and brought her up to sitting with him. He continued to suckle, nuzzle, until the yearning took up residence inside her bones and she was no longer herself.

"Look at you."

She turned her head as he had and confronted the full-length mirror she'd moved. When she stiffened, he ran his hand from the base of her neck to the base of her spine, softening her again with the soothing stroke. "Look at my girl," he said reverentially.

She saw them together. She didn't know where her body ended and his began. They weren't pieces that clicked. They had melded into one. Part of him. Part of her. "Look at *us*," she returned.

He made an approving noise. Then he turned his attention to the sensitive underside of her chin, jaw, ear. She watched their reflection as he ran his palm up the length of her thigh before wedging his hand between them to grip his erection.

"Stroke it," she murmured.

His hand pumped once, twice, again. She felt his body tighten against hers, heat.

"Again, Nick."

He groaned, his arm working, obedient.

"Again," she whispered.

He pressed his face against her throat, his neck red as poppies. She could see the outline of a vein. His jaw flared. "You've got me too excited. I might—"

She silenced him with a kiss, replacing his hand with hers. His moans filled her mouth. She echoed the strokes by sliding her tongue along his until he vibrated against her, on the brink of release. Relinquishing him, she planted her hands on his shoulders. "Watch," she said, waiting until his head fell back and his eyes opened to meet hers. "Watch me," she said again before she seated herself over him.

She parted over him, and his arm tightened around her to stop him from stretching her more. "Slow," he ground from between his teeth. "I've never… This is a first for me."

She tipped her mouth away from his. "Nick Malone, if you try to tell me you're a virgin right now, I'm going to kick your ass."

His unbidden laugh blew across her cheek. "No, baby. I've just never been…bare inside a woman before."

"Oh."

He kissed the curve of her cheekbone. "It feels right... you being the first."

"Yeah," she said, blinking at the wet sting behind her eyes. She'd never cried during sex. She wasn't about to start now.

Even if this didn't feel like sex. She'd had her fun. She knew what being with a man meant. But this... This felt like something else entirely.

A tiny ball of fear rolled through her, picking up speed. She ignored it when his hand closed around the back of her neck and the other settled on her hip, guiding her down over him. He filled her. She felt him pulsing inside her, and her thinking stopped abruptly.

"It's your turn to watch," he growled.

She steeled herself to meet his gaze and didn't blink as he guided her through the first stroke. His dark eyes dilated, and his lips parted beneath hers. Sensation chased friction as they rocked together. She could barely breathe. She arched, he plunged and she cried out in pleasure. All the while, she watched what their joining did to him, the intoxication that painted his face. It made her feel drunk on him. She reveled in the sound of their bodies coming together over and over until...

The ecstasy of free fall again. Echoes of a dream.

Only, in her dream, she hadn't been afraid to fall.

His body stiffened. She felt him spill himself inside her. They crashed to the quilt in an exhausted slump.

As they lay tangled like toppled branches, she realized the fall had already taken place.

And she was afraid. So very afraid she had changed things between them irrevocably.

Chapter 20

Rain fell in a pitter-patter throughout the night. Nick knew because he woke at several points in the guest bed, convinced what had happened between him and Sassy had been something he'd dreamed up. It would hardly be the first time.

Each time he stirred, however, he found his face buried in the dark cascade of her hair, his hand curved over her hip, her feet piled atop his. Nothing changed throughout the night beyond Riot joining them. He fit companionably in the space behind Nick's knees. The sound of his rumbling snores joined the chorus of raindrops on the sill outside.

It was difficult to sleep, even knowing he had somehow manifested the dream he'd harbored of him and Sassy together since he was too young to understand what that really meant. How many nights had he wished for this, the simple pleasure of sleeping beside her? The privilege of knowing what her skin felt like against his?

Twenty years was a long time to wait for the stars to align. How could he regret a single one when they'd led him here?

He sank back into sleep for the fourth time, afraid he'd wake again and believe even for a second that this was wishful thinking.

He roused again hours later to a mouthful of cat hair. He reached for his face, dislodging Rogue from her perch. She growled irritably before veering to the edge of the bed.

Sun stained the blinds a vivid gold. The spaces on either side of him where Sassy and Riot had been were vacant. He listened for them and heard nothing beyond the guest bedroom.

Leaning back on his hands, he eyed Rogue. "You like me well enough now to use my face as a pillow?" he asked.

Rogue merely glared at him, at once characteristically bored and malevolent.

Nick tossed his legs over the side of the bed, petting Rogue along her curved spine as he gauged the distance between his jeans and his shirt. He cuffed a hand around his wrapped wrist, rubbing. Last night's activities hadn't gone easy on the healing tissue.

His gaze seized on the mirror. There, he saw his sleep-tousled hair, running riot in messy curls. He traced the small series of scratches along the flexing of his shoulder. Not from Rogue. Love marks from her owner.

The smile that hooked the corners of Nick's mouth looked a little silly, maybe, but it wasn't going anywhere anytime soon. He tossed the sheet from around his waist and rose, gathering his things from the floor. After a quick wash in the hall bathroom, he used the unopened toothbrush he found under the sink to brush his teeth, then donned his jeans.

The house remained quiet. The television was off. She hadn't yet brewed a pot of coffee. The living room, dining room and kitchen seemed untouched from the night before.

For a moment, he eyed the closed door to her bedroom, hoping she hadn't risen to continue tearing the carpet up.

Then he heard the far-off sound of Riot's bark and followed it to the back door.

Through the glass, he found her standing on the porch at the rail, her back facing him. She wore a long *Rhythm Nation* tour T-shirt. Her hair fell long across her back, unbraided and unbrushed. Her bare feet were crossed at the ankles. The rain had washed away the muddy footprints on the porch boards, similar to the way Bly and Richie had scrubbed them off the carpet the evening before. Beyond the rail, he caught sight of Riot trotting from fence line to fence line, chasing squirrels up trees.

Nick opened the door and walked outside. She didn't hear him move in behind her and jumped slightly when he placed a hand on the rail on either side of her hips. "It's me," he murmured, wanting to meld into her rose scent. He lowered his lips to the curve of her neck and shoulder, gathering the fragrance in until his blood hummed. "You're up early."

"Riot had to make boom-boom," she replied, not turning around. She held herself upright as his arms banded over her belly.

He chuckled, watching the mutt balance on his back legs, paws waving in the air as if he thought he could levitate into the boughs of the tree. "Potty break's over, I take it."

Her hand fit over the wrap on his wrist, and they stood together in the dappled light from the treetops.

After some time, she said, "Nick?"

"Hmm?" he asked, opening his eyes. He hadn't realized he'd closed them, or pressed his cheek to her temple. He was lost and gone over her. What's more, he didn't care. She'd always had his heart. She just hadn't known it until last night.

Her touch traced the muscle in his forearm before falling away. "We should talk."

He stiffened, thinking about the promises he'd made hours ago. "I'll have the carpet in your bedroom out before noon. I can haul it off in my truck."

"No," she said. "Not about that…about last night. What happened between you and me."

A blip of uncertainty crossed the spectrum of pure bliss he'd found throughout the night. Half jokingly, he asked, "Should I be worried?"

She didn't turn or move or, he thought, breathe. The uncertainty sank further into his mind, causing a flutter of panic to arise.

"I think," she said then stopped and started again. "I think we may have made a mistake."

His body froze. The flutter grew to a gale. "What are you talking about? What mistake?"

"You don't think it was foolish?" she asked. "Jumping into bed like that with no thought for the consequences?"

"What consequences?" he asked. When she wouldn't answer, he unbanded his arms from around her and slowly turned her to him, afraid of what he'd see.

Her eyes didn't quite meet his as she rearranged her feet. She bit down on her lip. He automatically lifted his thumb to her mouth to soothe it with a stroke. Then he cupped her chin in his hand, raising it until her gaze collided with his.

There was doubt there and, worse, grief. As if what she was saying was a foregone conclusion already. "Talk to me," he said. "Tell me what's going on inside your mind."

She blinked rapidly, but not before he caught the glint of tears. Her eyes raced between his, seeking answers to questions she couldn't bring herself to say out loud. "I told myself, 'once.' 'Once and never again.' I wasn't myself. I didn't think about today or tomorrow or the next day. It was just supposed to happen one time."

"One time," he repeated. He shook his head. "Is that how you still feel this morning?"

"It shouldn't have happened at all. Nick, you're my best friend. Have I ruined this—what we have—because I asked you to take me to bed?"

"You haven't ruined anything," he assured her.

"Not in twenty years have we crossed a line," she reminded him. "How can we go back to what was when the line doesn't exist anymore? We practically painted over it last night. How are we supposed to find our way back?"

"Who says I want to?"

She narrowed her eyes. "What do you mean, you don't want to?"

He took a bracing breath, then unburdened himself. "Sassy, I've been in love with you since middle school."

Her expression blanked. Her mouth fumbled. "Wha… what did you say?"

"I've loved you for nearly two decades," he told her. "And not in a platonic way. Well, not always, I should say. But I can't remember a time when my feelings for you weren't complicated."

"Why didn't you tell me?" she asked.

"Because I've been avoiding this," he said, gesturing between them. "The questions. The doubt I see in you over whether we can make this work on another level." *The rejection*, he added silently. His stomach twisted at the thought of her shutting him out, after everything. He'd woken thinking his dreams had come to life. Had he really been stepping into his worst nightmare? "There is no me without you. You're part of me, my whole being."

Again, her eyes refused to meet his. "Then maybe we shouldn't."

He was losing her, as rapidly as he'd taken her to bed. "Shouldn't?"

She closed her eyes, hiding whatever emotions she felt. "It's best if we go back to being friends, right? Just friends."

He saw the pulsing at her temple, a nerve twitching. He couldn't help himself. He lifted his fingertips to massage it. "Can you let me say my piece before you decide for the both of us?"

Her eyes flashed, a spike of heat behind them. It cooled as she took in the serious mask of his countenance. She gave a nod.

"You know what I've realized these last few weeks?" he asked.

"What?"

"Why I've never been able to make a relationship with another woman stick," he revealed. "Because those relationships were a lie. Deep down, I've always known it would come to this."

"Do you hear yourself?" she asked tremulously. "Do you know what it is you're saying?"

"I do," he said, laying his hand on her shoulder. It moved in a caress down her arm until he found her hand. "I'm yours, Sassy Colton. If you tell me to stay or go, that's never going to change."

"I don't know what to say," she stated. "I don't know what to think or do or..." She released a breath that wasn't steady. Not even a little bit. "I don't want to make any mistakes. You mean too much to me."

He looked down at their joined hands. He ran his thumb across her knuckles. Twenty years he'd waited. It might hurt, but he could wait a little while longer. "You don't have to choose right now."

"Choose?" she echoed on a sudden sob. "Choose what? To roll the dice or walk away entirely?"

He shook his head. "There's no walking away from us. You're not getting rid of me even if you decide this isn't what you want. I'm not going anywhere. But I can't rest until you know for certain whether you feel strongly enough about me…about us…to take a leap with me. To spend every day of our lives side by side as partners, lovers, friends and all that that entails."

When he started to back away, her hand tightened around his. "Where are you going?" she asked, a tear slipping free.

He could no longer look at her and consider the possibility that she might decide against him. His fingers loosened from hers and he stepped back to the door. "To give you the space you need to consider." Riot trotted up the porch steps. Nick reached down to feel the familiar comfort of the dog's fur against his palm. "I'll call your cousins, see if I can't get one of them over to help with the carpet."

"You don't have to go," she said, her voice laden with emotions.

Nick lowered his head, telling himself it wasn't goodbye. There were no goodbyes between them. Nor would there ever be. Still, his heart splintered as he turned away from her. "I'll be here if you need me," he said in parting. Quickly, he and Riot left her on the porch before he could do something stupid like forget everything, all his good intentions, and sweep her off her feet.

Chapter 21

"Did you hear?" Ryan asked as he filed into the break room with a group of firefighters later that week.

Nick, who had received approval from his doctor to return to work the day before, looked up from the dirty nacho meal he'd ordered from the Mexican place down the street. It was the same one he and Sassy liked to indulge in with a pitcher of margaritas every Cinco de Mayo.

It wasn't Cinco de Mayo, and Sassy wasn't here. However, when Perez had offered to order something in for them from her family's restaurant, he'd been unable to think of anything but dirty nachos, the taste of salt on the rim of a marg glass and Sassy's cheeks pink with laughter as the pitcher got closer and closer to empty.

Nick set aside his fork. He'd been staring at his plate for so long the fresh-baked tortilla chips were going soggy underneath the weight of beef, beans, guacamole, pico de gallo, sour cream and tongue-kickin' fire sauce piled deliciously on top of them. The meal wasn't the same without Sassy. In fact, nothing was the same without at least communicating with her every day. He'd promised to give her time to think, but the radio silence on her end was nothing short of torture on his.

"Nick?"

He blinked away from his nachos to stare at Ryan. The man had turned a chair around and straddled it. "I'm sorry. Hear what?"

"About the gallery," Ryan said, reaching for a solo tortilla chip that had escaped its mushy fate.

Nick's heart woke, walloping his sternum. "What about it?"

"Detective Finbar saw fit to clear Zephyr and Sassy of all suspicion today in connection with known felon Weston Childress, aka Fletcher Ryder," Ryan replied.

Nick couldn't stop the grin from forming on his mouth. "About damn time."

"You're right about that," Ryan agreed heartily. "Word is a large group of business owners downtown were getting a petition together to file defamation charges against the Dark Canyon PD on behalf of Sassy and her gallery. They all vouch for her professionalism and clean business practices. The city council was going to throw its weight behind it, touting how much Zephyr's done for cultural affairs in the community. But since Finbar could dig up nothing on either Sassy or the gallery in any case, he made a public statement this morning, saying he was backing off both."

"I'm glad he came to his senses," Nick said. He could be glad his setup at the auction had led to Childress's eventual apprehension and also still feel guilty about drawing Finbar's attention to Sassy and the gallery in the first place. "I never wanted any of this."

Ryan snatched another tortilla chip and indulged. "Childress is out of the hospital and behind bars. That's all that matters, right?"

No, what mattered was that again Sassy wasn't speaking to him. Nick had put his heart on the line. Would this limbo he was in go on forever? If she was going to reject him, his dream of a future with her, he hoped she'd do so soon. He'd rather deal with a broken heart sooner than later and reconstruct whatever was left of their friendship in the wake of everything that had taken place over the last month.

"What's going on with you two, anyway?" Ryan asked, studying Nick's face as he wiped his hands on a paper napkin.

Nick shook his head. "It's nothing."

"I know you better than that, Malone," Ryan pointed out. "Don't forget, it was me who used to race you both down that big hill on Rocusso Street."

"If we know each other so well, why don't you talk about whatever's going on between you and Fern?" Nick tossed back.

Ryan buttoned up quickly, his expression shuttering. "There's nothing going on. She's in a fragile state. She doesn't have friends or family other than Sassy, Ava and me."

"Is that the only thing keeping you running back and forth to the hospital?" Nick asked.

Ryan lifted a brow. "You know what I think? You're trying to take the heat off you and my cousin by turning this around on me. Look, I care deeply about Sassy. I care about you, too. If something's going on between you, why hide it? You make sense together. You always have."

"Sassy thought you might be playing matchmaker," Nick recalled with a shake of his head.

"Tell me you don't love her."

"I do," Nick blurted. He took a deep breath to modulate his tone. "I do love her, all right? But she has to decide what to do with that before either of us can move on with our lives."

Ryan considered. He nodded slowly. "That's fair."

Nick studied his friend. "How long have you known?"

"That you're in love with her?" Ryan asked. "Since we were kids."

"Great," Nick muttered. "Who else knows?"

"To my knowledge, no one," Ryan said. "Bro code still counts for something, friend."

Nick could appreciate that. "Thanks."

An alarm sounded. Nick and Ryan moved away from the table at the same time. The last week of rain had been wreaking havoc on Dark Canyon's roads, especially in low-lying areas around the river near the rez, which had swollen its banks.

"They're calling us," Ryan said as Nick checked his pager.

"Us, too," Nick noted. "Bridge collapse on the highway leading to the reservation."

"The river?" Ryan asked.

Nick nodded confirmation, quickening his steps. "There were multiple cars on it."

"Looks like you and me may be getting wet," Ryan said before veering into the fire engine bay.

Nick cut toward the exit, where the ambulance was waiting for him. Rain pelted him as he pushed through the door.

"Come on!" Perez called, waving from the driver's door. "Boats came unmoored upriver and hit the bridge's support beams. There's people trapped."

Nick broke into a run. "Do we know how many?"

"Not yet," Perez said, "but I have a bad feeling about this callout." She waited until he was loaded in the passenger seat, soaking wet, to put on lights and sirens and peel out of the fire station parking lot. "Sorry, your welcome-back party'll have to be postponed again. This rain's keeping us busier than a cow's tongue at a salt lick."

"No problem," Nick said. If he couldn't eat dirty nachos, how was he going to hork down the ice cream cake he knew Perez had on standby? "I have a bad feeling about this call, too."

It was worse than either of them anticipated. Water was over the road leading to the bridge. Emergency vehicles had to stay back fifty yards. Officers already on scene had closed the road, set up barricades and were wading toward the scene of disaster.

The bridge had partially collapsed, half its supports gone on the north end closer to the rez. On the south side near Dark Canyon, the supports were hanging on. Cars were in the river. Several people had been swept downstream. Rescue boats and divers were already in the water.

"Stay back," a firefighter Nick didn't recognize cautioned as he waded through knee-deep water to Perez and Nick's position. "The whole thing's unstable. The rest of the bridge could go at any moment."

Nick pointed to the cars still on the Dark Canyon side of the structure. They'd slid into one another like dominoes. "Are there people in those vehicles?"

"We got most everybody out," the firefighter said, "but there's still one or two we haven't been able to reach."

"Because they're trapped or because they're unconscious?" Perez asked as she buckled into a set of waders.

"We've got one trapped between two other cars," the firefighter said, pointing to the chaos on the bridge.

Nick squinted through the rain. The vehicle in question looked an awful lot like... "Sassy," he said numbly, recognizing the same peace sign decal that had been attached to her Bronco until recently. "Jesus, that's Sassy's car!"

"Nick," Perez said, grabbing him by the arm before he

could move forward. "We haven't been completely briefed on the structural integrity of the bridge. If you go out there and that thing collapses—"

Nick shrugged out of her grip. Without waders, he fought his way through the floodwaters, milling his arms to make him faster.

Sassy's car was wedged between a Honda CRV and a dually. None of the doors could be opened from the outside of the vehicle or in. The bridge listed ominously to one side and had forced the CRV's driver's side into the low-hanging rail. The driver's door was open, just as the passenger side of the dually was. The drivers and passengers of both vehicles had escaped, leaving Sassy helpless.

Behind him, Nick heard Ryan shouting for him. Dilinger's voice joined in. He didn't stop. The floodwaters grew shallow as the pavement rose to meet the entrance to the bridge. He climbed the embankment until he was clear of the water and scaled the bridge to the break point, where asphalt had fissured and crumbled away. A drop of about two feet sloped toward the raging river. "Sassy!" he called, trying to see through her back window. Was there movement? Was she hurt? Was she conscious?

He looked around and found a chunk of asphalt as big around as his fist. Sliding down the slope, he left the relative safety of the embankment. He could feel tremors of instability underneath his feet as he dodged the vehicles still on the bridge, using his flashlight to check each one for drivers or passengers. As he neared the hatch of Sassy's car, he called, "Sassy! You in there?"

The outline of a hand pressed to the inside of the rear windshield. He closed the distance at a fast clip. Shining his light through the glass, he saw her pale features, her eyes as wide as caverns. The terror in them made his adrenaline leap. Scanning, he noted the sunroof on top of her car and motioned to it.

She shook her head. "It won't open," he saw more than heard her say.

The bridge swayed. The front tire of the CRV lurched over the rail. Sassy's car shifted. Nick gripped the roof of the Durango, planted his foot on the bumper and climbed. The frame groaned and metal shrieked as the dually shouldered heavily into the passenger side.

This chain reaction could only end in disaster. Nick had to get Sassy out immediately. Through the sunroof, he pointed to the right side of the back seat, then showed her how to cover her head.

She nodded and got into position.

Nick clipped the flashlight on his belt. With both hands, Nick used every ounce of strength he had to bring the chunk of asphalt down into the center of the sunroof. A crack spiderwebbed outward. He brought the chunk down in the same spot and felt the glass give way. It trickled into the cab below. He kicked away the sharp remnants around the edges before getting down on his hands and knees and peering into the back seat. "You okay?"

"I'm okay!" she answered.

He reached inside. "Take my hand!"

The bridge lurched. He grabbed the edges of the empty sunroof to stop his momentum. The Honda's headlights were now shining on the water beneath, seconds from going over.

"Nick!" Sassy cried.

He reached into the cab again. "Grab on, Sassy!"

Her fingers slipped over his. It took a moment to get a decent grip. He dropped the rock and wrapped his other hand over hers. "Watch your head!" he insisted, tugging.

Her head and shoulders emerged first. There was a cut on her temple that bled down the side of her face. He wrapped his arms around her waist and pulled her the rest of the way out.

Sobs racked her throat, but he had no time to hold her. They had to find a way out of this situation quickly. "Don't let go of my hand!" he told her as the rain beat down around them.

"Okay," she agreed, nodding quickly to show she understood.

"Can you walk?"

"I can walk."

"Good. Stay close. If the bridge shifts again, grab onto me," he instructed.

"I can do that," she agreed.

Carefully, they backtracked over the roof. The lights from the emergency vehicles lit the scene before them. Every vehicle had ricocheted into the weak support of the left rail. The supports underneath wouldn't be able to hold the combined weight of the cars for much longer.

As Nick shined his flashlight on the pavement, his feet came to a halt. The slope from the embankment had crumbled more, leaving a five-foot gap. He could see Ryan, Perez and others on the embankment, watching the scene play out. They couldn't get across.

He turned back to Sassy. Rain had washed away the blood on her face and plastered her hair to her cheeks. She looked to him for an answer, her hand locked firmly in his. "What do we do, Nick?"

He eyed the fall to the river. Branches and debris had been swept up in the current. He remembered the floodwaters that had killed his father. The situation was so similar, it raised the fine hairs on the back of his neck.

Nick turned to Sassy and took both of her hands in his. "Listen. You remember that summer after high school when we went crazy and decided white-water rafting was something we should do?"

She squinted at him. "What does that have to do with—"

"We both got tossed from the raft and swept downriver," he said. "We stuck together and made it out."

Realization dawned. Horror struck her face. "Nick. You're not thinking—"

"We can make it," he insisted.

"We don't have life preservers," she pointed out. "This isn't an excursion. This is our lives."

"I'm aware of that," he said, wrapping his fingers around her wrists and bringing her closer. "If I had any other way of getting you out of this, trust me, I'd take it in a heartbeat. But it may be our only chance, and we have to take it before the bridge goes out from underneath us. Are you with me?"

Her eyes milled between his before circling his face. "You won't let go?"

"Not for a second," he pledged. He kissed her brow. "We're good swimmers." He pointed downriver. "The river flows to the right. We'll make for the bank there."

She nodded, the muscles of her face firming in determination. "Got it."

There was a break between cars where the rail remained. Nick tested it with his boot. When it didn't give, he drew Sassy close to his side. "Hold on tight," he said. "We'll make it, all right?"

"I said I'd never white-water raft again," she stated, "but let's do it."

"On three." Nick counted it off. They launched themselves over the rail, jumping as far out as possible to prevent hitting any broken sections of bridge or vehicles directly underneath.

The surge swept them up in watery arms. Nick felt Sassy's fingers slip from his grasp as it closed over their heads. He kicked for the surface, reaching for her frantically. "Sassy!"

"Nick!"

The strangled shout was downstream. She'd already been pulled away.

"Head for the bank!" he called, kicking toward the sound of her voice. He couldn't see. Where was she?

Flashing lights from the shore blinded him. The current pulled and tugged. The swollen river threatened to close over him again. He was a breath away from becoming entombed in its shifting, wet heart. Blindly, he groped for something, anything, to keep from being pulled like a rag doll into the depths.

He grasped something soft. Fabric. Wrapping his hand up in it, he pulled it toward him.

Sassy gasped as she reached the surface. She sputtered and coughed. "N-Nick?"

"Here," he rasped. "I need you to swim."

"Something rolled over my head. A tree, maybe?"

He didn't like the lethargy he heard in her voice. "Just keep kicking for me, okay? The bank's just ahead."

"Nick…"

"Stay with me, Sassy," he said, tugging her along in what he hoped was the right direction. "Fight with me."

Her attempts to do so weakened with every moment they were in the water. Nick began to think they'd missed the bank and wouldn't be able to fight their way back to it. Exhaustion settled in his limbs like weights, making him that much more sinkable.

He couldn't let go of her and watch her slip away from him, as his father had done in Dark Canyon Wilderness years ago. It was his worst fears come to life.

A searchlight flashed over them like a strobe before it settled on their entangled forms. Shadows passed in front of it. Nick felt arms close around him. His arm torqued, trying to hold on to Sassy. "Her first," he gritted.

A bright orange inflated ring splashed into the water before him. "Grab on!" a voice shouted from overhead.

"Sassy," Nick said, working to keep his chin above the water level. He couldn't keep kicking. His legs were killing him. "Take the ring."

Her hand slid over the side of the ring and away. She tried again, making contact.

"Hold on," Nick told her. "They're going to pull you in."

She was too tired to protest. Using a rope, the people onboard the rescue boat tugged her toward the starboard side while the rescue diver stayed with Nick, buoying him by locking his arms around Nick's middle so his head stayed above water.

Two people maneuvered Sassy until her body was over the gunwale and safely inside the boat.

"Your turn, big dog."

The familiarity of the voice finally penetrated Nick's adrenaline-fueled mind. "Tony?"

Tony gave him a solid pat on the chest. "I can do more than dish up hot wings, and you've had more than enough heroics for one day. Let me take over."

"Gladly," Nick said and let Tony use the rope attached to him to bring them closer to the rescue boat.

"In you go," Tony said.

Nick grabbed onto the lip of the gunwale. Hands were

instantly there. They took him by the wrists, helping him drag himself out of the floodwaters.

Nick collapsed on deck, relieved to find Sassy already there beside him. He fought for air and rolled toward her, sweeping the hair from her face. "Still with me?" he asked faintly.

"Mmm-hmm," she managed. She shivered violently and turned her face into his throat, burrowing into him for warmth.

He held her close, realizing that head-to-toe shivers had taken him over as well. He ran his hands over her for friction and heat as the river tossed the boat and the captain fought the waves.

Blankets were thrown over them. "This'll keep you warm till we get you two to the hospital."

"T-Tony?" Sassy said, squinting for the person behind the voice.

"Surprised, Colton?" he asked, tucking the blankets in around her for good measure.

"I—I think we're ready for those h-hot wings now," Nick quipped.

Tony laughed, patting them both on the back. His hand moved in circles, doing his best to generate heat for them. "There'll be a wait on those, folks."

"N...no...problem," Sassy murmured through chattering teeth.

The searchlights cast everything around them in stark detail. Nick's focus narrowed on Sassy until the boat bumped against the bank and they were transferred into the waiting arms of paramedics on shore.

Chapter 22

Sassy woke to bright white light and warmth she wanted to ball herself into and never leave. A protest from her raw throat prevented her from sinking back into sleep, as well as memories from the floodwaters. The inertia of dreams felt far too much like the current she'd escaped.

Her mother sat at her bedside. She straightened when Sassy blinked at her, adjusting the shawl over her shoulders. "You're awake."

Sassy tried clearing her throat and winced. Had she swallowed the whole river? "Where's Nick?" Her voice sounded like someone else's, fractured and deep.

"He's in the room next door," Bly noted. A partial smile slid over her lips. "I told the RN you wouldn't be separated for long." Just as quickly, the smile slipped away as she lifted a cup of water at the bedside and brought it to Sassy's lips. "Oh, Haseya. What were you doing crossing the river during a storm? Haven't you been through enough danger lately?"

Sassy swallowed the water. Strange how the thing that had nearly killed both her and Nick felt miraculous against her throat. "I didn't think the bridge would fail. As soon as I got the word that Finbar had closed the investigation into Zephyr, I needed to see my artists on the reservation to check in, make sure they were okay after everything that happened..."

"You were worried more about their reputations than yours." Bly shook her head. "We all nearly lost you and Nick today."

"Did everyone make it?" Sassy asked urgently. "From the bridge? I saw some people go into the water when it happened..."

"Everyone has been accounted for," Bly assured her. "Some are here, and it's a miracle none of them were fatally injured, including yourself."

"Nick said we'd make it," Sassy said, laying her head back against the pillow, finding comfort in the starched cotton of the pillowcase. Her limbs were still so tired, she could barely lift her arms and legs. "How is he always right?"

"Shh," Bly said, brushing her fingers through Sassy's tangled tresses. "Rest awhile longer."

"Mom?"

"Hmm?"

"Ayóó áníínishní."

Bly sighed. A kiss touched down on the top of Sassy's head. "I love you, too. I'll find you something to eat while you sleep."

Something to eat. Sassy felt her lips curve even as she drifted away, following the pull of the dark back into slumber.

When Sassy roused again, dark pressed against the windows and she was alone. A to-go container from the Sauce Spot sat at her bedside, along with a spray of flowers in a crystal vase. The sound of rain on the windowpane made her shiver.

She vaguely remembered her mother saying she was

going to visit Fern. Ryan had been in to see that she was all right, along with Ava, Chay and her father. They'd all left so she could continue resting and to check on Nick in the room next door.

Nick. The need to clap her eyes on him made Sassy kick off the blankets. She gripped the side of the bed, testing her legs. The muscles were no longer cramping, though they protested when she pushed herself up to standing.

She spent a few minutes in the bathroom. The woman staring back at her in the mirror had dark circles under her eyes and was a shade pale. The cut on her temple wasn't as vicious as it had felt before the nurses had cleaned and bandaged it. Relieved to see that her mother had brought her toothbrush and robe from home, she used the first then sidled into the second, tying it at her waist.

Her hospital socks gripped the tile floor as she left her recovery room and wandered down the hall to Nick's.

No sooner had she lifted her hand to knock than it opened.

He stood on the other side, his wavy hair a halo of messy curls over his head. His lion eyes stood out from his fair complexion. They arrested on her. "Sassy," he said, hoarse. "I was just coming to check on you."

Of course he was, she thought. His robe was white. The hospital logo was printed on one side of the chest. "Did my mom buy that for you?" she asked knowingly.

He reached for the tie at his waist. "She did. I thought it'd be better than wandering around in a backless gown."

"I'd have liked to see that," she teased. Her mirth faded swiftly. "You saved my life, Nicholas."

"We saved each other," he said, sobering. "Tony, too."

"I think we owe him a meal this time," Sassy contemplated.

"You're right about that." His hand lifted to the bandage on her brow. "How's your head? You said something in the water hit you."

"It's fine," she said, closing her eyes at his touch. "They did a scan. Nothing to worry about."

"When Ryan stopped by, he said you were sleeping. I held out for as long as I could."

"I wanted to see you, too." Sassy made a noise in her throat. "They should've just put us in the same room and saved us the trouble."

A smile pulled at his lips as he continued to scan her. "You're really okay?"

She nodded. "You?"

"I'd have walked out of here by now if you weren't still here and the doctor would sign off on it," he revealed.

She thought about it. "So why don't we?"

"What?"

"Walk out of here," she prompted. "Right now, together."

"Has the doctor said anything about you being released tonight?"

"I don't care," she told him, shuffling closer so she could place both her hands over his heart. "You've got medical training. You could take us home. We could take care of each other."

His features livened with a laugh. "That's a terrible idea." The laughter tapered off slowly and his eyes glimmered. "Which exit should we sneak out through?"

She didn't move, focusing on the soft *thump-thump-thump* of his pulse under her palm. He was here. They both were. The solace she gathered from that healed her in so many ways. "This is not how I wanted this day to end. I planned to visit the artists on the rez, then I was going to grab some hot wings and stop by your apartment after your shift."

His expression softened as he tucked her hair behind her ear. "Yeah?"

She nodded. "I really miss Riot."

He cracked a grin. "He misses you. I think he misses Rogue, too, believe it or not."

"Maybe they should have another overnight," she said. She tugged at his lapels, wanting to nestle underneath right up against the heat of him where she knew she'd be safe forever. "I see dozens of them in their future."

"That would make coparenting easier."

Expressing her true feelings to him had seemed so scary this morning. After everything that had happened on the bridge, it felt right. "We can make this work, can't we?"

"You and me, Colton," he said warmly, "we can make anything work."

"We've taken care of each other for twenty years, prioritized each other... You've never failed me. I don't ever want to fail you."

"We won't fail," he promised. "I've fallen in love with you a hundred times, and I'm going to keep falling in love with you for all the time we have left."

She did nestle up against him. Lifting her mouth, she sought the sanctity of his and melted into the righteousness of his kiss. When they both came up for air, she lifted her pinkie between their tight-knit bodies. "Swear?"

His lips curved against her cheek. He linked his pinkie with hers. "I'm yours, Sassy. Always. I swear."

Epilogue

"Are you slicing that cheese or eating it?"

"Both," Sassy answered handily. She ducked to avoid her mother's swipe. Stuffing another pinch of shredded cheddar into her mouth, she backed away from the prep counter where she and Bly had been working for some time. "Come on. I'm starving."

Bly shook her head, raising the mixing spoon gripped tight in her fist. "You never learn, Haseya."

Perhaps not. But she loved the sight of her mother in her kitchen. Her smile faded swiftly as her mother's eyes warmed in understanding.

There had been talk amongst her parents for weeks about her selling the house after the break-in. However, Sassy had finally made the two worrywarts see her side of things.

She'd had dreams for this house—dreams she hadn't made happen at that point, and she wanted them to come true.

In the weeks after the flood, she had convinced Nick and Riot to move in with her. On the outside, the transition seemed speedy. Anyone who knew the two of them, though, had no trouble understanding why they'd done it. Their bond was ironclad, they'd already built a solid footing on top of which they were now actively constructing a lasting relationship, and after everything that had happened between Ryder and the storm, Sassy found sleep difficult to achieve without burrowing into the safety of Nick's arms every night.

They'd recently moved back into her bedroom now that the carpet had been replaced by warm-toned hardwood floors and the mattress even had been hauled off to make room for its new memory foam replacement.

They'd picked out sheets together. It wasn't china patterns, but they'd taken the task seriously regardless.

Then they'd spent the next few days christening each new set of linens properly.

The idea of having her family over at the end of what had been the house's extensive reno period had come after she and Nick put the last coat of paint on the living room walls. It had been part of her dream, after all, to have all the Coltons under one roof.

Nick had agreed the house was ready for company. After they'd cleaned up the paint supplies, they'd collapsed on the couch, fought over the remote, playfully switching between the cooking show she'd started watching to glean culinary inspiration (they couldn't very well eat takeout for the rest of their lives) and old sci-fi series reruns he enjoyed winding down to.

After spilling beer and popcorn, Sassy and Nick had spent the rest of the night...well, not fighting.

The memory brought her smile back in full force. She glanced over her mother's shoulder to the woman stirring a pot of mashed potatoes on the stovetop. "How's it coming, Aunt Sherry?"

Sherry held up her large stirring spoon with a cheery grin. "If it sticks to the spoon, it'll stick to your ribs."

"Just the way I like it," Sassy said.

Ava came into the room, Gracie snug against her shoulder. She set a bottle on the edge of the counter and began gently patting the baby's back. "Fed and changed," she announced. Touching a kiss just above Gracie's tiny ear, she rocked side to side. "Chay set up the pack-and-play in your room for naptime. I hope that's okay."

"That's perfect," Sassy murmured, leaning in to get a better look at Gracie's heavy eyelids and contented expression. "Are you sleepy, baby girl?"

Gracie mimicked Sassy's smile and cooed.

Ava laughed quietly. "She likes you. Maybe you and Uncle Nick can babysit soon."

Sassy loved the sound of *Uncle Nick*. She enjoyed the fact that her family had accepted him into the fold. Not one of them had questioned their leap into cohabitation. None of them had seemed surprised, either. Her parents in particular were thrilled, and Ryan had been claiming credit for the whole affair.

"Want me to take her?" Sabrina asked, wiping her hands on a dish towel. She had finished arranging fresh flowers in two vases—one for Fern and another for Margot. "You can take a break. Try some of that sangria Sassy made. It's actually pretty good."

"Hey," Sassy said in mock-offense. "I make things."

Ava chuckled as she transferred Gracie into Sabrina's arms. She draped her baby blanket around her. "The last thing I saw you make was boxed mac-and-cheese."

Bly picked up the conversation. "It burned."

Sherry shook her head. "How do you burn boxed mac-and-cheese, Sassy? The instructions are right there in front of you."

"I got distracted," Sassy pointed out.

"By the packet of cheese," Ava remembered, "which you

consumed while the pasta burned." She wrapped Sassy in a sidelong hug to soften the impact of her teasing. "Though I will say, I think you did the whole thing just to make me laugh."

Sassy mimed zipping the corner of her mouth. At the time, Ava had been enduring the loss of a loved one. Sassy had known she couldn't make her a gourmet meal. Hence, the mac-and-cheese incident. "We should take this pitcher of sangria out to the boys."

"Excellent idea," Ava agreed, pouring herself a glass. She poured one for Sassy, too. "Let's see if their glasses are empty."

They carried the drinks out to the porch where the grill smoked and smelled deliciously of pork rub and smoked baby back ribs. Sassy's mouth watered as she set the sangria pitcher in the center of the outdoor table. "Where is everyone?"

Ava took her glass to the porch railing. "Oh. Oh, my."

Sassy joined her. Her eyebrows shot toward her hairline. "There's something you don't see every day."

The men had abandoned the sacred duty of manning the grill to engage in what looked like an intense game of Shirts and Skins with her uncles and Noah in shirts and the other men—Nick, Ryan, Jacob and Chay—without. It had rained again recently, not enough to cause the river to spill its bank again and wreak more havoc. But enough to muddy the yard. They were each coated with enough muck for Sassy to assume they had decided against touch football but had opted for the real deal.

Ava beamed when Chay spotted her on the porch and extended a wave. She waved back, sipping her sangria. "My money's on one of the uncles breaking a rib."

"Mine's on burnt ribs," Sassy chimed, watching Nick

take a tackle into a mud puddle like a champ. She was going to have to help him wash that out of his hair. Dual showers were another benefit of coupledom she was enjoying immensely. Just thinking about the both of them sliding up against each other under the steaming hot spray thrilled her. "Let's go, Team Skins!"

Richie planted his hands on his knees, winded. "Betrayed by my own daughter."

"I don't know, Sassy." Nick tossed the football into the air and caught it. "Your old man hits like a sack of bricks."

"Old man," Richie muttered. On the next play, he targeted Nick, tackling him into a particularly gooey patch of earth.

"Oof," Ava said, wrinkling her nose. "Bly won't let either of them inside."

Sassy cackled as her father and partner struggled to stand in the slip-and-slide ooze. They toppled, going down in the mud once more. "You men need help?"

"They're beating us," Ryan complained, slicked with sweat and breathing heavy. He put his hands on his head. "Twenty-four to seven."

Nick beckoned her. "Sassy. We need you."

She debated, examining the messy yard, the messy men, and the messy dog prancing around them like it was the best day of his canine life. Riot barked, as if inviting her into the fray. She sighed and handed her favorite cousin her sangria glass. "Ava... I'm going in."

"Oh, boy," Ava said with a fond shake of her head.

Sassy stripped off her t-shirt, revealing the sports bra underneath. As she came down the porch steps, Chay, Jacob and Nick applauded while Ryan called out, "Secret weapon!"

"This gives you kids five," her uncle Sam said, spinning

the football between his hands, "but we'll still kick your butts." He high-fived his brothers.

"Bring it on," Sassy invited. She clasped Nick's outstretched hand and tugged him out of the mud.

His front buffered hers as he came to his feet and she steadied him with her arms around his middle. Mud transferred from him to her, but she didn't give a hoot. He was dirty and sweaty, mud caked over half his face, and his tawny lion eyes shined at her under a halo of tousled dark hair. "Dad, you're going to want to close your eyes now," she told Richie. Then she linked her arms around Nick's neck and pulled his mouth down to hers.

Her cousins made gagging sounds as Nick responded readily, his arms twining around her waist and pressing her against him until mud and urgency welded them together. She could never get enough of this.

She *would never* get enough of this. Him. What they'd made and would continue to make as their future spread out before them like a banquet.

Nick grinned as her fingers combed through his damp hair and her nails breezed across his scalp. "How am I supposed to concentrate on beating these guys when you're here looking like..." He gestured to her sports bra and exposed navel. "Well, like my next meal."

God, she liked the sound of that. "Save some for later," she suggested, disentangling herself from him. She pointed to Ryan. "You throw. I'll run it in. The rest of you hold back Noah. He's carrying Team Shirts over there."

"Insults!" Richie called from across the line of scrimmage.

"I've been running it in," Jacob claimed.

"You're on the line," she said. She leaned toward him,

eyeing the ranks of Team Shirts. "If Dad comes for Nick again, hold him off."

"I don't want to hurt him," Jacob hedged.

"He's tougher than he looks," she said. "And if he sprains Nick's wrist again, Mom won't let him play football anymore."

"Got it," Jacob said with a nod.

She patted his shoulder then set herself up behind Ryan's quarterback position as the others crouched at the line. Ryan called out the play and she shimmied forward to slap Nick on the rump. "We've got this, Skins!"

Nick laughed. "Yeah, we do." He glanced back at her, and his mischievous grin took her back to past games of Shirts and Skins—to joint science fair projects and high-speed bicycle races.

To kissing outside the honky tonk and countless meals shared.

The fun wasn't over. It would go on just as they would. For that, she had never been more grateful.

* * * * *

Get up to 4 Free Books!

We'll send you 2 free books from each series you try PLUS a free Mystery Gift.

FREE Value Over $25

Both the **Harlequin Intrigue®** and **Harlequin® Romantic Suspense** series feature compelling novels filled with heart-racing action-packed romance that will keep you on the edge of your seat.

YES! Please send me 2 FREE novels from the Harlequin Intrigue or Harlequin Romantic Suspense series and my FREE gift (gift is worth about $10 retail). After receiving them, if I don't wish to receive any more books, I can return the shipping statement marked "cancel." If I don't cancel, I will receive 6 brand-new Harlequin Intrigue Larger-Print books every month and be billed just $7.19 each in the U.S. or $7.99 each in Canada, or 4 brand-new Harlequin Romantic Suspense books every month and be billed just $6.39 each in the U.S. or $7.19 each in Canada, a savings of 20% off the cover price. It's quite a bargain! Shipping and handling is just 50¢ per book in the U.S. and $1.25 per book in Canada.* I understand that accepting the 2 free books and gift places me under no obligation to buy anything. I can always return a shipment and cancel at any time by calling the number below. The free books and gift are mine to keep no matter what I decide.

Choose one:
- ☐ **Harlequin Intrigue Larger-Print** (199/399 BPA G36Y)
- ☐ **Harlequin Romantic Suspense** (240/340 BPA G36Y)
- ☐ **Or Try Both!** (199/399 & 240/340 BPA G36Z)

Name (please print)

Address   Apt. #

City   State/Province   Zip/Postal Code

Email: Please check this box ☐ if you would like to receive newsletters and promotional emails from Harlequin Enterprises ULC and its affiliates. You can unsubscribe anytime.

Mail to the **Harlequin Reader Service:**
IN U.S.A.: P.O. Box 1341, Buffalo, NY 14240-8531
IN CANADA: P.O. Box 603, Fort Erie, Ontario L2A 5X3

Want to explore our other series or interested in ebooks? Visit www.ReaderService.com or call 1-800-873-8635.

---

*Terms and prices subject to change without notice. Prices do not include sales taxes, which will be charged (if applicable) based on your state or country of residence. Canadian residents will be charged applicable taxes. Offer not valid in Quebec. This offer is limited to one order per household. Books received may not be as shown. Not valid for current subscribers to the Harlequin Intrigue or Harlequin Romantic Suspense series. All orders subject to approval. Credit or debit balances in a customer's account(s) may be offset by any other outstanding balance owed by or to the customer. Please allow 4 to 6 weeks for delivery. Offer available while quantities last.

Your Privacy—Your information is being collected by Harlequin Enterprises ULC, operating as Harlequin Reader Service. For a complete summary of the information we collect, how we use this information and to whom it is disclosed, please visit our privacy notice located at https://corporate.harlequin.com/privacy-notice. Notice to California Residents – Under California law, you have specific rights to control and access your data. For more information on these rights and how to exercise them, visit https://corporate.harlequin.com/california-privacy. For additional information for residents of other U.S. states that provide their residents with certain rights with respect to personal data, visit https://corporate.harlequin.com/other-state-residents-privacy-rights/.